Shadows of the Past

By

Hilda St. James

To: Gertrud
Hilda St James
It was nice working
with you (Sabeena)

This book is a work of fiction. Places, events, and situations
in this story are purely fictional. Any resemblance to actual
persons, living or dead, is coincidental.

ISBN: 1-4107-9751-1 (e-book)
ISBN: 1-4107-9750-3 (Paperback)

This book is printed on acid free paper.

1stBooks - rev. 11/10/03

Chapter 1

Sarah looked around the spacious bedroom that would be hers until Brandon regained the use of his legs. Her eyes settled upon a painting of a tall woman wearing a simple, low cut black dress. She had beautiful hands, with long, slender fingers, like Brandon's. Her face was hidden by a veil and in one corner was written, 'the faceless woman'. It was signed, 'Brandon'. Her thirty year old patient certainly had great talent. Why did he call her the faceless woman, she wondered and continued to stare at the painting.

"Help! Somebody help!" Brandon screamed.

Sarah jumped, her heart pounding with both fright and surprise. She spun around, yanked open the door and darted to Brandon's room just across the corridor from hers. He was lying in bed and for a moment he looked at her in surprise as though he had forgotten all about her.

"Brandon, everything is fine," she said gently, looking into his frightened blue eyes. His chest was rising and falling rapidly. "Do you want to talk about it?" she asked, forcing herself to stay calm. He nodded and motioned her to sit on the edge of the bed. She sat down and Brandon's cold, damp hands clamped around hers tightly. His eyes settled upon her face but he remained silent.

Compassion flooded through Sarah when she saw the desperation and fear in his eyes. There were beads of perspiration on his forehead and she could only imagine the emotional storm raging within him. She

1

didn't really know how to handle this situation. His emotions were in distress, far worse than any physical pain which could be relieved by medication.

"Before you say anything, I want you to close your eyes and take three deep breaths," she said softly, her eyes holding his.

He squeezed her hands harder, closed his eyes and took three deep breaths. After a brief moment of silence, he said, "The night of the accident, I was trapped in my car. My legs were pinned down. I saw the woman…but I couldn't get to her. Her head was on the steering wheel and there was a child…she looked like Lisa…at the orphanage. The woman died. Why did she have to die? Tell me why! I don't like to see children suffer. Why did I have to be involved in an accident? Why me?" He looked at her expectantly, as though she had the answers he was looking for. She looked into his blue, expressionless eyes, but could give him no answer.

She searched her mind frantically for every bit of information she had learnt about situations like Brandon's. In the four years of her nursing career, she had never dealt with a case like his.

"A while ago, I relived the entire accident and I couldn't stop my mind from taking that direction. I had no control whatsoever. It scares the hell out of me! Help me. Please."

His grip on her hand was becoming painful. "I wish I could help you, Brandon. There is not much that I can do. You must talk to your doctor." She watched as the fear in his eyes changed to anger. She had to at least help him to remain calm. If he panicked, it would only make things worse. "The accident was not your fault. The woman went through the red lights and she had way too much alcohol. Her death is something very difficult to accept but there is one thing you must keep in mind. The accident was not your fault." She hoped desperately that she was saying the right thing. He did not answer nor showed any signs that he had even heard what she said. "Brandon," she said softly.

He stared up at the ceiling, his face tense. Finally he looked at her. "I keep telling myself it's not my fault but part of me refuse to be convinced. I feel so guilty. Why couldn't I do something...anything to avoid the collison?" His voice fell to barely a whisper. "The child was so scared, Sarah. Sometimes I could still hear her screaming, 'mommy'. Her terrified face haunts me. I wonder where she is now. Does she have a family? Damn me! I took her mother away from her!" He fell silent, his eyes mirroring his tormented spirit.

The only sounds in the room were his noisy breathing and the persistant ticking of the clock. Sarah gently removed her numb hand from his. He looked much calmer now and she hoped that he would remain that way throughout the night. He continued talking about the accident but didn't mention the orphanage again.

"Am I ever going to be normal again!" he suddenly shouted. His desperate eyes searched hers and Sarah felt completely helpless.

"Brandon, at this time you probably think that your life will never be normal again but that's not true. It takes time to heal. Unfortunately, you can't swallow a pill and make it all go away. Time is the best medicine. You will have a normal life again."

He propped himself up with his elbows. The white sheet slipped to his waist. Her eyes settled upon his sculpted shoulders and broad chest. For a split second she had the urge to reach out and caress his shoulders. She stood up, shocked and afraid of the emotions she felt. Where on earth did that come from!

He continued talking about the accident and his stay at the hospital. Sarah listened to him intently. She felt that talking about the accident would do him good. Everytime he fell silent, she asked a question so he would continue talking. He was breathing normally now and for the first time he smiled. Sarah smiled in relief. The tight knot in her stomach disappeared.

"I'm so tired, Sarah. I'd love to get one whole night of peaceful sleep. No nightmares. I'll take a tranquilizer and try to get some sleep." He laughed, a flash of embarassment crossed his face. "I'm usually in control of myself. It's just...things are different right now"

She reached for the bottle of tranquilizers on the bedside table, opened it and gave him one. He popped it in his mouth and took the glass of water she offered him.

"Shock and stress can do rather strange things to people," she said gently, taking the glass from him.

He settled back into bed, wincing with pain. "Did my dad hire you through a nursing ageny?" he asked.

"Yes." Austin had interviewed her and offered her the job. She pushed the thought of Austin's cold, hard eyes from her mind. Sarah caught herself staring at Brandon's chest again and quickly looked away. She hoped that her action had gone unnoticed by him.

This was the first time she had worked in a private home and her patient was a young handsome man who she felt terribly attracted to. She didn't like what she felt. It was something she didn't want to feel, and certainly not with her patient. Whatever went on between the two of them had to be strictly professional and she intended to keep it that way. Sarah shifted her weight from one leg to the other, finding the silence rather uncomfortable.

Her heart skipped a beat as she realized what he was doing. His eyes were slowly examining the length of her body and he didn't seem aware that she was looking at him. She stood there, stuck in the same spot, surprised and embarassed.

"Are you feeling better," she finally stammered, hoping to take his attention away from her body.

"I feel better. I hope that your first night at work wasn't too unpleasant," he said softly, his eyes sweeping over her again.

She suddenly remembered what she was wearing. Her nightdress was no more concealing that Saran wrap. No wonder Brandon's eyes were stuck on her. Sick or not, the man was no angel either. Instinctively, she reached out and switched off the bedside lamp, grateful for whatever privacy the semi darkness offered her. She crossed her arms over her chest and swore to herself that she wasn't going to wear this nightdress again as long as she worked here.

"Try to get some sleep," she stammered. Sarah saw the smile on his face before she turned around and headed for the door.

"Leave the door open," he called out after her.

She closed her room door, leaned against it and buried her face in her hands. "Oh no," she groaned. She still couldn't believe that she had gone into Brandon's room dressed like that. What was he thinking about her right now? She wondered how well he was able to see with only the bedside lamp on. She hadn't expected that he would call out for her during the night.

She picked up her small suitcase, flung it on the bed, pulled out sweats and a T-shirt and changed. If he called out for her again, she would be properly dressed. She pushed the suitcase into the closet and climbed into bed.

Thought the king size bed was comfortable, Sarah kept changing positions. She just couldn't sleep. Her mind was a playgroung for questions. He had told her about an orphanage, but he was a rich man's son. When he had spoken about Lisa, there was so much pain in his eyes. Who was Lisa?

She took a deep breath and rolled onto her left side. The air was fresh and clean. There was no disgusting smell of stale beers and overflowing ashtrays that she was so accustomed to. Brandon was lucky to grow up in a home like this. She envied him.

The next morning, she awoke to the music of her radio alarm. She climbed out of bed, humming along with Phil Collins, her favorite singer. She changed into a white uniform and pulled her chesnut, shoulder length hair into a pony tail. Picking up a box from the counter, she opened it and took out a pink ring. "You will forever live in my heart," she murmured and slipped it onto her finger. She took out a few more rings and hurriedly slipped them on.

As she stepped out of the bedroom, the first thing she saw was Brandon's smiling face. The memories of the previous night sprang to mind. She felt her pulse quickened.

"Good morning, Brandon. Did you sleep well?" she said, trying to sound professional. She moved the wheelchair closer to his bed.

He sat up in bed. "I slept a bit," he said, trying to swing his legs over the side of the bed. "This hurts!"

"Let me help you," she said moving towards him.

He held up a hand. "No! I have to learn to do this on my own!" With clenched teeth, he slowly swung his legs over the side of the bed, swearing under his breath as his feet touched the floor. He flung aside the sheets and Sarah was grateful that he was at least wearing boxers.

She supported him as he moved from the bed to his wheelchair.

"Get me something from the closet," he said, examining the long scars on his legs.

She was certain that if his voice could have been touched, it would have been icy cold. He wheeled his way past her, his face a frosty mask, to look out the bedroom window.

Sarah opened the closet. Everything was well organized. Shirts, pants and ties were seperated. His shoes were neatly placed in the bottom and in one corner there was a pair of ladies shoes. She took out a blue shirt and grey pants and made her way over to him.

Brandon took the shirt and slipped it on. "I'll need help with the rest," he said.

7

She nodded, bent down beside him, slipped on his socks, then his pants. She helped him to stand up, her arms around his waist as she pulled the pants up. They were close, much too close. Their bodies were almost touching and his warm breath caressed the side of her neck. She was aware of only her unwanted feelings and their closeness. She wondered what it would be like to be kissed by Brandon. She forced the thought away, reminding herself that this man was her patient and nothing more. Once he was sitting in the chair, she squatted beside him and tied his shoelaces. She stood up, relieved to finally put some distance between them. He looked at her keenly and she wondered if he had somehow sensed what she was feeling.

The gurgling sound of the percolator and the smell of freshly brewed coffee reminded Sarah of how empty her stomach was.

"I always program the coffee maker at night. I like my coffee ready when I get up in the morning," he said as they entered the spacious, sunny kitchen.

"What would you like for breakfast?" Sarah asked.

"Coffee. About three cups." He looked up and smiled. The anger she had seen in his eyes just moments ago was gone, and he looked quite calm compared to the previous night.

"I rarely eat in the mornings," he called out as he wheeled his chair around the living room and pulled back the curtains. "The snow is almost gone." He went back to the kitchen and poured himself a cup of coffee. "It's kind of strange to wake up and find someone else at home. It's been a long time since anyone stayed overnight. Do you feel comfortable here?"

8

She closed the refridgerator and turned to face him. When their eyes met, she couldn't utter a word. There was no mistaking the attraction she saw in those blue eyes. Those looks must have something to do with last night, she thought. Feeling uncomfortable beneath his gaze, she turned towards the window and pretended to watch something interesting. "I'm quite comfortable here," she finally answered. She didn't like the way her feelings were becoming out of hand. Brandon effortlessly disturbed emotions within her that she would rather not feel. She turned around, ready to fight her unwelcome feelings, she had every intention to smother them, to make them die.

"Why did you take this job?" he asked, a puzzled look on his face.

His question took her by surprise. She needed a job and this one payed well, so she had taken it. It never once crossed her mind that she might be attracted to her patient. For seven years she had not allowed herself to become emotionally involved with anyone. She had concentrated on finishing high school and then nursing school.

"Is there any reason I should have refused?" she asked.

He smiled, a hint of amusement in his eyes.

If only he knew what he was doing to her emotions. Just the way he looked at Sarah awoke in her that desperate need to be loved, a need that she was determined to deny.

He sipped his coffee and studied her in silence.

Why didn't he just look somewhere else? She hated it when people made her the center of their attention.

"I like having you around. There is just one thing I want to ask you." He poured more coffee in a cup that had a grumpy face painted on it.

"What is it?" she asked, her defences up. This man was a total stranger and her past had taught her never to trust easily. She looked at him suspiciously, pulled out a chair beside the counter and sat down.

"Your white uniform, well, could you put it away and wear something else. It constantly reminds me of my helplessness." His voice was as bitter as the coffee she was sipping.

"That's not a problem." She sighed.

"Good. Make yourself some breakfast. Have a seat and enjoy it," he said pointing to the sturdy mahagony table in the dining room.

"I'm not very hungry. I'll grab something later on."

He picked up a stack of letters from the counter and started going through them. He placed them into two different piles. After a while, he said, "I thought nurses followed all the rules, like taking a good breakfast before starting the day."

"Well, you made a mistake."

"Yes, I did," he answered as he tore open an envelope.

"You have a beautiful house," she said, changing the subject. "I love the furniture."

He looked up at her. "This used to be my grandparents home. All the furniture is mahagony. There are some beautiful chairs upstairs that he made. He also made the bed in your room."

"The artistic streak comes from your grandfather? Your paintings are beautiful. I love that one in the room with the woman wearing a veil.

10

His looked at her, anger clouding his eyes. He turned and went back to the living room. She had no idea why he reacted that way. She didn't say anything wrong.

She went to the living room and sat down on the sofa opposite him. There were some things that she wanted to ask him.

He looked up from the letter he was reading. "I can smell a question. What is it?"

"Did you talk to the doctor about your nightmares?" she asked playing with the rings on her fingers.

"No. The first two weeks after the accident, it was horrible. I had nightmares all the time. It's better now. I don't think I need to talk to my doctor.. His gaze slid from her face to her busy hands. He wheeled his chair backward, putting some distance between them.

"Something strange happens," he continued. At times I feel like I want to cry but I just can't. It's like something inside of me has shut down. It's normal to cry when someone dies. A woman died in the accident and I haven't shed a tear." He stared down at the darkly polished floor. "I become angry for no reason at all. I'm scared of so many things. I'm not the same person. Sometimes I wonder if I'm becoming crazy." He looked at her, his eyes full of fear. "I'm not the same person and that scares the hell out of me."

"You are not becoming crazy. You should talk to a psychologist. You'll have answers to your questions and you'll understand what you're living with."

He looked at her, eyebrows raised. She could tell he was one of those people who thought that you had to be crazy to see a psychologist.

"Who? Are you joking?" He shook his head. "Not me."

She was tempted to tell him that a psychologist would probably hurt his ego but heal his emotions, but held back her comment. "Not knowing is the worst part, Brandon. When you know what you are dealing with, it helps the healing process."

"I know you mean well." He placed the stack of letters on the coffee table and picked up a Times magazine.

"You told me about an orphanage. Was it in your dream also?"

Brandon's head shot up, his eyes full of rage. "Don't ever ask me about that! Do you understand! It's none of your business!" He flung the magazine into the greystone fireplace at the other end of the living room, sending a cloud of ashes into the air.

Sarah instinctively moved back in her chair. Had he punched her in the face she wouldn't have been more surprised. She just sat there and stared at the angry man in front of her. She couldn't understand why such a simple question had provoked such a violent reaction. She was only trying to be helpful. If she had known that he would have reacted that way, she would have never asked that question. Conflict was the last thing she wanted.

"Don't ever talk to me like that again!" Her voice was flinty. "You do that one more time and I'm out of here! Understand?" Their eyes held. No one looked away from the other, like two people sizing up each others strengths before going to battle.

Brandon finally looked away. Sarah stood up and walked over to the window, questioning her decision to take this job. She should have asked more questions about Brandon. The man seemed to have about six different personalities. She knew that she should have controlled her temper. She needed this job to achieve her goal. She walked back towards Brandon. "I'm sorry about the question. I didn't mean to upset you. I was just trying to help." Sarah's throat was tight from pent up tears. He had insulted her and she didn't like a minute of it.

After what seemed like a lifetime of silence, he finally said, "I'm sorry, Sarah. You have nothing to be sorry about. I know that you asked that question out of kindness. I shouldn't have reacted that way. Please, let's forget this little incident. I didn't mean to hurt you." He gave her hand a gentle squeeze, made his way over to the door, pulled it open and went out on the patio.

The icy wind made her shiver. Brandon was sitting there in the cold and her heart went out to him. The agony in his eyes just before he had turned away didn't go unnoticed. She suspected that somewhere in his past there were very unpleasant events. She got his coat and joined him on the patio.

"If you want to stay out, you should at least put this on," she said, holding out the coat. The cold wind bit through her uniform. He did not take the coat. She knelt beside him and he turned to face her. Their breath fogged the air between them. "I really didn't mean to upset you," she said gently.

He took the coat, slipped it on and Sarah went back inside.

Back in her room, she changed into jeans and a denim shirt. She felt sorry for Brandon. She got the impression that he had been terribly hurt in the past and that he was still a prisoner of his past. She saw a tiny bit of herself in him. The past had a way of coming back to haunt people, she thought, pulling back the lace curtains. Sunshine washed over the room and for the first time, she noticed the beautiful carvings on the head of the wooden bed. She sat down and looked at it. It was a picture of a couple sitting in a garden full of smiling children. With the tip of a finger, she traced the outline of a little girl and her heart swelled with love.

Suddenly she heard a noise and Brandon swearing loudly. For a minute Sarah felt afraid and uncertain. She hurried back to the living room.

"Are you okay?"

"Yes. My finger got caught in the door." He turned on the tap and ran water on his finger.

Sarah picked up the african voilet on the counter top and picked off a dry leaf.

"I'm not a very easy person to deal with at this time. If you ever feel like quitting, go ahead." He let out a long, weary sounding breath. "I don't mean to scare you or make things difficult. These days I have problems figuring out what's going on. That is why the four nurses before you quit after a few days." He closed his eyes and massaged his temples.

She walked over to Brandon and took his hands in hers. "You should see a psychologist. You need help." For a moment she was afraid that he would become angry again.

Surprisingly, he smiled. "Promise me, Sarah. If you can't handle this job that you'll let me know. He looked calmer now. It seemed like he had temporarily made peace with whatever was bothering him.

She nodded, feeling confused at his emotional swings.

"My turn to be curious. The way you spoke about the accident gave me the impression that you are quite familiar with psychology. Are you?"

"I don't know much." She pulled out a chair and sat down. "It fascinates me. I plan on going back to school. I want to become a child psychologist." Just mentioning her dream stirred an intense joy within. In one year she would be ready to go back to school. She saw the admiration in his eyes and felt proud of herself. She couldn't remember ever being this proud in her life. She wasn't accustomed to having people look at her that way.

"I'm sure you'll make a good psychologist." He moved closer to her. "Why child psychology?"

She didn't like his question. It was a bit too personal. Maybe if her life had been different she would have seen it as a normal question. They looked at each other in silence.

"Maybe my question was a bit too personal. If you don't want to talk about it, that's okay." He reached out and covered her hands with his. Her heart drummed in her chest and to her surprise she found herself enjoying the tenderness in his eyes. The warmth of his hands slowly inched it's way up her arms. She pulled her hand away. Brandon had seen part of her that she did not intend to reveal to him. That weak, vulnerable side that was supposed to stay behind the brick walls she had built.

"No. It's not too personal," she said, smiling. I really like child psychology and, of course, children. She turned sideways and pretended to examine the african voilet. "I think that there are too many children who have problems that they shouldn't be having. Many of them desperately need help and they never get any. I think it leads to drugs and teenage pregnancies. Maybe those problems could be avoided if they get help while they are still young."

His face was tense. "You have a point," he said. He fell quiet for a while, dark shadows in the depths of his eyes.

She wanted to ask him if he was okay but on second thoughts decided not to. She didn't want to provoke another angry outburst. Why the sadness, she wondered. He seemed to have it all; a respectable family, wealth and a good job.

"What do you think of teenage girls who give their children up for adoption," he asked, his voice cold.

Sarah felt like she had just been slapped in the face for no reason at all. Why did he have to ask her a question like that? They both seemed to have the gift of asking each other questions that they should not. It was a question that she really didn't want to answer. It suddenly struck Sarah how crazy her reaction was. Whatever this man thought of her didn't matter. He was just a stranger passing through her life.

"A child is a big responsibility and most teenage girls are not ready for that." She fought to keep the pain and anger out of her voice. I think adoptive parents could offer those children, loving, stable homes. Children are so innocent, so sweet. They

16

deserve loving, caring parents." She let out a long nervous breath.

"I think those girls take the easy way out! They have fun and they don't want the responsibility after!" His voice was harsh and cruel.

Their eyes clashed. Who was Brandon to judge those girls? His judgement was harsh and cruel. He had absolutely no idea what he was talking about. For a moment, Sarah couldn't think clearly. Pain and anger were mixed together in her mind. She yanked off the leaves from the african voilet without realising it. Unable to control her anger anylonger, she snapped, "Did you ever notice that it takes two to make a baby! Where are the fathers in all this? They walk away from those girls. They want fun and no responsibilities."

His eyes moved from the plant to her face. "You have one thing right. It takes two to make a baby. The fathers should not walk away. If you see it from my point of view...never mind," he said waving a hand in the air.

Whatever he was going to say didn't interest her. She had heard enough from the self righteous stranger. She promised herself that in the future she would steer away from such subjects. Sarah stared at the plant. She hadn't been aware that she had stripped off all the leaves.

"Maybe one day I'll tell you why I feel the way I do. We have different opinions on this subject."

"I guess I over reacted a bit," she said nervously. She was angry at herself for losing control and reacting the way she did. She couldn't help but wonder what her reaction would have been like if someone other than Brandon had asked her that question. Why did she feel the need to keep her life such a secret from this man? What on earth was going on with her? Why was it so important what Brandon thought about her?

Brandon studied her keenly for a minute. "We make a nice pair. How many times did we have misunderstandings today?"

"I guess if we stay in the same house for too long, someone will scalp the other."

"Luckily, you're here for just a short while so, we'll be fine."

"Yes. When my contract is over we will not see each other again. I doubt that our paths will ever cross in the future."

Chapter 2

The doorbell rang. Brandon ignored it, fought back the surge of anger and continued reading his letters. Whoever it was, could just go away for all he cared.

Sarah got to her feet and before she could answer, the door swung open and a well dressed man in his early fifties, with a receding hair line, stepped in.

"Good-morning, Mr. Chase," she said.

He strode past Sarah as though she was invisible, his head held high, his dark eyes, chunks of ice.

"Hello, dad. You're early." Brandon moved towards him.

"I have some free time this morning. How are you doing?"

"By the way, dad. Did you see Sarah when you walked in?" Brandon looked from his father's icy face to Sarah. She looked uncertain and rather uneasy.

"I didn't come here for a fight. It's all we've been doing lately." He unzipped his coat.

"I'd like to have a word with your nurse." He turned to Sarah, "Follow me to the study." His words were not an invitation, they were an order. She followed him down the corridor to the study and closed the door behind her. He sat down in front of the sturdy wooden desk and motioned to Sarah to sit opposite him. Austin fixed her with cold keen eyes, silently examining her face. Sarah shifted uncomfortably in her chair.

"I hope things are going well so far," he said, leaning foward on the desk.

"Yes it is. If there is a problem, you'll be the first to know." She rubbed her sweaty palms on her jeans.

"Good." He leaned back in his chair and crossed his legs. "There is something I want to make clear. My son is a young handsome man and you are a pretty girl. Everything that goes on here must, do you understand me, it must be strictly professional. Brandon is engaged to Stacey and will be married shortly." He fell quiet for a while, then he stood up. "If ever you decide to fling yourself at my son, that's your problem!"

"Why would I want to fling myself at your son?" Mr. Chase, you hired me through a nursing agency, not on the street corner or a hotel! Don't ever forget that!"

He walked around the desk and looked down at Sarah. "I see we understand each other quite well."

She stood up. "Is there anything else? Do you want to know how your son is doing or did you come here to insult me?"

"Cool that temper of yours, young lady!"

"Don't tell me how the hell I should act!"

He walked back to the other side of the desk and sat down, a twisted smile on his face. "Don't you dare talk to me like that! You need my money to live!"

"Is there anything else?"

"I expect you to be very careful when you drive Brandon to the hospital for his appointments. Don't use your car. Take Brandon's, it's much more comfortable."

She started to walk out of the room, her hands balled into fists.

"By the way, did Stacey stop by?" he asked.

Sarah stopped and slowly turned around to face him. "No, she didn't." Sarah's eyes swept across the walls of the study, decorated with photos of Brandon's stunning bride to be.

Austin watched her in silence, then said, "Beautiful, isn't she?"

Sarah glowered at him but remained silent.

"Beautiful, intelligent, well-bred. What more could a man ask for?"

She strode to the kitchen, grabbed her coat and turned to Brandon. "I'm going to the pharmacy to pick up a few things." He nodded and looked from Sarah's angry face to his dad. Brandon wondered what had happened in the study.

"She has quite a temper," Austin said. "How is it going with you two?" His eyes never left Brandon's face as he waited for an answer.

"Quite well," he said, nodding. "What did you say to her, dad? She looks really angry."

"Nothing that she should be angry about." He sank down on the couch, pulled out a pack of Benson and Hedges and lit one.

"What did you say to Sarah to upset her that much?" Brandon insisted. "I want to know."

Austin sat stiffly in the chair, blew out smoke then said, "I told her whatever goes on in this house must be strictly professional."

"Why did you say something like that. She's a nurse not a …" Brandon stopped talking and let out a weary sounding breath. His mind drifted back to this morning when she had helped him to get dressed. She was so close and for one crazy instant he had wanted to take her in his arms. From the moment he had laid eyes on her, he had felt the first spark of attraction.

21

"Brandon," Austin's voice pulled him back to reality. "What's going through that head of yours?" He pulled the ashtray closer.

"For a minute you lost me. It's not fair the way you treated Sarah! Why do you do that to people? Just for the fun of it?"

"Employees must know their places! Have you seen Stacey lately?"

"First, don't ever do that to Sarah again! Now the question part. I haven't seen Stacey for a while! I don't feel like talking about her right now."

"She's probably too busy with the wedding plans. There's lots to be done," he said, grounding out his cigarette.

"Too busy to include the man she is marrying! I called her place and the boutique several times. She's never there. I left messages with the saleswoman but my calls were never returned. She probably found a guy who can walk," he said bitterly. He knew that Austin would protect Stacey as usual. In his eyes, Stacey was perfection stamped with dollar signs.

"Come on Brandon. You're being childish!" Austin got up and walked to the fireplace. "Stacey will come by later. I spoke to her this morning."

Brandon did not miss the foxy smile on his dad's face. What was he up to this time? Brandon loved Austin dearly but detested his constant need to be in control of everything. If Austin was not in control of his business and family, he was terribly unhappy. Brandon wished that his father would let go, he was tired of being controlled. Austin was slowly becoming a heavy weight on Brandon's shoulders.

A long time ago, Brandon had made a promise to himself that he would never do anything to hurt Austin. That promise was made with all the sweet, pure innocence of a child. Now Brandon wasn't so sure that he could keep that promise and it made him feel guilty. How long was he going to let Austin control his life? How long was he going to obey Austin's every command. He was torn between wanting to please Austin and taking control of his own life.

"Did she tell you that in person?" A suspicious thought settled in Brandon's mind and he felt anger stirring within him. Did Austin hire a young, pretty nurse with the intention of making Stacey jealous?

"What's your game?" Brandon snapped.

Austin slowly turned around. "What game?"

"Okay dad. You hired a young pretty nurse. You know Stacey is terribly jealous. Is it your way of bringing Stacey back?" he shouted. Brandon knew his father well. Austin was a master of manipulation and he got some weird sense of satisfaction from it, too.

"I hired Sarah because she is competent! I'm not playing games. How dare you Brandon!"

Brandon buried his face in the palms of his hands, wondering if he was wrongly accusing his father. He finally looked up at his dad. "I'm sorry about the things I said." Brandon didn't feel like fighting with his father. He would leave that for his younger brother, Christian, the rebel. Once more, he just let himself be part of Austin's game. "I think Stacey is having second thoughts. When I was at the hospital, she hardly ever visited and since I'm home, she stopped by twice."

"She's just shaken up by the accident. It's probably very hard for her to see you like that."

Brandon listened to Austin. He was a heart beat away from screaming at his dad. Austin always took Stacey's side.

"Brandon, are you having second thoughts?"

"No," he lied. Since the accident, he didn't see life the same way and he wasn't sure that he wanted to spend the rest of his life with Stacey. All she thought about was money, everything else was secondary. She was so much like Austin. Brandon wanted love, a family and a quiet life.

"Why don't you put the wedding date forward, Brandon?"

"Why should I? Why do you always try to control my life? You hired someone to do a double job! To take care of me and to make Stacey jealous! I don't want to marry Stacey and I don't want a nurse! I don't need you to make decisions for me. Have you noticed that I'm not mentally retarded?"

"What the hell is wrong with you? Have you lost your mind?" Austin's face went white. He looked from Brandon to the door that had suddenly swung open, grabbed his coat and strode out the house.

Brandon breathed a sigh of relief as he watched Austin driving away. He deeply regretted what he had said to his father and it weighed heavily on him. He had never spoken to his father that way before.

"I hope I didn't...well...come in at a bad time," Sarah said.

He did not answer. A dull throb started at his temples and his neck was stiff with tension. There were so many things he wanted to tell Austin but he just did not have the courage to. Why couldn't he be more like Christian?

Brandon switched on the television and stared at it, not really hearing what the person was saying. Anger still churned within him and he really needed to talk to somebody about his dad and Stacey. He looked at Sarah sitting quietly by the window and for a while contemplated talking to her. It wasn't such a good idea. He hardly knew her. He wondered how much Sarah had overheard when she walked in earlier. Her short stay was certainly no vacation. First, he was not very nice to her, then Austin walked in and insulted her for his own twisted reason.

There eyes met and held. Her eyes went from being uncertain to shy, then she looked away. Sarah's eyes were mirrors of her soul. He liked that. How different from Stacey's he thought. Stacey's eyes rarely showed her emotions. His eyes slid down to the base of her throat and settled upon the throbbing pulse. He decided to wait a bit more before confiding in Sarah. She had had enough already.

"I'd like to go outside. Would you mind coming with me?" he asked.

"Not at all," she answered, without hesitation. "It's not as cold as this morning. A perfect afternoon to go for a walk." She pushed back her chair and stood up.

They slipped on light coats and went outside. Brandon wheeled himself forward, his head lifted to capture the gentle warmth of the sun. There were a few birds here and there, and tiny blades of green grass dotted the lawn.

Brandon felt a sense of calm settle upon him, something that had been gone for so long that it now seemed alien. He wanted to hold on to that calm feeling and never let it go. He glanced sideways at Sarah. It was funny the way she had walked into his life and his heart. He felt very comfortable with her, as though he had known her for years.

They walked past apple trees, weeping willows and the entrance to the garden. When they reached the far end of the lawn, where the land sloped down, he said, "Go take a look."

Sarah walked past Brandon, stood between two trees and looked down. There was a slim stretch of beach. "It's so beautiful! I can live out there!" she said.

Brandon's smile brightened his face. "I have a tiny bit of Casco Bay. When it warms up, we could go there sometimes." They looked at each other for a while. "I'll race you down there," he joked.

"I love a challenge." She smiled down at him. "I'm certainly going to win."

"I'm not so sure." Brandon felt strangely disappointed. By the time it warmed up Sarah would be gone.

"Do you swim there?" Sarah asked.

"Not often. Stacey and I like to swim. She prefers the swimming pool so I go with her. By the way, Stacey is my fiancé. She will come by later today." Refering to Stacey as his fiancé just did not sound right anymore. Recently, she had been ignoring him.

Their eyes met and Brandon saw the sadness that briefly lingered in the depths of Sarah's.

She walked past him and stared down at the stretch of beach. Brandon joined her. He had seen the way she looked at him a few times and it was surely attraction he had seen in those eyes. Did mentioning Stacey upset her? He dismissed the thought. They barely knew each other. He wondered if Sarah was seeing someone? Brandon could not deny that he was attracted to her.

His mind drifted back to Stacey. Why was Stacey hiding from him? Did she really change or was his imagination playing tricks on him? The wheelchair probably scared her. Stacey was so proud, so perfect.

"It's so quiet, so peaceful here. I just love it." She did not look at him.

Brandon stared at her delicate profile and he couldn't help but wonder who this woman was. He longed to ask her questions about herself but he felt that he had no right to. She was his nurse. He wanted to take her hands in his but she probably belonged to someone else.

"I love it here, too. Stacey dosen't. She likes to live downtown because that is where all the action is. Parties, friends. I like parties but when it is over I like to come to my quiet home." Do you like going to parties?" His voice was gentle.

She plucked off a dry twig from the tree and broke it to bits as she spoke to him. "I like parties. Recently I haven't had much time for fun stuff but that will come."

"Me neither." He laughed and looked up at her. "I don't see myself dancing anytime soon."

She tucked her hair behind her ears. "In a few months, yes. Certainly for your wedding."

They started back towards the house.

Brandon wasn't sure that he wanted to spend the rest of his life with Stacey. He wondered if his feeling was an indirect result of the accident. And his newborn, very real attraction to Sarah, was it just a phase he was going through? Strangely, these days he was no longer looked forward to Stacey's visits or phone calls. For a moment, he felt completely confused, like his mind could no longer tolerate all the questions storming around. Sarah was right, he should see a psychologist. How many times had his emotions taken him on a roller coaster ride? How many times had he tried to figure out what he was really feeling but just could not? He could just picture the horrified expression on Stacey's face if he told her that he was going to see a psychologist. She would consider him weak. He didn't realise that he was pushing his chair faster and faster.

"Brandon." Sarah's soft voice slid into his confused world. "Are you okay?"

He stopped for a moment, breathing hard. "Yes." He was grateful that she interupted his thoughts. It was too much to handle.

She knelt down beside him. "Were you thinking about the accident again?"

Her soft voice and the gentleness in her eyes touched him deeply. "Not the accident." He sighed, then continued, "Sometimes I feel so confused. I think my mind has become…sort of weak."

She placed one hand on his. "Please don't be angry with me for saying this. You should see a psychologist. When you are physically ill, you go to a physician. Right now, you're not doing well emotionally. Why don't you go see a psychologist? There is absolutely nothing wrong with that."

"I will think about it," he smiled.

When they got into the house, Brandon went over to the fireplace, put some kindlings and paper at the bottom and lit it. The fire slowly came to life. He rubbed his hands together and forced himself to think of pleasant things instead of what was bothering him. Sarah walked over to Brandon and gently reminded him it was time for his exercise. He nodded, moved back a few spaces and slowly stood up with Sarah's help.

He winced and swore softly as he took a step foward. He had the feeling like electrical shocks were going up his back and down his legs. Their bodies touched, Brandon chose to ignore how close they were and how nice it was just to hold her around the waist.

They looked at each other, their faces just a few inches apart. Brandon's eyes settled upon her lips and for a second he had the urge to kiss her. He tore his gaze away. What was wrong with him? He was engaged to another woman! When they walked past the window in the living room, he stopped for a while and looked out, wishing that he could go jogging.

Sarah supported him as they continued to walk around the house. He glanced sideways at Sarah's tense face and wondered what she was thinking.

Brandon eased himself back into the chair, tired but happy. It was the first time he had walked so much since the accident. He threw another log into the fire and smiled. This time the smile met his eyes, it was genuine, from the heart.

He watched Sarah in silence as she set the table for two. No one had bothered to switch on the lights and the glow of the fire threw a soft, warm light through the house. He leaned back in his chair, his hands folded behind his head. He felt happy and desperately hoped that it would remain that way.

When dinner was ready, he switched on the lights regretfully and went to the dining room. Sarah was playing with her rings again, that meant she was nervous. He looked at her out of the corner of his eyes and wondered what made her so nervous. He had seen the sadness in her eyes quite a few times. She was young, definitely pretty, had a career and good goals in life. Why the sadness?

Brandon tasted the chicken Sarah had prepared. He forced himself to chew and swallow. Whatever spices she had put in it was horrible. He looked up at her, she was eating and seemed to be enjoying it. He couldn't help laughing.

"What's so funny?"she asked.

"Your chicken. What did you put in it?"

She looked insulted then shy. "I'm not very good in the kitchen. I did my best."

Brandon's body tensed at the sound of a car pulling up in the driveway. If it was Stacey, she may as well just leave. He did not want to see her tonight. There were too many things they had to talk about and he didn't have the energy to do so. He made his way towards the door and Sarah pushed back her chair and stood up. Brandon opened the door, a wave of relief washed over him. It was his mom, Elizabeth. She walked in, hugged Brandon and turned towards Sarah. "Hi dear. How are you?" She walked over to Sarah and they shook hands.

"Fine, thank you, Mrs. Chase," she answered.

"Call me Elizabeth. Are you comfortable in your room?" She glanced over at the table. "I'm sorry, I interupted your dinner. Go ahead and finish eating."

"Join us for dinner," Brandon said.

"If there is any chocolate cake left from the other day, I'll have a piece." She filled the kettle. "Would you like some tea, Sarah?"

"No, thank you," Sarah answered.

He looked at his mom moving around the kitchen quietly. She looked so small and delicate, like if you touched her, she'd break How could such a sweet person put up with a man like Austin. Was it love? He always wanted to ask her if she had a happy marriage. She joined them at the table.

"I hope you like your room," Elizabeth said to Sarah.

"I like my room. This place is beautiful, especially the little beach at the back."

"I played there quite often as a child." She tucked her dark hair behind her ears and turned to Brandon.

"I think I'll leave you two to chat in private," Sarah said.

"There's lots of books in the study, if you'd like to go there," Brandon offered. Sarah left the living room. Brandon's eyes followed Sarah until she turned and went into the study. When he looked at his mother, he realized that she was looking at him thoughtfully, her chocolate brown eyes, warm and gentle. He did not know a more loving and caring person than Elizabeth. He loved her and never wanted to do anything to hurt her.

"Mom, have you seen Christian recently? It's been quite a while since I saw him." Christian and Austin had never gotten along. Contrary to Austin, Christian believed that everyone had the right to make their own choices. Christian held firmly to his belief and that

31

drove Austin crazy. He had certainly inherited Elizabeth's iron will.

"I spoke to Christian this morning." She sighed wearily. "I wish he would come home but he refuses to. He said when Austin cleans up his act, he'll come home, not before. He works at a garage and he is staying at Jim's place. You remember, Jim?"

Brandon nodded. "He will be fine, mom. Maybe dad is too tough on him."

Elizabeth sipped her tea. "Austin goes about things the wrong way at times and he is as stubborn as a mule. I can understand why Christian is behaving the way he does."

"The next time you talk to Christian, please ask him to come see me. Mom, why did you stop by so late? I know you don't like driving at night." He was tempted to ask her if it was Austin's idea but didn't. He did not want to hurt her feelings. Besides, why should she pay for his dad's mistakes?

"It's a long time since I came to see you. I miss you and I wanted to see how you were doing. How is it going with your legs?"

"I'm doing much better. I walked quite a bit today, with Sarah's help, of course."

"Everything is going to be fine. You'll see."

He couldn't help smiling. Those were her favorite words. Words that had comforted him countless times. They had been talking for about thirty minutes when she finally said, "I don't want you to think that I am spying on you. Austin…well…he wanted to know if Stacey was here." She fell quiet, twisting her purse straps around her fingers.

"There is something else, mom."

"It's hard for me to tell you this." She leaned closer to him and her voice fell to a whisper.

"Austin thinks that there is something going on between you and Sarah."

"What!" Brandon balled his hands into fists. "What's going on with Austin?" I can't imagine why he told you that!" He moved closer and gave her a kiss on the cheek. "Don't feel bad about anything, mom."

When she finally looked up, there was a thin film of tears in her eyes.

"There is nothing between Sarah and me. Stacey did not come by. I haven't seen her for a while. I really don't care if she comes by or not." He caught a glimpse of fear in his mother's eyes. "I think she is having second thoughts."

"I just want you to get better. Think about yourself and when you are better you can deal with Stacey," she said gently. She stood up. "I'd better go. It's getting late." She kissed him on the forehead. "See you soon." Looking down the corridor, she called out, "Bye Sarah."

Sarah came out of the study and hurried towards Elizabeth. "Bye. It was nice meeting you."

"Your mom is such a nice person," Sarah said, as they watched Elizabeth pull out the driveway.

"I couldn't have a better mother."

The weeping willow by the window shook restlessly in the wind. Brandon looked up at the sky, the full moon barely shone through the dark, opressing clouds. He hoped that Elizabeth would get home before the storm broke. She was scared of storms. He glanced at the grand-father clock, standing in the corner. It was eight-fifteen. She should be home by eight-thirty. He decided that he would call and check on her.

Sarah went to the fireplace. All that remained of the cheerful fire were glowing embers. She threw a log in and watched as the smoke curled up, disappeared and was replaced by small flames.

Brandon was still sitting beside the window, a thousand things going through his mind.

What would Austin do If he decided not to marry Stacey? Brandon did not even want to think of his dad's reaction. He pondered on his childhood promise, that he'd never do anything to hurt his parents. How could he keep that promise and choose his own paths in life? Impossible. It had to be one or the other. He went over to the desk in the living room, opened a drawer and took out photos of two children, a boy and girl of African descent. He placed the photos on the television. Sarah half turned and looked from him to the photos.

"My World Vision kids," he informed Sarah. Brandon had sponsored two children through World Vision. When he had first recieved their photos, he had proudly decorated his desk with them, but had put them away because Stacey didn't like to see the pictures. She had told Brandon that he was wasting his money. There was a sudden, blinding flash of lightening followed by roaring thunder. Rain pounded against the widow panes. Out in the darkness, the trees were just trembling shadows. Brandon picked up the phone and dialled his parents number. Austin answered in a business like voice.

"It's Brandon. Mom is home?"

"Yes. She just got in."

Brandon's nervousness disappeared. "Good-night, dad," he said and hung up the phone. He went to look out the window and Sarah joined him. The rain came down harder and the trees bent foward beneath it's force as though begging for mercy. They watched the storm in silence and from time to time Brandon's stole glances at Sarah. The sky lit up and a low growl of thunder followed. They looked at each other and Brandon noticed how tired Sarah looked. She had eyes that told it all. He had an irresistable urge to take her in his arms. His eyes slid down her body and back to her eyes. She looked shy, embarassed.

She turned away and stared out the window.

"Are you tired, Sarah," Brandon asked. The rain had ceased and he opened the window a bit, enjoying the fresh,clean air.

"No. Are you?"

"I'm ready to go to bed." He headed for the bedroom and Sarah followed him. He pulled the curtains close, pulled off his T-shirt and bent foward to untie his shoe lace. He winced and straightened up.

"Let me help you," Sarah said, squatting beside him.

The fury of the rain had died down to a whisper. The thunder had ceased but lightening still lit up the sky. Brandon looked at her and the beginning of a different kind of storm started to build within him. The only thing he was aware of at that moment was his feelings. That urge to hold her in his arms and to kiss her. He ran his fingers through his hair and let out a nervous breath. She slipped off his shoes and looked up at him. Silence hung between them.

Brandon leaned foward and took her face in his hands. He hesistantly lowered his head until their lips touched. He felt her move just a bit closer to him. He pulled away from her. She stared at him in surprise.

"Sarah," he said, running his fingers through his hair. "I'm sorry. I promise that it wouldn't happen again."

She stood up and wiped her hands on her jeans. "What were you thinking!" Her voice was cold. "I am your nurse and nothing else! If you feel like kissing someone I suggest you go find Stacey! Don't ever do that again!"

She had reason to be angry. He was totally out of place and though he felt embarassed, he could not deny that he had enjoyed the brief kiss. Brandon's heart hammered in his chest as he fought to control the desire raging within him.

The blare of loud music got their attention. They both headed out the room when they heard the door open.

"I'm sure it's my brother, Christian," he said to Sarah. "There is nothing to be worried about."

"Brandon. Anyone home?" a male voice called out. "Wake up, it's party time."

Brandon looked at his younger brother standing beside the door, soaking wet and wearing a black cowboy hat. He had Elizabeth's warm brown eyes and easy smile and it was clear that he had had too much to drink. Christian was only twenty but he looked older.

Christian turned his attention to Sarah. "You must be the new nurse." He examined her for a minute, then said, "You're too pretty to be a nurse." He stuck his hands in his pants pockets and laughed. "Did you ever meet my dad and Brandon's girlfriend?" he asked Sarah. "I hope you didn't. They are really weird."

"That's enough, Christian! You're drunk. Why are you driving?" Brandon asked angrily.

"Are you going to invite me in or what?" He completely ignored Brandon's questions. "I see. Are you asking me to leave?" He half turned and started to open the door.

"Christian!"

He closed the door and turned back to face Brandon. "Just kidding. I'm not going anywhere. Or maybe I will." He turned back to the door.

"Go get some dry clothes!" Brandon snapped. He went over to the window to see what car Christian was driving. The car was pink. What in the world was wrong with his brother? He looked at Christian and asked, "What's that thing you're driving?" Brandon laughed until tears were rolling down his cheeks.

"That's an insult," Christian said, walking to the window. "It's pink but it's not a Cadillac but it looks like one. And guess what? Every day I drive past the store just when Austin is going in. It makes him freak. I just love it. If I get out the car I'm sure he'll kill me." A puddle was starting to form on the wood floor where he was standing. He looked down at it and said, "I'll wipe it up. I really need to get out of these wet stuff. Oh Sarah, would you mind leaving the room. I want to take off my wet clothes. If it was Stacey, it would be okay to change in front of her. But you are a lady and that's why I'm asking you to leave."

"Shut up, Christian! Go get changed and after that get the mop."

"Okay." He sprinted down the corridor, leaving a trail of water.

Brandon could just picture the horrified expression on his dad's face when Christian drove by with that car. If only he had some of Christian's courage!

"The car lights are still on," Sarah said.

"Don't tell him anything. He'll push it down the road tomorrow."

Christian emerged from the corridor wearing Brandon's clothes and holding a mop. He started mopping the water from the floor. "When are you going to get rid of Stacey," he looked at Brandon. "She's no good for you. Stacey is Austin's clone. Somewhere into the experiment, something freaked out and the clone became a young female."

Brandon glared at him angrily. "Shut up and go to sleep!"

"How come you're not wearing a shirt?" Christian asked, looking from Brandon to Sarah.

"He was just getting ready for bed," Sarah said. Christian left the mop beside the door, announced that he was going to bed. He started to go up the stairs, stopped half way and came back down. He looked at Brandon and asked, "Why do you let Austin control your life? How can you live like that?" He leaned against the wall, his eyes never leaving Brandon's face. "Don't marry Stacey. I know what I'm saying and I know I had too many beers. You're too good, Brandon. Get up and be bad."

"Can we talk about this another time," Brandon asked. "And Austin does not control my life!" Christian had touched a very sensitive spot deep within

Brandon. It was so true, so many aspects of his life was controlled by his dad eversince he could remember.

"You're way too nice Brandon. Not because you were....."

"Shut up!" Brandon interupted his flow of words before he could say anything else. He didn't want Sarah to hear that.

"Christian, your brother is very tired. Why don't you finish this conversation tomorrow?" Sarah said gently.

"Thanks for letting me stay the night," Christian said and went upstairs.

Brandon was tired and Christian had said things that really upset him. He went to his room and Sarah joined him.

"Sarah, I hope that whatever was said here tonight will remain here," Brandon said coldly as she helped him into bed. He realized how much he sounded like Austin and hated it.

"Who do I look like? The town's gossip?" she asked angrily.

"Good-night, Sarah," he said, ignoring her angry question. It was better to end the conversation before they got into a fight. Brandon and Sarah had the gift of saying the wrong things to each other.

She spun around, switched off the light and left the room. He watched her until she closed her own bedroom door behind her. He was sorry about what he had said to her. It was not fair. When the emotional storm within him stopped raging, he still could not fall asleep. He had to take drastic measures to change his life and doing so would mean putting Austin and Stacey aside.

Brandon loved the comfortable life he had but did not share the same overwhelming love for money as Stacey. He wanted a family and a quiet life. Stacey wanted money, power and a glamorous life. The gap was too large, he could not meet her halfway.

He listened to the water running in Sarah's room, then saw the light go off. There was something a bit mysterious about her, something that he had never seen in anyone before and it attracted him.

Chapter 3

Over the next two weeks, there was a great change in Brandon's condition. He had taken Sarah's advice and started seeing a psychologist. His nightmares became less frequent and he started to regain some emotional control.

She stood on the patio, sipping coffee and enjoying the peace and quietness that comes with dawn. The morning fog was gently lifting off of Casco bay and in the far distance, she could barely see the dark stumps of tiny islands.

It was two weeks of happiness for Brandon and two weeks of struggle for Sarah. He was regaining control of his emotions and she was starting to lose control of hers. She constantly fought against her feelings for Brandon. She had made a deal with herself a long time ago and had managed to keep it, until now.

She went back inside, walked softly towards Brandon's room and peeked in.

"I'm awake," he called out and laughed softly.

"Good morning. Did you sleep well?" Her expression was serious and she tried not to show any emotion. She walked over to the bed, careful not to look at him.

"Why are you so serious?" he asked.

"Am I?" She pushed the wheel chair closer to the bed.

"Why do you answer a question with a question?" He swung his legs over the side of the bed, bit down on his lip and took a deep breath. "Damn it."

41

Sarah supported him as he made his way over to the chair and helped him to get dressed. Being this close to him, feeling his warm breath caressing the side of her neck, made her nervous. She dared not look up at Brandon, afraid what she may see in his eyes, and he, in hers. His warm hands closed over her arms as he eased himself back into the chair.

"Sarah, I have to take a shower. I can't manage that on my own. I need your help." He let go of her arms.

Sarah stopped moving. She felt like someone had just splashed icy water in her face. She didn't answer. She had assisted lots of patients to take their showers and it never bothered her. Why should it be any different with Brandon? It's not like she had never seen a naked man before. Since she had been there, Mark, a male nurse, came everyday to assist Brandon with his shower. Why couldn't he skip his shower one day?

"If it makes you uncomfortable, I'll just try on my own."

"I'm not uncomfortable. It's part of my job. After breakfast will be okay?" The tremor in her voice betrayed her emotions. Brandon wasn't just another patient. He was a good looking man whom she felt terribly attracted to and she had noticed that the feeling was mutual. She had to constantly remind herself to be careful. Brandon was awakening dangerous emotions in her. Emotions that she had pushed down and kept a firm grip on were suddenly surfacing and she could not do a thing about it. She was angry that she had such feelings for him. He was engaged to another woman and would be married in a few months. Was she falling in love with him?

Brandon belonged to another woman and he was in love with the other woman, she reminded herself. If she wanted to get hurt again, then Brandon was the perfect candidate.

She opened the cupboard and took out two cups, trying to ignore the restless drumming of her heart. How much help did Brandon actually need in the shower? She took the cup of coffee from his outstretched hand. "Christian is still sleeping, I guess." He made his way over to the window and looked outside. "The car is not there. We are alone. He must have sneaked out during the night." After breakfast, Sarah took out towels from the cupboard and placed the mat at the bottom of the bath tub. Brandon came in and closed the door behind him. Sarah's throat went dry and her hands were cold from nervousness.

Brandon took off his shirt, held on to a metal bar and slowly stood up. Sarah draped a large white towel around his waist and he started to slip off his pants. She helped him into the bath tub and just before he sat, she removed the towel.

They did not look at each other, they did not talk. Brandon sat down. There was just an uncomfortable silence that hung between them. Sarah was angry at herself for being so nervous and embarrased. How many times had she done this before and her patients had undressed in front of her. When she finally looked at him, she could tell he was trying hard not to smile.

"I can manage from here. When I'm ready to get out I'll call you," his said lightly.

She nodded and left. She knew that she could leave him alone for a while and there was no danger. There were bars on the side of the bath that he could use to support himself if he wanted to stand up. She went to her room, sat down and tried to block out the image of a naked Brandon. She knew that her attitude earlier was more immature than proffessional. She told herself that Brandon was no different from any other patient but part of her refused to be convinced.

The water stopped running and he called for her.

Walking into the bathroom,she smiled nervously at him. "I can see all went well." She picked up a towel and started drying his back. He grabbed the bar on the side of the bath and stood up.

"I'll help you out," she said gently, supporting him as he got out. Though it wasn't her intention, her eyes ran over his body. Luckily he hadn't noticed. She continued talking about anything that came to mind, her work, the weather, her friends.

Brandon didn't say a word, he just listened and smiled. She saw the smile, ignored it and started telling him about a film The thought crossed her mind that she might be sounding silly but at the moment she didn't care.

"Sarah, I prefer to get dressed in my room." He placed a towel on his lap and started out the door. "I'm sorry if you're embarassed but I need your help."

"I'm not at all embarassed. I do this kind of stuff quite often," she answered, following him into the room. He looked amused.

He took the navy blue shirt that she held out to him, started to put it on and suddenly stopped. His eyes widened as he stared past her at the door. Sarah pivoted around slowly, not knowing what to expect. She didn't hear anyone come in. She recognised the woman standing in the doorway. Stacey. Sarah thought that she looked like one of those women in Calvin Klein's advertisement. Her black hair hung in silken confusion and her grey eyes were made up to perfection. The short skirt hugged her long, shapely legs.

Stacey's cold eyes swept over Sarah then settled on Brandon, naked except for the towel on his lap.

"I didn't hear you come in," Brandon said to Stacey.

"I can see you're having fun and naked as well. Let me see," she said, placing a finger on her lips. "You call that naked fun. No, you call that fooling around with your dumb nurse!" She walked past Sarah and stood in front of Brandon. "I dont like what I'm seeing!"

Sarah started to walk out of the room. It would be better to leave them alone.

"Where are you going, miss? Your job isn't finished!" Stacey snapped at Sarah.

Stacey's choice of words and her tone of voice sent Sarah's mind reeling back into the past. Sarah spun around. Memories that she would rather forget stormed her mind. Their eyes clashed.

"I refuse to take orders from you!"

"So, let me see." She placed a well manicured hand on Brandon's bare shoulder. "You take orders from him, and what else? You were surely having fun with a naked stranger!"

Sarah's body trembled with anger. "How dare you!" Sarah's hands were balled into fists.

Stacey looked at her and mockingly and said, "I'm sure you're nothing but a cheap little bitch! Did you

45

buy your nursing licences, dear? With money or something else?"

"Shut up Stacey," he said, pushing her hand away. "What's wrong with you?"

"I'm sorry, Brand. I just couldn't see you naked in front of another woman." She ran a finger along his arm.

Sarah stormed out of the room.

"Are you crazy, Stacey? Why were you hurling insults at Sarah? What did she do to deserve the bitchy side of you?" His voice was flinty. He buttoned his shirt and struggled to put on his pants. "As long as she is here, you're going to treat her with respect!"

"I hate the woman! And don't tell me how to treat her!"

"Enough!" Brandon stopped her flow of words. Let's forget Sarah for a while and talk about you. If I remember clearly, you were supposed to stop by two weeks ago."

"My summer collection arrived at the boutique. I was loaded with work. I'm sorry, dear."

"Are you allergic to the phone or did you forget my number?" he asked coldly.

"You don't have to be so mean! For the past month I have been working like crazy!"

"What's going on? Having second thoughts?" He looked her in the eyes. "Are you afraid to be tied to a man in a wheelchair?"

"Brandon, I think that you are overreacting." She knelt down in front of him. "Nothing has changed," she whispered. "I'm not afraid of the chair and I'll never stop loving you."

"How stupid do you think I am?" he asked, fixing her with a cold stare.

She sprang to her feet. "You're being impossible," she shouted angrily.

Sarah stood on the patio, her arms folded tightly in front of her. A heavy weight filled her chest. Stacey had treated her like she was some horrible insect who shouldn't be there. She thought that such treatment had stayed in her past and would never come back. Sarah wondered if the past had a will of it's own and would always come back to haunt her. The chilly wind was starting to numb her body but she didn't want to go back in the house. Not now, she was still too full of rage. She couldn't afford to lose her job and the things she wanted to say to Stacey was a sure way to do it.

She turned around at the sound of the door opening. "Sarah, why don't you wear this." Brandon asked, holding out a coat. "I don't know where is yours, so I brought mine."

"I'm fine." Stacey was standing at the door, her face looked like it was sculpted from ice.

"You'll catch a cold. Please take it," he said softly as he made his way over to her.

She reluctantly took it and watched as Brandon went back to his fiancé. She slid on the coat, sprinted down the short flight of stairs and headed in the direction of the beach.

"Why did you give her your coat?" Stacey shouted as Brandon made his way into the house. She was stupid enough to go out without a coat. Why should you take one for her?"

Stacey looked at the fire place and back to Brandon. "Did you two spend a romantic evening in front of the fire?"

"So what if we did?" he sighed wearily. "The answer to your silly question is no."

The cell phone in Stacey's handbag rang insistently but she didn't answer. She continued to glare at Brandon. He picked up her handbag and started to open it. "Don't!"

"You never minded me answering your phone. Why the sudden change? Hiding something?"

"Your mind is playing tricks on you, Brandon. As long as that woman is here, I'm not coming back. Get rid of her!"

Why are you really here? Why do you act like Sarah is a threat to you? I know you, Stacey. Your behavior is just a cover for something that you don't want me to know."

"Okay, Mr. Know it all. I'm out of here." She grabbed her handbag and dashed out the door.

Sarah was sitting on a small bench at the far end of the lawn when she saw Stacey approaching. Sarah stood up and walked towards her. She wasn't afraid of Stacey.

"Pack up your bags and get the hell out of here!" Stacey shouted as she stopped just a few inches away from Sarah. "When I get back I don't want to see you here!"

"I already told you that I will not take orders from you. I haven't changed my mind." She calmly said. Why did Stacey hate her so much? She felt like a child again, being punished for something that wasn't her fault. Her pain changed to anger but her voice did not show it. "I'm not going anywhere, Stacey. Not until my contract is over."

She could see that Stacey was growing more and more furious by the second and Sarah actually enjoyed making her furious. In a strange way, it made Sarah feel stronger. Earlier Stacey had made her feel so small she had thought that she would just disappear.

"Get out!" Stacey's eyes were grey storm clouds.

Sarah stared at the other woman and her mind drifted back to another time. How many times had she been sent away from a friend's house because her dad was an alcoholic?

"Sorry to spoil your day. I'm not going anywhere," she said, surprised at the strength and determination in her voice.

"You piss me off."

Those words and Stacey's lady-like looks didn't match at all. "Exactly what I was hoping to do," Sarah answered calmly.

"You cheap bitch. Austin told me that you're one of those air-heads who is out to hook a rich guy. I believe him. Before you can hook a rich guy like Brandon, there are certain things you have to change." She circled Sarah. "Just look at your clothes. Sears liquidation. Eighty percent off. And where did you find your car, honey? In the dump?"

Sarah spun around and faced her. "I've worked damn hard for what I have and I'm proud of it. Why do you want me to leave?" She stuck her cold hands into her pockets.

"I just hate you. That's all," she answered swiftly.

Sarah looked at the satisfaction in Stacey's eyes and she felt something crumble within her. She had used up every bit of enery in her possession to stand up to this woman, but she was no match.

Her eyes filled up, she walked past Stacey and headed towards the house. A feeling of worthlessness swept over her. Why did Stacey hate her? The woman didn't even know her. She wiped her eyes before pushing open the front door.

Walking past Brandon, she headed for her room, feeling like she had fallen into a world that had suddenly gone mad. First, it was Austin who came after her for no reason at all and now Stacey. For a moment, she considered leaving.

There was a soft knock on the door and Brandon asked, "Are you okay?"

"I'm fine." Her voice sounded like a croak.

"No you're not. I'm sorry about what happened. I need to talk to you. Please."

"I'll be out in a few minutes. I know it's time for your exercise."

"I wasn't even thinking about that. I'm worried about you."

"Don't be." She didn't want his sympathy.

A few minutes later, she slipped off the coat that Brandon had lent her and went to join him in the living room.

Suddenly, there was a loud screech of tires and a noise of metal crashing against metal.

"Did…you hear it too?" Brandon asked. His face was white with fear.

"I did," she said firmly, realizing that the noise had pulled his mind back to the accident.

He let out a long, nervous breath, shook his head and asked, "What on earth was that?"

They both moved over to the window.

"No," Sarah said, pressing her hands against her mouth. The right side of her Toyota was badly dented and one of the headlights had fallen off. "Why did Stacey do that?"

"She has gone crazy!" He buried his face in his hands for a while, then looked up at Sarah and took her hands in his. "I will take care of the car. It's the first time I'm seeing this side of Stacey. I'm really sorry about all this."

The rocking chair beside the window creaked as she sat down. She had had more than enough for one day. What woman in her right mind would just crash her brand new Mercedes into an old worthless Toyota on purpose?

"I'll call the garage and have someone pick it up. I'll take care of the bill." He went to the phone.

"Why should you pay for her mistakes?" On second thoughs, she said. "I shouldn't have asked such a question." It was none of her business and she was sorry about her question.

"You're right. I should not pay for her mistakes, but I know Stacey. She would never pay for the repairs."

He dialled a number and spoke quietly into the phone. He asked someone to come get the car, gave his name and address, then hung up.

They sat in silence for a long while. Sarah could see that he was really embarassed. She wondered if he was being honest when he said that it was the first time he was seeing this side of Stacey. Probably just lying to cover up for her Sarah concluded and got to her feet.

51

She could hardly wait for the week-end. She would have two days away from this crazy job.

"Time for your exercise,"she said.

Brandon nodded, muttered something that she could not understand and started to get up. They walked around the living room, and along the corridor several times. When she told him that it was time to stop, he said that he wanted to continue. He winced with pain, but kept pushing himself. Finally Sarah insisted that he stop and he agreed with her.

Brandon pointed to the window and she turned to look out. Her car was being towed away. "They'll take care of it," he said, breathlessly. "Really, I don't understand why Stacey reacted the way she did." After a moment of silence, he said, "I don't want to see her for a very long time."

She was surprised by his statement. Stacey would be his wife in a few months and judging from the abundance of her photos around the house, Brandon seemed madly in love.

He looked at Sarah and hesistantly asked, "Would you like to go for dinner? A small quiet restaurant."

Sarah was skeptical. What if they ran into Austin or Stacey?

Brandon chewed on a fingernail. "I really need to get out for a while. And we have to eat anyway. If Stacey comes by, I don't want to be here. Please say yes," he said gently.

"Okay." The thought of going out for a while was enticing. "I don't know Freeport well, so you'll have to be my guide."

"Where are you from?"

"Scarborough."

She picked up his coat from the coffee table and went to hang it in the closet, hoping that Brandon would not ask further questions. Sarah didn't feel like talking to him about herself. She turned to face him, a stiff smile on her face. He looked at her keenly, as though trying to read her mind or facial expression "Christian's latest heartthrob lives in that area so he goes there often." He moved towards the fridge, took out two cans of Pepsi and offered one to Sarah.

Once Brandon was comfortably seated on the passenger side, Sarah climbed in the car. Leaning over, she reached under the seat, caught hold of the lever and moved the seat foward. She pulled out the driveway and they both half turned to look at each other at the same time. There was a hint of nervousness in his eyes and Sarah was quick to reassure him. "I promise not to drive too fast and to be really careful."

He nodded and smiled.

She made her way around the huge puddles that had formed from the melting snow. The snow banks had turned into tiny heaps that would be gone by the next day. When they arrived at the intersection of the main street, she asked, "Left or right?"

"Right. Two corners from here, there is a big antique store, you turn right again."

She nodded. In the distance, the top of the lighthouse came into view, barely a shadow against the darkening sky. The sidewalks were crowded with people obviously taking advantage of the warm spring evening.

"Sam's antique store," she mumbled and turned right. "Is that the restaurant you are talking about?" she asked, pointing to a lighted sign announcing lobster dinners.

"Yes." He straightened up in his seat and took off his seat belt when she brought the car to a stop.

Sarah instinctively looked over the parking lot before she helped Brandon out of the car. She certainly did not want to run into Stacey or Austin. Their cars were not there and she felt relieved.

She pulled open the heavy wooden door and followed Brandon into the cozy restaurant. He stopped to examine a large oak wine cabinet. "This is beautiful. If they want to sell it, I'll be first in line. Look at all the good wine in there, too."

"I don't know why people like wine. It tastes bad."

"Tell me you're joking."

They went to a vacant table beside a large window. Brandon moved aside the wooden chair and fitted his wheel chair perfectly in its place. With an outstretched arm, he pulled out the chair beside his. "Sorry I can't do it the way it should be done."

"It's perfect Brandon." She sat down. "Thank you."

"What would you like to eat," he asked, opening the well worn menu. "I'm hugry."

Running a finger along the list on the menu card, she said, "I'll have caesar salad."

"That's all?" He looked at her, one eyebrow raised. She nodded.

"You have to try the lobster. It's delicious. Want to try some wine? Maybe you'll discover why people like it. Try just a little bit."

"Okay."

A smiling, middle aged waiter stepped forward. He turned his attention first to Sarah, then to Brandon, scribbled their orders on a note pad and left.

"It's nice to be away from home. A welcome change. Especially after all that happened today."

She was tempted to tell him not to mention today's events again. She wanted to forget it. "It wasn't your fault so don't feel bad about anything."

The waiter arrived with a bottle of wine, filled their glasses and left.

"Don't drink it if you don't want to." He raised the glass to his lips.

As the evening wore on, Brandon's smile became more spontaneous. The sadness that she often saw in his eyes was gone. This was a different man and her attraction to him bordered on dangerous. He lit the candle on the table, his head bent.

Sarah moved aside her glass, making space for the waiter to put her plate. After a brief conversation, he left.

Over dinner, Brandon told her stories about his grandparents and his job at Austin's clothing store. "The part I love the most is preparing the catalogs. This year I did not do the spring catalog. Can't wait to go back to work." He turned his attention to the plate of lobster. "Want to try some?" He looked up at her and smiled. "It is delicious."

"No, thank you." She took a sip of wine. The layers of caution she had so carefully wrapped herself in was quickly falling off. She found herself chatting easily with Brandon, enjoying his company and the clear interest she read in his eyes.

Just knowing that the man sitting at the opposite side of the table was attracted to her, made Sarah's heart sing. It had been such a long time since she had let herself go this far and it felt damn good. She knew that it could have a short life span but for the moment she didn't care.

Mind and emotions warred. The man opposite her belonged to another woman, another world and she was conscious of that. The one thing she hungered for was love and in the past it had brought her only pain. Her eyes rested on his lips for a second and the memory of their brief kiss came to mind. If only it had lasted longer.

"Sarah, where are you," he whispered.

She laughed softly. "I tend to drift off into my own secret world at times."

"Is your secret world a happy place?" He dipped a piece of lobster in garlic butter.

"Mostly happy," she lied. She had no desire to tell him about her personal life. Whatever image he may have built of her seemed good and she wanted it to stay that way. She tore her gaze away from his face.

"Do you have a private little world where you lose yourself sometimes," she asked, curious to know more about him.

"Yes." His hand covered hers.

"Is it a happy place?"

Sadness lingered in his eyes briefly and she was sorry that she had asked such a question. "My salad is good," she remarked, hoping to change the subject.

"It is happy and sad, but I intend to do something about the sad part." His eyes lingered on her face tenderly.

She turned to look out the curtained window at the traffic on the narrow street. Emotions were overpowering her mind and will. Why did Brandon so effortlessly knock down her walls of defence? She turned to face him.

He took her hands in his and brushed them lightly with his lips. She knew that she should put a stop to it right now but she didn't. The warmth of his mouth tingled it's way up her arm.

"Why is love so important to the human heart? Why do we constantly search for it?" he asked, his eyes never leaving hers.

His question touched a sensitive chord in her. Was he desperately yearning to be loved too? Impossible. He was really good-looking and apparently wealthy. He shouldn't have problems finding love. She decided that she misunderstood him completely, after all he was getting married in a few months.

Sarah slid her hands out of his as the waiter approached with thick slices of chocolate cake. When the waiter left, Brandon reached for her hand again, softly caressing it. This has to stop, she told herself as she glanced out the window.

The trees trembled and she heard the first whisper of the wind. She did not like driving in storms and judging from the dark, swollen clouds, there was going to be one.

"We had better get going," she said, turning to look at the clock. It was ten-fifteen.

"Not yet," he pleaded.

Sarah's mind struggled to control her heart. She wanted to stay longer, wanted to see the tenderness in his eyes. She swallowed, her mouth suddenly dry. For the last seven years, she had been chasing away any man who seemed interested in her. Why was she encouraging Brandon?

"If you really want to leave, then we will," he said gently.

On their way home, the first raindrops began to fall. Brandon slid a CD into the player strains of saxophone music filled the car and the rain came down harder. Sarah kept her eyes on the road.

"Do you like saxophone?" He asked.

"I prefer Madonna," she answered, eyeing the windshield wiper dancing in front of her.

"You don't look like the Madonna type."

"Am I under a microscope?"

"Yes and I like what I see."

"What do you see? No, forget I asked that question." Her fingers clutched the steering wheel.

"I see someone who is scared." His voice was barely a whisper. "What are you afraid of?"

She let out a noisy breath. "I'm not afraid of anything."

"You don't strike me as Superwoman, either."

Fear wrapped icy fingers around her heart. Soon they would be alone. She would have to help him undress. Could she trust her emotions that had suddenly become a traitor? For seven years, she had kept a firm grip on them and now they were threatening to run free.

They rain was coming down furiously and by the time they got inside the house, they were soaking wet.

Sarah switched on the light and followed Brandon to his room. She dreaded having to help Brandon undress and get into bed. Their bodies were always so close, much too close. She made up her mind that no matter what, her emotions were not going to win.

Brandon switched on the bedside lamp and a soft glow spreaded throught the room. He started to pull off his T-shirt.

Sarah watched him. Her legs shook beneath her and she couldn't go towards him. Desire surged through her and she was momentarily confused at her feelings. Taking a deep breath, she covered the distance between them. Their eyes held. The desire in his eyes only made hers stronger. They were two consenting adults, who shared the same desire, alone on a stormy night. What was there to stop them?

In the minutes that followed, the air popped like fireworks, with tension. She helped him remove the rest of his clothing and slip into a dry underwear. She knelt down beside him and started to put on his pyjama.

Brandon reached out and caressed her lips with his fingertips. He slowly lowered his head until his lips brushed hers lightly. His hand slid up the back of her neck and pulled her closer. She caressed his bare chest and gave way to his probing tongue. He murmured something that she could not understand and his kiss became urgent. She let her head tilt backward as his mouth slowly caressed her throat.

It had been such a long time since she had felt anything this intensely. She felt herself being swept away by passion and willingly let herself be. Her entire being tuned itself into him.

"Sarah," he whispered against her ear.

She pulled away and got to her feet. What the hell was wrong with her? Looking at his surprised face, she tried to think of something to say. "Don't ever do that again! I'm your nurse and nothing more!" Her words sounded stupid to her own ears. She had been a willing participant in all this.

Brandon leaned back in his chair. "I got the impression that you liked it as much as I did." He stared at her angry face. "I'm sorry I kissed you." He moved closer to her.

She took a step backward. "Don't ever touch me again!"

"Sarah, you kissed me back. You touched me." He looked up at her in surprise.

She searched her mind, looking for something to contradict his statement. "You are imagining things Brandon." She instantly regretted her words. A look of confusion crossed his face. She knew that emotionally, he was fragile and she should have never said that to him. He had enough questions and uncertainty stalking his mind.

"What are you trying to do to me?" he asked.

Unable to look at the pain in his eyes, she turned away.

"Please help me over to the bed," he said.

She helped him over to the bed. He lay back and pulled the covers up.

"I'm sorry about what I told you. Your mind was not playing tricks on you. I really kissed you back." That was the toughest confession she had ever made in her life.

"Good-night," he said.

"Have a good night." She turned and left the room.

Chapter 4

Brandon felt strength surging through his veins. He was ready to take the reins of control that Austin had never allowed him to hold. Last night, he had spent a long time evaluating his life and he had every intention of changing it. Austin played a mixed role in Brandon's life, Austin the dominator and Austin the father. It was Austin who made all the decisions whether or not Brandon liked it. Brandon obeyed, he felt like he owed Austin his life. During his childhood, Austin had never allowed him to forget where he had come from. He had only stopped mentioning certain heart wrenching things once Christian was old enough to understand. Fortunately, Elizabeth was always waiting with comforting arms, always had the right words to make him feel better. Bitter anger bordering on hatred rose within him towards a woman who he called, 'the faceless woman'. He muttered a curse and closed his eyes. He hated her, and all women who gave their children up for adoption.

Things could have been worse. What if Austin and Elizabeth had not walked into his life? He shuddered at the thought.

Brandon knew that his decisions would lead to a nasty fight with his dad, but that didn't bother him. Not this morning.

Stacey was the second on his list. He had decided to call off the wedding. Over the last year, she had changed too much, all she ever talked about was money. It had become an obsession and he wanted no part of it. If her recent actions were anything to judge by, she would be happy about his decision. It certainly looked like she was searching for a way out.

"You look well rested," Sarah said, walking into the room.

With a jolting movement, he turned to look at her. A flash of embarassment flitted across his face then, he smiled slowly. "I didn't hear you come in." He sat up in bed.

She turned away and walked over to the closet, her face serious. "What are you wearing today? You have an appointment for physiotherapy at ten-thirty."

"Grey pants, blue shirt." What was going on with Sarah, he wondered, watching her searching through the closet. She looked rather angry.

He carefully climbed out of bed. His legs were shaky but the wheelchair wasn't far away. He took a few unsteady steps, grabbed onto the chair and sat down. "Today is definitely a great day. I did it alone." Sharp pains spreaded through his lower back and down his legs but it was nothing compared to the satisfaction he felt. He had gone from the bed to his chair - alone.

Sarah turned around and started towards him. "Brandon! Don't do that again! If you wanted to try on your own, you should have at least waited until I was beside you."

Brandon took the shirt she held out to him. "I wanted to try on my own," he said. "By the way, since when do I need your permission to do things?" He grinned at the frustrated look on her face. "Okay. I promise to follow the rules."

He took the pants from her, leaned foward and started to put it on. The pain was not too bad, he could endure it. He desperately wanted his independance. There was only one problem, it would mean that Sarah would leave and he didn't want that. His feelings for her ran pretty deep. He finished tying his shoe laces, straightened up in his chair and looked at the woman standing in front of him. He had to find a way to keep her.

Over coffee, he looked at Sarah out of the corner of his eyes, she looked nervous. She was probably thinking about their kiss last night, he thought. She had kissed him back just as passionately. Why did she tell him that his mind was playing tricks on him? He sliced a bagel in two and popped it into the toaster.

"Brandon, I'm sorry about what I said to you last night. It was cruel. Your sense of judgement is very good." She looked at the toaster while she spoke.

Her honesty shot through him like a bolt of lightening. It must have taken a lot of courage to admit that she had kissed him back. He pulled the bagel from the toaster and started spreading cream cheese on it.

"I can understand if you are angry with me. You have the right to be. I'm a nurse and I know that you are emotionally fragile right now. I should have never said those words. He offered her the bagel and she shook her head.

"You had the courage to tell me that my mind was not playing tricks on me. I admire that. Sarah, I'm not emotionally fragile. Please don't say that to me again. I said some mean stuff to you when you first got here. So, we're even. I was just wondering, why did you say that? What are you afraid of?" He realised instantly that the last question was all wrong but it was too late.

63

Her eyes grew hard with anger, her fingers clamped around the cup she was holding. "What am I afraid of?" she said heatedly. "What were you hoping for? That I'd jump into bed with you? I'm not a bed-hopper! I lost control. That happens to people. I'm sure you will agree with that. And just in case you forgot, you're engaged to another woman!"

"I don't think that you're a bed-hopper," he said, embarassment splashed across his face. "I had no right to ask you what you're afraid of. I'm sorry and yes I'm engaged to another woman. Promise, I'm never going to touch you again." He felt guilty for the pain he saw in her eyes. He'd hurt her with his dumb question and there wasn't a thing he could do to change it. "I'm truly sorry about that question."

She drew in a deep breath and stood up. "We have to leave soon."

He nodded, surprised that such anger could come from such a tender person.

Half an hour later, Sarah pulled out the driveway.

"Have you seen the film, Titanic?" he asked. "Everyone is going nuts about it." He wanted to see her smile again, to see the pain disappear from her beautiful eyes.

"I saw it. Great film. Did you see it?"

"I didn't have time. Too busy." He laughed, settled back in his seat and stared out the window. It seemed like the trees had turned green overnight.

"I can go with you if you would like."

"Is it, well, kind of girl stuff?" He glanced over at her.

"Let me see. The film is divided into two parts. Love story for girls and special effects for boys. You'll love it." She chuckled softly.

"Nice answer. I'll give you an 'a' plus."

Someone was furiously honking their car horn. Brandon half turned and looked behind him. The bright flash of pink told him it was Christian. "It's my little crazy brother," he said.

Christian changed lanes and drove alongside them. Brandon rolled down the car window. "Why don't you come by later? You're becoming a stranger."

"Going to Scarborough to see my girlfriend. Maybe tomorrow. Hi Sarah."

Sarah waved at him. When they arrived at the stop lights, Christian changed directions.

"I like his car," she said, changing lanes.

"Are you joking?"

"No. I like Christian, too. He's a nice kid. Something about him reminds me of my brother, Timothy."

"Do you have lots of brothers and sisters?"

"No. Just Tim and me," she said, a tender smile on her face.

Sarah followed Brandon into the hospital as the wide electric doors swung open. They went down the white wall corridor and turned into a small room. He hated the smell of antiseptics that lingered in the air. Brandon went over to the receptionist and after a few minutes he came to join Sarah in the waiting room. "Why don't you go out for a drive instead of waiting around in this place with strange smells?"

"I work in places with strange smells. Remember?" She picked up a magazine.

"Good Housekeeping," he murmured. "Do they have recipe in that book?" he teased. He felt happy, free, like barriers had suddenly fallen away.

"My food?"she asked.

He tried not to smile but couldn't help it. "Yes." He picked up a National Geographic and they both fell silent.

Brandon glanced around the room, the chairs lined along the walls were half empty. Some of the people spoke in whispers that still somehow managed to echo across the room.

A young girl, maybe ten years old, wheeled her chair into the room, followed by a woman. The child's eyes swept over the room and settled on Brandon. They were the only ones in wheelchairs. She moved her chair close to his.

Brandon looked up and met a pair of curious blue eyes and pouting, pink lips.

"Mister, you have a strange watch," she said.

"Lisa, don't bother anyone." A tall, well dressed woman said and turned to Brandon. "My daughter talks all the time."

That name and those blue eyes flung him back into the past, to another world and another Lisa. He used to call her his sister. She was so pretty, but often very sick. He wondered where she was now or if she was still alive. Anger rose to his throat.

He smiled at the child who seemed to be waiting for some kind of answer. "My watch. I almost forgot. What's so strange about it?"

"There are strange drawings on it," she said, leaning closer. "The roman stuff."

"Roman numerals. It's a boring watch. Not like yours. Let me see." He leaned foward to look at her watch. "I bet your watch beeps, lights up in the dark and stuff like that. I'd like to have one of those." He winked at her.

"Yeah? Why didn't you buy one like mine?"

"Bad choice. Want to exchange watches?"

"No way! Mine is nicer." She rubbed her small hands together.

"Why are you in a wheelchair?" she asked, looking him in the eyes.

"I had a car accident. You?"

"Got hit by a car, last summer. I walk a bit but it hurts."

"I can walk a bit, too. I bet by the end of the year we will be able to run."

She pouted her pink lips and shook her head. "It will take a long, long time."

Brandon desperately wanted to tell her something to make it easier for her, something to encourage her, but there were no words. A long time ago, with another Lisa, he always seemed to have something encouraging to say. A thought suddenly popped into his mind. "The trick is to keep yourself busy, that way you don't think about your problem all the time. Play with your barbie, stuff like that," he said, pleased with himself.

"I don't play with barbies. I'm ten years old!"

"Oops. Sorry."

A nurse called out to Brandon. He waved good-bye to Lisa and glanced at Sarah. She was looking at Lisa, her eyes wide, and in their depths, he saw something disturbing. Torment. She was not aware that he was looking at her, she just stared at the child.

He went to the small room for his exercises. Jason, his physiotherapist, greeted him with a smile. "How is it going, Brandon?"

"Much better. I can't wait to go jogging." He pushed himself up with his arms and moved to the small black bench as Jason started pulling electrodes from a box.

"It's going to be cold," he said, smearing a transparent gel on the electrodes.

"When are you going to stop telling me that?" he joked.

"When your treatment is over." He stuck the small electrodes to Brandon's lower back.

"How many volts today?"

"How many do you want? One or two hundred?" he teased.

"Maybe four." He felt the first tiny stream of warmth creeping through his back.

Jason opened a brown folder and started a familiar series of questions that Brandon knew by heart. Brandon answered and Jason scribbled hurriedly. He finally closed the folder, took off his glasses and asked, "Are you trying to walk on your own?"

"I walked quite a bit this week. My legs are getting stronger."

"Cooperating with your nurse?" Jason unfolded a metal walker.

"Yes. She is really nice." His cold stare slid to the walker then to Jason. "I hope that thing is not for me." He eyed the walker with contempt.

"You'll need one like this. It's not just for senior citizens. Use it to go over to the bed." He moved the walker closer to Brandon then started to remove the electrodes.

Brandon stood up and moved pass the walker without touching it. Once Brandon was lying down, Jason started the usual motion exercises. Brandon was quiet, his mind on the piece of metal not far from the bed. There was no way he was going to use that. He just wanted to kick it through the open door.

"You have to let go of the chair soon," Jason said. "And stop hanging on to your nurse. Use the walker. I know it's much more interesting to hold on to the nurse for support." Jason chuckled. He helped Brandon up and over to his chair. "You'll need a bed handle, as well." Jason plucked a curved piece of metal with nuts and bolts from a box. "This will be adjusted to your bed, so you'll be able to get out alone. You can get a very good walker and bed handle at Home Health Care." He scribbled something on a paper and gave it to Brandon.

"When I get out of this chair, I'll walk on my own. I don't mind using the bedhandle but I'm not going to use that piece of thing over there." He said coldly, pointing to the walker.

"Up to you." Jason answered impatiently.

"Do you think that I will really be able to walk again? You know, without stuff to help me?" he asked hesistantly. Brandon was afraid of the answer. What if he ended up having to use a cane or something else to help him get around? He just wanted to walk again, on his own, without the help of anything or anyone.

"Yes you will."

"Thanks Jason." He wheeled himself out of the room, contemplating whether or not to give the prescription to Sarah. He stopped, stuck it in his pants pocket and went to join her. The thought of Sarah seeing him with a walker made him feel embarassed.

On their way home, she half turned, glanced at him briefly, "Are you tired?"

"Just a bit." He rolled down the car window. "It's like an oven in here. But it's a good sign. Summer is comming. Or, maybe it's not such a good sign." He stared out the window. He'd have to talk to Stacey very soon and ask the Printery not to print the wedding invitations. Icy fingers of fear clawed at his heart, and he could picture Austin's angry face. His dad would certainly fight back with every weapon he owned. Brandon pushed those thoughts out of his mind. He didn't want to deal with that right now. Why don't we stop and get some lobster rolls?" The delightful smell of Sam's restaurant made his mouth water.

"Sounds good and smells good." Sarah pulled into the small parking lot, filled mostly with motorbikes. She grabbed her purse, sprang out the car. "My turn to buy lunch."

Brandon watched her dash up the small flight of stairs and into the restaurant. His attraction to her was becoming stronger, and he wanted to tell her the way he felt. How could he? He was engaged to another woman?

He watched Sarah walking towards him, smiling. There was so much he wanted to ask her but dared not. Earlier, when she had looked at Lisa, there was torment in her eyes. Why? Her personal life seemed to be a secret and there were times when he could see that her heart was swollen with pain, especially after the phone calls to her family.

"I'm hungry," she said climbing in beside him.

"Sarah" His throat felt dry. He wanted to tell her that he had fallen in love with her. He swallowed. The words were in his mind but he just couldn't say them. Was it wise to do so? He hardly knew this woman.

She looked at him, a coldness crept into her eyes, as though sensing something she did not like. "What is it, Brandon?"

"You are doing some strange things to my heart. When you look at me, I feel like I'm being drawn into a strange, sweet world. A place I don't want to come back from." His words sounded silly to his own ears, but he meant it. She was doing things to him that no other woman had ever done. Not even Stacey.

Her eyes widened, she blinked several times in the space of a heartbeat, then turned away.

"Sarah."

She started the engine and pulled out the parking lot without even looking at him.

He had made her angry. She was like a stone wall, silent, cold and hard. He should have taken the cue. She was his nurse and nothing more, but why did she kiss him back? Her silence was unbearable. He wished that she would say something. She remained a piece of ice. The silence was thick, uncomfortable.

"I'm sorry if I have upset you. I didn't mean to. I know that I'm engaged but in my heart it's over with Stacey. Maybe there is someone in your life. Someone you love." He felt a twinge of disappointment.

He looked at her. She said nothing.

71

"Sarah, please say something." He closed his eyes and ran his fingers through his hair.

"I'm your nurse! Keep that in mind! There will never be anything between us. If you're lonley, go see Stacey or some other woman! Is this your way of trying to get me into your bed? Sorry pal. This isn't going to work!"

Brandon felt insulted. He wasn't the kind of man who jumped from one woman to another. "I don't go around taking advantage of women."

"I don't care what you do with your life. It's none of my business. Back off!"

Brandon half turned and looked at her. He had seen her angry when he had kissed her, but she'd never spoken to him that way. He ran his fingers through his hair.

Sarah parked the car on a quiet street corner and turned to face Brandon. Her eyes were shining with tears. "I'm sorry about the way I spoke to you. I believe that you are a nice, decent person, but there will never be anything between us."

"Why all the bitterness, Sarah?"

"My private life is my business!"

Brandon nodded and remained silent. He had caused enough waves in perfectly still waters. When they pulled into the driveway, Sarah noticed that the garage had brought back her car. She helped Brandon from the car to his wheelchair and went to examined her car.

"Why did they repair the rust spots?"

"It's a little gift of appreciation. Thank you for putting up with me." He smiled up at her.

"I can't accept that. I'll pay for it."

"No you will not. I'll stay out for a bit. I need to be alone for a while." He pushed his chair forward and headed toward the back of the lawn.

"Please phone the garage and let me know the price for fixing up the rust spots," she said.

"No Sarah," he answered firmly.

"Then I'll do it myself," she called out.

He was suddenly very nervous about his decisions. He'd thought about ways to change his life but not the consequences that would certainly follow. He had to talk to someone. The fear and uncertainity of standing up to Austin was slowly consuming him and doubts began to worm their way into his mind.

He didn't want to go to Elizabeth. She was a kind, loving mother, but she wanted the family to stay together, to live in harmony. Christian had already walked out. She would certainly advice Brandon not to go against Austin . Brandon knew that Austin was like garden weeds, give him a little space and soon he will be everywhere.

Brandon hadn't given much thought to Elizabeth. How was she going to handle all these changes? He didn't want to hurt her, but it was inevitable. Elizabeth didn't deserve this and he felt guilty for the pain that he would cause her.

Out of the corner of his eyes he saw Sarah sitting on the steps. Her reaction hung heavily upon his heart. What did he expect? He was still engaged to Stacey. Once he called off his wedding, would Sarah have a change of heart?

Sarah joined him under the elm tree.

"Are you okay?"she asked.

"Yes."

73

"I'll be inside."

"Do you mind staying out with me for a while?"

"I don't mind."

She walked beside him. "It's a nice day."

"Yes. Too bad I can't go down to the beach. It feels so good to just sit there and stare out at the bay. It helps me to forget and that's exactly what I want to do right now."

"I know what you mean."

He wanted to take her hands in his, to hold her close and to taste her lips. He reminded himself that he'd promised never to touch her again. They looked at each other. Her eyes held a guarded look, like a sentinel on the watch for intruders.

He leaned foward and picked up small branches lying on the lawn from last night's storm.

"Let me help you with that." Sarah took the branches from him.

"Just dump it behind the apple trees over there."

He watched as Sarah flung the branches behind the tree. He liked her a lot. She had helped him to understand a lot about his emotional problems, she had spent hours talking to him, trying to make him feel better.

Sarah held open the heavy oak door for Brandon, he made his way past her to look out the window. He sat there for a long time, trying to decide if it was wise to ask Sarah's advice. Talking to her about the accident was quite normal. Involving her in his personal problems was another thing but he really needed to get it out. It was so unbearable. He muttered a low curse, frustrated at himself for feeling like a weakling. He used to be so strong.

Brandon spent most of the afternoon on the computer, checking classified ads. He had to find another job. Austin was certainly going to fire him. He glanced at Sarah who was sitting on the couch, completely absorbed in a book. For the entire afternoon, they had hardly spoken to each other, except during his exercise.

"Nice work," she said, breaking the silence.

"What?" he asked, turning to face her.

"I was just saying that your work is really good." She held up a catalog.

He went to the kitchen, filled the kettle and plugged it. "Coffee?"

"Sounds good." She joined him in the kitchen. "Is everything okay? You don't look too well." She said gently. "Did you have bad news at the hospital?"

"I had good news, except for the walker Jason wants me to use."

"There's absolutely nothing wrong with using a walker. You're getting better."

"There's some other things."

"Do you want to talk about it."

"It's some pretty serious things. I'm not sure you want to hear it."

A quick flicker of nervousness crossed her face. "If something is bothering you so much, I'm more than willing to listen."

"I'm going to call off my wedding."

"When two people are in love they can always work things out."

"I don't love her anymore." Brandon saw so much in Sarah's eyes, disappointment, fear, then something

75

so cold, it made him shiver. He unplugged the kettle and poured hot water into two cups.

"Give it some more thought."

He sipped his steaming cup of coffee. "I've made up my mind."

"You're the only one who can make that decision."

"I don't want to hurt Stacey. I've known her all my life. She's the daughter of Conrad, my father's business partner. Austin expects me to marry Stacey."

"You have the right to make your own decisions."

Sarah fell silent, toyed with the rings on her fingers. "Why don't you invite her over this week-end and have a talk. I will not be here and you two will have the place all to yourself. She probably does not want to come because I'm here. If she really wants me to leave, I will. Maybe it will make things better for you two. If she's jealous then my being here does not help." Her eyes roamed the room, never settling on Brandon.

"I think that she's using you as an excuse." He rubbed the back of his neck, it was stiff with tension. "If I call off the wedding, I'll be in really big trouble with Austin. If Stacey and I get married, the company stays in the family. If I don't, Conrad can do whatever he wants with his half."

"I think that you should put your hapiness first. You're a grown man and you have the right to make your own decisions."

"Not when your father is a dictator! And, well…there is something else."

"What does he say about Christian?"

"He can't control Christian. I agree with my brother's actions. The situation with Christian and I is not the same." It's strange, after all these years, he still felt so different. It was like he didn't belong with the Chases' family. There was always an invisible barrier that seperated him from them. He wondered if he would ever be completely free of his past. Impossible, he thought, the past was part of his life and he just had to accept it.

"You look so sad. If calling off the wedding is doing that to you, then you should reconsider things."

"It's not that. Maybe one day I'll tell you. It's a long story."

"I'm going home for the week-end. Is someone going to stay with you during that time. I don't think that you should be alone."

He wanted to ask her to stay, he liked her company but it was her days off. "My mom's housekeeper will come by . Big plans for the weekend?"

"No. I'll go out with my friends Saturday night. Nothing special."

"You must be longing to see you boyfriend." She had made several calls during the week but never said any thing about it and she had always used the study.

"You want know if I have a boyfriend, right? No, I don't. I don't have the time to spare."

Brandon was happy to hear that she was single. He smiled at her. "You don't have the time. Maybe you just didn't meet the right guy as yet. When that happens, I don't think that you'll be able to escape."

"I don't think that such a man exists or will ever exist," she said, a hint of anger in her voice.

She got up, went to the kitchen sink and rinsed her cup. He could tell she wasn't as tough as she pretended to be. The kiss they had shared was proof.

Brandon half smiled and went over to the fireplace. He started a fire and Sarah joined him. She sat on the rug beside his chair. "Why don't you call up a friend on the week-end and go out a bit. It will be good for you," she urged him.

He was happy to see her smile again and he wanted it to stay that way. No more questions he told himself and no more confessions of love. She looked even more beautiful in the soft glow of the fire.

"I have other things to do." He threw another log in the fire. "I must talk to Stacey tomorrow. I have to tell her it's over. I'm sure she'll go running to dad and then he'll come charging over here like a raging bull."

"I'll call you tomorrow night to see how you're doing."

"I'll be waiting for your call."

She just sat there hugging her knees and smiling up at him. Did she even realize what she was doing to him? It took every ounce of courage that he possessed not to touch her. He'd be contented just holding her hands. Unconsciously, he brushed a strand of hair away from her face. She took his hand and gently caressed it with her lips. Brandon felt like his heart was going to explode. She ran her hands up his arms.

He looked at her, stunned. Was this the same woman who had just told him that she had no place in her life for a man? He felt his body trembling with emotions gone crazy. He leaned sideways and she moved closer. Their lips touched lightly at first and grew into a deep, passionate kiss. His mouth slid to her throat and a soft moan escaped her lips. His mouth captured hers again in a hungry kiss.

Damn the chair, he thought. He couldn't get her any closer. She slid around in front of him, pressing her body closer.

"Sarah," he murmured against her lips.

"We have to stop," she said, moving away. She buried her face in her hands. "No, Brandon. It's crazy. There could never be anything between us."

"Why Sarah?"

Chapter 5

The wet, grey road unfolded like a never ending carpet in front of her. The picture of lonliness stamped on Brandon's face when she had said good-bye, lodged itself in her mind, causing a sense of sadness. Why did she care this much for a stranger? Why did she feel that twinge of pain when she had left him?

She didn't want anything or anyone disrupting her carefully mapped out life. For years she had stuck to her plans. Now she had a real threat to her well thought out life. She had tried to stifle her feelings for Brandon, to ignore them, but they were now unleashed, wild and powerful. Last night, she had hoped that he would touch her, kiss her. When he'd brushed away the strand of hair, she could no longer control her emotions. She just had to kiss him, to feel his body close to hers. Where was the Sarah she had worked so hard to create? Why did she have to fall in love with him? The one thing that she didn't want.

Uneasy thoughts wormed their way into her mind. Why did Brandon show such feelings for her? Was it because he was lonley or were his feelings real?

He didn't strike her as a liar. He seemed so sincere, so caring. He did many small things that made her feel special.

Familiar houses floated into sight. She parked her car in front of the small brick house, climbed out and sprinted up the short flight of stairs. She fumbled in her oversize handbag, found her keys and let herself in.

The house was quiet and she hoped that her dad, Edward, was not around. She tip-toed up the steps to the second floor and peeked into her parents room. Edward was sprawled across the bed, sound asleep. For a few minutes, she watched him in silence. He was more like a stranger than a father. A half bottle of vodka, and a few beer bottles stood on the bedside table and several ashtrays were scattered around the room.

How many years had she spent longing, hoping, that he'd stop drinking and be a real father to her? A hope that would never materialize. A father was one gift that she was never going to have. She turned around and went back down the stairs. Why did her mom, Anna, stay with him?

She wondered where was her mom and Tim. Maybe Anna was working. Sometimes she worked week-ends because she didn't want to be around her drunken husband.

Sarah started clearing away dishes from the countertop. It felt good to be home, even if her family was not perfect. At least, here, the world she had built for herself did not stand threatened.

The door creaked open and Anna walked in, her arms loaded with grocery bags. Sarah hurried over to her, took a few bags and fetched them over to the kitchen.

Anna looked tired but she was still an attractive woman, an older version of Sarah.

"Worked again today, mom?" She dropped the bags on the counter.

"Yes. How is your new job?" Anna pushed aside items in the cupboard to make space for the bag of pasta in her hand.

"Everything is going well. Brandon is very nice. Where is Tim?"

"He left early this morning. I don't know where he went. I finally took your advice. Tonight I'm going to the restaurant with Vicky and Jane and we're going to play bridge after."

"Good for you, mom. You should have started that a long time ago." She planted a quick kiss on her mother's cheek. "I hope you'll do that at least once a week. It's going to do you well. Why sit around here and watch dad have all the fun?"

"And you Sarah? When are you going to stop hiding?" There was sadness in the depths of her eyes and in her voice.

"Mom, I don't want to talk about that. I'm happy with my life."

Heavy footfalls brought Sarah's gaze to the stairs. Edward came down, dressed in his usual housecoat. It was probably twenty years old by now, Sarah guessed. Edward and Sarah looked at each other. She didn't know what to say to her father and that hurt her.

"Look who's home," he sang, walking towards the kitchen.

"Want a coffee, dad?" Sarah asked.

"Not a straight coffee?" His eyes seemed to be mocking her. "Add some whiskey to it, honey. How is that man patient of yours?" He broke out in a fit of laughter.

Sarah set down the cup of coffee in front of him, ignoring his question. Why did he have to hurt her? Did he even realize how much he made her suffer?

"Pass me the vodka, Sarah! Now!"

"Get it yourself!" she screamed at him. No matter how hard she tried to be nice to him, it just didn't work.

"Edward, stop it," Anna said.

He picked up the cup and fixed Sarah with cold eyes. "Hope you not messing around with that man patient of yours. Remember what happened last time you messed around with a man? You gained forty pounds of belly!"

Sarah felt hurt, insulted and very angry. Why did he always remind her of her painful mistake? If he had been a father to her, maybe she would have never made such a mistake. She wanted to tell him that she was just looking for love, the love she never had at home.

"Don't start picking on her! You always do that! Why?"

He turned to Anna. "Make me some breakfast woman! Why do you always take sides with her? Warn her about the man she's babysitting."

"Whatever I do is my business! You know something, dad? I'm intelligent enough to learn from my mistakes. Do you learn from yours? No. Will you ever learn from yours?"

"With a track record like yours, I would shut up!" He slammed his fist into the wall and sprang to his feet. He took a step toward Sarah and she backed away.

Anna grabbed Edward's arm. "Sit!"

Edward looked from Sarah to Anna, his eyes bright with fury. "This is my home and she had better show me some respect. Don't talk to me like I'm a dog."

"You should start showing her some respect," Anna said firmly.

Sarah opened the door and left. The chilly wind stretched it's cold fingers deep into her shirt but she continued walking. A deep void settled in her chest. She loved her father. Why couldn't he love her back? Why did he constantly remind her of her mistakes?"

With her head bent, she continued along the sidewalk, hoping that she wouldn't see familiar faces. What she needed right now was a quiet place to cry her heart out. As she came closer to Mary's café, she caught sight of Tim's car parked in front.

Tim was sitting beside a window and motioned to her to join him. She walked into the quiet café and took a seat beside him. He looked so much happier these days and he had gained a bit of weight.

"Hi sis." He leaned over and kissed her on the cheek. "Had a fight with dad?"

"Yeah. I can't handle him anymore, Tim. If I rent an apartment, then I'll have to put off my studies for another year. Besides, I don't want mom to be alone with that grouch."

"Mom can handle him." He ordered coffee for Sarah. "Tell me about your new job." He studied her carefully, as though trying to find out if something about her had changed.

She filled him in on the details, hiding nothing, except her feelings for Brandon.

"They sound like a bunch of crazy people. You should quit that job. Get something else.

You can always start your psychology course a year later."

"I can take care of myself, Tim. You worry too much." She looked at Tim's anxious face. There was a time when she didn't know how to stand up for herself, and the neighborhood kids had tortured her with insults. Luckily, Tim had been there for her. He had assumed the responsibilities that Austin never did. Tim was her brother, father and best friend. Anna was always working, it was her way to escape her drunken husband. She was so drained, emotionally and physically, she had nothing to give to her children.

"I can't help worrying. You never kow what could happen over there."

"Don't be worried. Where is Allana?"

"In Boston with her parents."

"Do you miss her?"

"Of course I do."

Sarah listened to Tim talking on and on about Allana and their plans for the future. She was very happy for Tim.

Tim grinned. "I have news for you. We're planning to get married next year."

"Wow. I think I'm going to faint." She looked up at him, "What am I going to wear to the wedding?"

"You have one year to find a dress." They looked at each other and laughed.

"And you Sarah? Still want to remain a spinster?"

"I have my life all planned out. I want to keep it that way and yes I want to remain a spinster." Memories of the kiss she shared with Brandon flashed across her mind. She half turned, stared out the window, not daring to look Tim in the eyes.

"You have a secret. I can see it."

She swung her head to face him. "I have no secrets."

"Yes you do." He stood up. "Feel like sharing it?" For a moment, he looked worried

"Spit it out, Sarah," Tim said as the walked out the café.

"There's nothing to spit out. Your mind is working overtime."

She longed to talk to him about Brandon, to tell him that her feelings for her patient scared her, threatened her and that she was falling in love. If she wanted good advice, Tim was the person to talk to. Sarah looked at her watch, she wasn't going to bother Tim with her problems. She would do everything in her power not to become involved with Brandon.

"By the way, did mom tell you she's going out with her friends tonight? I wonder if she has a boyfriend." He turned to Sarah with a mischevious grin on his thin face.

They stopped, looked at each other and laughed.

"You're bad Tim. I don't think mom has a boyfriend."

"Before she goes out, get out your war paint kit and paint her up a bit."

She slapped him on the back playfully. "It's not war paint. You're being nasty.

By the time they got home, Anna had already prepared lunch and Edward was finishing up his bottle of Vodka. He did not join them at the table. Sarah looked at Edward out of the corner of her eyes as she sat down. Over the last year, her father had been fired from so many jobs. She was certain that every employer in Scarborough knew him.

"No one can make a meat loaf like you, mom," Tim said, eating another piece.

"Eat. You need to put some flesh on those bones. When I look at you I see only arms and legs." Anna looked at him with motherly concern.

"We're lucky Sarah didn't make us her famous chicken." Tim joked.

"There's nothing wrong with my chicken. I made it at work. Brandon chewed, swallowed and politely asked me not to make it again." Sarah laughed until her cheeks were hurting.

"You didn't," Anna said in disbelief.

"I think it's good."

"Anna," Edward called out. "There's something you don't know." He got up and walked over to them, placed his hands on the table and leaned toward Sarah.

"What is it Edward?" Anna asked, frustration clouding her eyes.

"Your daughter only knows how to jump in the sack with a man!" He looked down at Sarah and laughed. "That's what you do best, isn't it?"

She drew back, the cruelty of his words slammed into her like a fist. Why did he constantly remind her of her mistakes? Why couldn't he forgive her? Why couldn't he see all the efforts and sacrifices she had made?

"Edward! Stop that right now!" Anna grabbed his arm and led him to the door. "Go for a walk."

He glared at her, yanked his arm away and bellowed, "Are you trying to throw me out of my own house?" He moved closer, looked down at her and laughed. "Try again."

"Dad, why are you so cruel to Sarah? Everybody makes mistakes. I made a lot. I took drugs, ended up in prison but you never say anything about it. Why are you doing this to her?" Tim's voice shook.

"Why? I'll tell you why. I didn't want another child! She's not wanted! Guess what? The unwanted child wanted to bring her unwanted child into this home!"

"Shut up!" Sarah screamed. Pain conquered the anger that was bubbling within her. She felt crushed. Was she really an unwanted child? That would explain Edward's cruelty.

"That's a nasty lie!" Anna yelled. "You wanted another child as badly as I did!" She held the door open, "Go for a walk, Edward!"

Sarah cried. She didn't try to be strong nor to stop the tears. Edward had just ripped her soul into tiny pieces. She was barely aware of Tim's comforting arms around her. Was her father serious or just being cruel?

"He does not mean it. He's drunk," Tim whispered.

Edward stepped out the door, swearing as loud as his lungs would allow him.

"It's not true, dear. He is being cruel. He was crazy about you. He talked about you all the time." Anna said

The word, 'was', stuck in her mind. It was all in the past. Now, her father hated her and there were no words to ease her pain.

"Please, mom. I need to know the truth. Am I an unwanted child?" Their eyes held.

"He's lying, Sarah. I swear to you. It's not your dad talking, it's the alcohol. I will tell my friends I can't make it tonight and we'll go somewhere together."

"No. I want you to go out with your friends. I'll go down by the lake with Tim and the old gang."

Edward finally came back in, ignored everyone and went sleep on the couch.

Around four o'clock, Anna said good-bye to her children.

Sarah watched until Anna's car disappeared around the corner. Anna was finally learning to live again and Sarah was happy for her.

The beach was deserted when Tim and Sarah got there. There were the remains of a fire and empty beer cans scattered aound. Tim and Sarah headed off to the wooded area, each taking a different direction. She started picking up dry branches and the thought of Brandon slowly invaded her mind. She missed him. He had been in an exceptionally good mood yesterday. Was it the real Brandon or did he hit an emotional high? Was Stacey there with him right now? Were they working things out? Jealousy, anger and pain shot through her. She was angry with herself for feeling the way she did.

Tim was pulling part of a broken tree trunk along the beach. He stopped and looked at the bundle of dry branches she was holding and called out, "Stop being lazy or you'll freeze little sister. Find some firewood."

"Gathering firewood is a man's job."

"Not anymore."

She walked slowly towards Tim. So many memories lived on this stretch of beach. She'd found solutions to many of her problems, right here, with Tim by her side. It was here, on this beach, that she fell in love with Jake and made the biggest mistake of her life. She put down her bundle of firewood and walked into a small clearing among the pine trees. She had come here so often with Jake, the father of her child. He was sixteen and Sarah, fifteen. Sarah was in love with him. He didn't laugh at her because her dad was a noisy alcoholic who woke up the entire street. He had respected her. He had made her feel wanted, loved. He had comforted her after her fights with Edward.

One day after a particularly nasty fight with her dad, she was really in pieces and couldn't find Tim anywhere and her mom was at work. She had joined Jake on the beach and they had talked for a long time about Edward. Jake had taken her in his arms, rocking her gently as she cried. They had ended up making love. Even now, she could remember how lonley and unwanted she felt and how comforting Jake's closeness had been. The power of those feelings made her shiver. She had become pregnant and when she had told Jake, nothing could have prepared her for his reaction. He had just looked at her and screamed, "It's not my child! I never want to see you again!"

She had begged him not to walk away but he had left anyway. Sarah had no choice but to give her baby up for adoption. She had cuddled her daughter for a few minutes and even now she could still feel how warm the baby was, still feel the little mouth searching her bosom hungrily. Her legs felt weak. Her heart swelled with grief and guilt. If only she could have kept her baby.

She started back down the beach towards Tim. Four months into her pregnancy, she had met Ralph. It had started off as friendship and he had later told her that he loved her and was going to take care of her and the baby. She had fallen in love with him and they had become lovers. Because of him, she would be able to keep her child. Two months later, she had found out that he was married and had a child. She was devastated but she did not cry. Instead, she had pushed it all deep into her mind and decided to change her life. She forced herself to stop thinking of Ralph, too many unpleasant things had gone on between them. She felt ashamed, cheap. "Stop it!" she said to herself. "It's the past." How she hated Ralph.

Sarah flung the dry branches beside Tim. "That's all I found," she said.

Tim squatted, struck a long wooden match and started the fire. "You're lazy." His eyes searched her face for a minute. "What's wrong? You look like you just saw a phantom."

Sarah piled branches on the fire and watched it come to life. "Why did you say something like that? I'm fine." She held his gaze.

He shook his head in disbelief. "When are you going to face those things that haunt you?" His voice was soft, full of concern.

"Tim, I appreciate all you have done for me. I'm a woman now. Please stop worrying about me. You have your life to live."

"You will always be my baby sister," he whispered.

Mike and his girlfriend Paula were the first ones to arrive, putting an end to their conversation.

"Boy am I glad there's a fire," Paula said, walking over to Sarah. "Good to see you out. You have to take a break from those books." She slipped on her mittens. "We have a lot of catching up to do."

"No books today. You look great, Paula. We have to go for lunch soon."

"Tim told me you were coming and I just had to see you." They smiled at each other.

"Lunch next week-end?"

"That sounds good."

A tall boy who seemed to be all arms and legs walked towards them, singing the theme song from the film, 'Titanic'. The others laughed.

"You're spoiling a good song, Randy," Sarah called out.

"I sing what I want, my lady. You're as pretty as ever. Do marry me, Sarah." He knelt down in front of her. "Please, say yes." He looked at Tim and back to Sarah. "Do I have to ask Tim for your hand in marriage, my lady?"

"Where's the new girlfriend of yours?" Sarah asked, amused by his outrageous actions.

"She couldn't make it. Strange, everytime I invite her out, it seems like she can never make it." He laughed. "Figure out the rest." He stood up and faced Tim, "The others are not coming. They said it's too cold. Bunch of chickens! Can you believe that? Too cold."

"I hope he's not going to make us play 'wheelbarrow', Sarah whispered to Paula. "What a game." She had known Randy and Mike for as long as she could remember.

Mike grinned. "I prefer to play 'wheelbarrow', than listen to Randy imitating Pink Floyd.

Everyone huddled around the fire. The wind had died down a bit but it was still cold. Mike opened a cooler and passed some beers around. As usual, Randy entertained everyone.

Sarah listened to the boys teasing each other while she tried to dodge Paula's questions. It felt so good to be here with friends she'd known all her life.

Sarah looked at Paula's pixie-like, familiar face. "Question for you, Paula."

"Shoot." They grinned at each other.

"I know you and Mike are in love. Everyone can see that. If you wanted to stop loving him, could you make yourself do it?"

"Why would I want to?" Paula looked puzzled. I don't think that's possible. Why such a question? Falling for someone and you are scared?"

"I'm not falling for anyone." She traced a circle in the sand. "It was just a psychology question." She longed to confide in someone. She was scared of her feelings, scared to fall prey to them.

"Still bent on becoming an old woman with two cats to greet her when she gets home?"

"For now, yes."

"When you meet the right guy, you'll never be able to escape."

"That's what you think."

Mike reached out and pulled Paula close to him. She rested her head on his shoulder and they spoke softly to each other. Sarah turned and stared at the other end of the beach, it was dark and deserted. She preferred looking in that direction than at Paula and

Mike. Seeing them so much in love only reminded her of how empty her life was. She had shut herself off from relationships because of Jake and Ralph. She had tasted deception even before she was ready to handle it. It still hurt today to know that she had loved people who were never able to love her back.

Her mind drifted to Brandon, the way he looked at her, the way he had kissed her and her heart drummed in her chest. What would it be like to become his fiancé, she wondered.

A sudden thought struck her mind. Was he like the others? Interested only in her body. No, it can't be. Life would not be that unfair. Something had to be different.

She wondered if Brandon had taken her advice. Was Stacey over there with him right now? She had promised to call Brandon but decided not to. What if Stacey answered the phone?

Randy's singing brought her attention back to the crowd. He was singing a song by Pink Floyd and Tim was begging him to shut up.

"I've been watching you all night," Paula said. "You look like a woman fighting off something. What's going on?" She smiled, then continued. "You can tell me anything."

"I don't know what you are talking about." She looked at Paula, one eyebrow raised. "Your imagination is really running away with you."

"What does your patient look like?" She looked expectantly at Sarah.

"Not bad. If it wasn't for his crooked nose, he would be, well, sort of good looking." Sarah wanted to laugh, she had killed Paula's curiousity. "Besides, he's engaged and getting married pretty soon."

"I see. Nothing going on there."

By the time Sarah got home, she was exhausted. Anna's car was in the driveway. Sarah opened the door and crept up the stairs. Anna was asleep and Edward's side of the bed was empty. She went to her room and closed the door behind her.

Chapter 6

The morning fog clung to her face and bare arms, it fell like a soft blanket upon the trees. Sarah shivered and folded her arms across her chest. There was something mysterious about the foggy morning, as mysterious as the unchartered future awaiting her. She walked deeper into the fog, towards the beach, hoping that her quiet walk would shake off those unpleasant feelings that clung to her like leeches. Feelings that Edward's cruelty had inflicted upon her. Alone with nature, in this quiet place, heightened Sarah's awareness of how she really felt. She was hurting and so lonley. She stopped under a tall elm tree, the thightness in her throat grew stronger and finally she allowed herself to cry. She felt so unloved, so unwanted. She brushed her tears away and told herself that once she started her psychology course, she wouldn't feel this way anymore.

Sarah spun around at the sound of a whirring noise coming from behind.

"Sarah, are you okay?" Brandon asked, his eyes searching her face with concern.

"Oh my eyes. Just allergies. I thought you were still asleep." She pretended to examine the elm tree. "Quite big, isn't it?"

"You don't have allergies and you're not really interested in that tree. Look at me, Sarah."

She looked Brandon in the eyes, ready to convince him that she had allergies, but the tenderness in his eyes shot through her heart like a bolt of lightening.

She had the sudden urge to open up to him, to tell him how she really felt. She took a deep breath and told herself that wasn't such a good idea. She would just lock it away, pretend that it was not there, like she had been doing for such a long time.

Brandon pushed himself up with his arms and took a step towards her.

Sarah's arms circled his waist and they walked in silence. She felt comforted by his closeness, his kindness. Why was this man capable of doing such things to her?

"Sometimes you look so sad. Why Sarah?"

They both turned their heads at the same time, their faces barely a few inches apart. Sarah heard the pounding of her heart and was shocked by her sudden desire to kiss him.

"Maybe talking would help. Don't you think so?" he asked. "Let me be your friend."

She turned away. His words were so gentle, like soothing balm on an open wound. She didn't want to talk about it, she would just break down, become weaker. A sense of unease settled upon her. She had been feeling exactly the same way, weak and broken, the day she had ended up making love with Jake. Back then, she was in many ways still a child. Today she was a grown woman and making such a mistake a second time would be foolish. The thought of falling into Brandon's arms made her shiver. She forced herself to be strong, to show this man that she did not need his help.

"That's so sweet of you, Brandon." With her head held high, she smiled at him.

"But you don't want to share it. Right?"

"I feel better now. I don't want to think about it anymore." He had seen through her lie. A tendril of anger slowly formed in her mind. Why did she have to show him her weakness?

"You know what they say about hiding things in the human closet?"

"No I don't" To her annoyance she sounded weak instead of strong and confident.

"Those things become big, strong and take over your life."

"Why don't you sit on the bench. I'll get your chair." She just ignored his last sentence, even if it was true. The subject was closed. She didn't want to talk about it anymore. She got the wheelchair and walked towards him, smiling like all was well. He looked at her, a puzzled expression on his face.

"It's not good to run from the things that bother you. Stand up and face them." His voice was as gentle as the wind that caressed her bare arms.

"I guess so."

"I went to see Stacey on saturday. I told her it was over. She was not happy but I am. Austin did not show up as yet. When he does, it's not going to be nice."

"You just have to be strong," Sarah answered absently, shocked at the joy that shot through her. Why should it matter if he stayed with Stacey or not? There could never be anything between her and Brandon.

Sarah held the wooden door open and Brandon made his way in the house. It looked different now that all Stacey's photos were removed. She was happy for Brandon, he was taking care of his life and his hapiness. She looked at him pouring coffee into the cups. He was quiet and for a moment, then said, "I was disappointed that you didn't call on the week-end." he said, his eyes lingered on her face.

"I had so many things to do and time went so fast. I'm sorry." Once again, the lies just rolled off her tongue.

The doorbell rang. Sarah put down her cup and hurried to the door. A young man was standing there with a bunch of red roses.

"Sarah Taylor?" he asked with a quick flash of white teeth.

"Yes," she finally answered. Who on earth had sent her flowers at Brandon's place? Her eyes moved from the delivery boy, to Brandon, and back to the flowers.

"Roses for you," he said, holding the flowers in outstretched arms.

She took it, threw him a puzzled look, then pulled out the card from the tiny envelope. It read, 'I missed you while you were gone. Dinner tonight? Please say yes. Brandon'.

She watched the delivery boy walk back to his car, then turned and closed the door. Leaning against it, she looked at Brandon, who was looking at her nervously. Sarah was deeply touched by his gesture. This was the first time in her life a man had given her roses, the first time a man had told her that he missed her. She looked away from Brandon. How was she supposed to react? What was she supposed to say? For a moment she felt rather confused.

"Please say yes," Brandon said softly.

She didn't answer. Sarah wanted to say yes but it scared her. What if she fell hopelessly in love with this man? 'Impossible. I'm stronger than that', she told herself.

"Sarah

"I have never been asked out in such a nice way. Yes, I will go."

She just stood there holding the flowers and looking at Brandon. He took the flowers from her, unwrapped them and put them in a vase.

"It's true. I missed you." He smiled slowly, his eyes warm and happy.

What did you say to a handsome guy who just sat there and told you that he missed you? She didn't know if she should be honest with him or not. She had missed him too and could hardly wait to see him.

"Sarah, I'm not trying to replace Stacey if that's what you are worried about." He sounded and looked so sincere that Sarah believed him.

"I didn't say that.

"I know. If you thought about it, it's quite normal."

She picked up her cup, it slipped from her moist hand and crashed to the floor. She was mad at herself for being so nervous. She squatted and started to pick up the pieces.

Brandon leaned foward and helped her. "Do I make you that nervous?" he asked, his mouth close to her ears.

Her body stiffened, her hands stopped moving. Was she that easy to read? "You make me nervous. You did that from the moment I first saw you." She got up and went to put the broken cup in the garbage can. She regretted saying those words. They were a sign of weakness, something she couldn't afford to harbour.

"You did things to me from the first second I laid eyes on you. I can't tell you about that right now."

"What did I do to you?" Part of her really wanted to know but common sense told her it was better to leave it like that. "Forget I asked that question."

"Good idea. I don't want you breaking up the house." He laughed. "Did you know that you blush?"

"I don't."

"Yes, you do." He looked at her, amused.

"Where are we going?"

"That's a surprise." His eyes lingered on her lips and she turned away.

"You will have to give me directions." She avoided his eyes, the tenderness in their depths kept pulling her, like a strong current on a stormy sea.

"If we take a taxi, we both get to look at the scenery and hold hands," he said, smiling.

"Where are we going?"

"I get the impression that you are scared. There's nothing to be scared about."

"I'm not scared." She laughed nervously. "Any reason I should be?" Her voice held a tinge of challenge.

"Sarah, you're a mystery. I'd pay a milloin bucks to know what's going on in that head of yours."

"Don't do that. It's scary."

Sarah saw a piece of crumpled paper on the floor and went to pick it up. As she unfolded it, she noticed that it was from the physiotherapy department.

"Give that to me, please."

Sarah had already read it. She could tell that he was not pleased that she had seen it. "You probably hate these things but they're part of your recovery program."

"I will not use those things." He reached out for the paper and she gave it to him.

"Why? I can go pick it up."

"No. Not today!"

"Don't you want your independence? Don't you want to go jogging again? It's time to get out the chair."

"I don't want you to see me with a walker. Not before our date. I know it's somewhat stupid. I'll get it in a few days."

She looked into his angry eyes, not really seeing the anger. He had used the word, 'date'. Until now, she had just seen it as going out for dinner.

"Sarah, I don't want you to see me with a walker right now. Tomorrow I'll get it."

She nodded, not really paying attention to what he was saying. Sarah was caught up in her own thoughts. She had to be careful with Brandon. She had let things go too far already.

"What's going on, Sarah?"

"Just trying to figure out why you are ashamed of a walker," she lied. "I'm going to make sure you buy those things and use them."

"Really?" He looked at her determined expression and laughed softly.

"I'm serious."

"When I get out this chair, I'm going to walk without that stupid piece of metal!" His voice was cold, determined. He took the piece of paper, stuck it in a drawer and turned his attention to Sarah.

"I'll drive you to Health Care tomorrow to get the walker and bed handle."

He rubbed his hands together and stared out the window. "I hate the walker!"

"I'm sure you do, but you need it." She wanted to tell him that putting his pride aside wouldn't kill him, but held back from doing so.

"I'll get those things tomorrow."

At five, they climbed into a taxi. Brandon was dressed in a black turtle neck sweater and grey pants. Sarah gave him an appreciative glance then looked at her blue jeans self consciously.

Sarah was curious about where they were going, and questioned him, but Brandon kept his vow of silence. They talked for a while about music and the latest films and then he became quiet, slipping into his own world.

She caught sight of the young taxi driver looking at her in the rearview mirror. They smiled at each other.

She didn't know why Brandon's mood had suddenly changed and she was disappointed. They had spent a pleasant afternoon together and he was fine. She wondered if he was thinking about Stacey. Was he sorry that he had broken up with her?

She turned her attention to the store lined street, crowded with shoppers. It was one of her favorite places to hang out as a teenager when she came to Portland on week-ends.

The sound of paper crunching drew her attention to Brandon. He was crumbling a piece of paper and his face had not lost it's grim expression. Sarah felt a hint of anger. He had invited her out and now he was completely ignoring her.

He stared straight ahead and was not even aware that she was looking at him. She wondered if he was sorry that he had invited her out. Was he cursing himself this minute?

"Brandon," she said softly.

"Yes." Their eyes met, a stiff smile on his face as he tried to hide the paper behind his back.

"If you want to go back home, it's okay. I don't mind." For a minute, she held her breath, afraid of his answer.

"That's not it. I was lost for a while. I was thinking about Austin. That's all." He forced a smile. "I'm sorry about that."

'Austin', the name fell on her like a hundred pound weight, sending fear through her heart. If Austin found out they would both be in trouble.

The driver turned onto a narrow street lined with pine trees and a line of sailboats floated into view. There were small cottages nestled among the trees.

"Turn left," Brandon said.

Hidden among the trees, was a beautiful countrystyle home with a balcony overlooking Casco bay.

"Here we are," he said to Sarah.

"It's beautiful here," she said, climbing out the car and looking around.

Brandon took slow steps up the short flight of stairs and once they were inside, he sank down on a chair . Sarah opened the patio door and went to stand on the balcony and a few minutes later, he joined her.

"This place is heavenly," she said.

"My friend Robert and I bought this place a year ago. Follow me," he went toward a large window at the back of the house. "Take a look."

She looked out the window. There was a small strip of beach hidden among the trees. "You want to rent that piece of beach?"

"No. But you can come here as often as you want. Go have a look. I can't get down there."

"I'll have a look at it later. Your friend, Robert, does he come here often?"

"He's in Europe so he wouldn't stop by today. Come with me."

She followed him to the balcony, where they sat side by side. He looked at her for a long time, then brushed the wind blown hair away from her face. Brandon's tenderness touched something sensitive within her. She did not look him in the eyes. She was taking tiny steps into a forbidden world. A place she had sworn never to go again, but it felt so good. Why were forbidden things so enticing?

"This isn't just an invitation for me. I love you Sarah." He kissed her hand.

She felt as though her heart had swollen and filled up her entire chest and suddenly came back to normal all in a split second. She knew that he had feelings for her, but love, that was such a strong word.

"I don't expect you to tell me the same thing," he said. "The other day you told me that you had no place in your life for a man. I guess I'll just have to worm my way in."

He had already done that but she wasn't going to tell him. This was dangerous. She had fallen in love with him. Brandon didn't know her at all. He fell in love with an image, an illusion. She stared at him not daring to say what she really felt.

"Please don't run away from me." He squeezed her hands gently.

"You hardly know me and you've just broken up with Stacey."

"Sarah." He took her face in his hands. "Emotionally, I split with Stacey a long time ago. I'm not trying to replace her."

The crunch of gravel in the driveway announced someone's arrival. Sarah felt her body go stiff. "Who is that?" She sprang to her feet, scared that it was Austin or Stacey.

"Hey, don't be nervous. It's dinner." He chuckled softly and went to answer the door.

Sarah watched as the young man fetched in some boxes and listened to the friendly conversation between the two.

"Hungry?" Brandon asked as the young man left.

"Not really." She walked into the dining room.

"I'm hungry."

"You are always hungry," she teased.

"And you're too skinny. I'm trying to fatten you."

"I see. I'm never going to get fat with sea food." She joined him beside the table. "There's always the garlic butter. I'll give you mine. I ordered chicken for you. I don't think you like sea food."

She grimaced. "I don't."

"Candles and music will be good." He opened a cupboard, took out two candles, lit them and set them down on the table.

"Madonna," she said.

"Out of luck. Mozart?"

"That guy doesn't know anything about music." She laughed softly.

"Are you joking?"

"Do you really listen to Mozart?" What taste in music, she mused. Something had to be wrong with this man.

"Sometimes." He went through a pile of CD and slipped one into the player."What's so wrong with liking music by Mozart," he said defensively.

Strains of piano music filled the room, the candles flickered as a gentle wind blew in from Casco Bay. He pulled out a chair, sat opposite her and filled her wine glass.

"This chicken is good," Sarah said, looking up at Brandon. It seemed like he didn't even hear her and that tormented look that she had seen so often in his eyes was back. She didn't like to see him like that.

"Brandon. Where are you?" She wished that she could erase his pain, make things better for him, but that was impossible. He had to do it for himself.

"What did you say? I'm…I was lost for a minute."

"What's wrong?"

"I'm sorry about that. I wanted this to be a fun evening. I told myself that I would not think about my problems but it keeps nagging at me. When Austin finds out that I called off the wedding, he is certainly going to pay me a visit and it's not going to be nice."

Sarah put down her knife and fork and stared at the flickering candle. "It's your decision to make." She saw the tension on his face. "It's your life to live."

"It's not that simple. Stacey's dad, Conrad, and Austin are busines partners. Dad wants the business to stay in the family. If I don't marry Stacey then Conrad can do whatever he wants with his half of the business."

"Austin can offer to buy Conrad's part of the business."

"It already belongs to Stacey. She would never sell it to Austin. She would rather sell it to a stranger just to get back at me. Why am I dumping my problems on you?"

"It's okay. Talk to me. It's not good to keep all those things bottled up inside of you."

"Sarah, I'm not pyschic, but I know you have things bothering you too. You don't need anything added." He reached across the table and took her hands in his.

"Let's try to forget what's bothering us. At least for this evening," she said.

"Good idea. I'll go down to the beach with you."

"No. I'm afraid that you'll hurt yourself."

"I want to go with you."

Later that evening, they made their way down to the beach. Brandon was exhausted and Sarah could see that he was in pain.

"Beautiful, isn't it," he said, sitting on a rock.

"Yes, it is."

"It's so peaceful. It's like I'm in another world," he whispered.

The tranquility of the night hugged them softly. Sarah sat down beside Brandon and stared out at the bay. In the distance, the light from the lighthouse, swept through the darkness. A gentle wind played in the trees, producing a soft, rustling sound.

His arm slid around her waist, her body stiffened and he let go of her. Sarah knew that she was threading on dangerous grounds. Why didn't she put a stop to it before? Once Brandon found out about her, he would run like the devil was at his tail. Her life was far from perfect. Would he be able to accept her? Out of the corner of her eyes, she noticed him studying her keenly, and stood up, hating to be so closely examined. She had to put an end to it. Turning towards him, a bright smile on her face, she said, "Let's go for a walk."

He stood up, a gentle smile on his face as he took her hand in his. "I feel like you're trying so hard to shut me out. Why?"

She plucked a dry leaf from the nearby tree and crumbled it. "I've been hurt before. It takes time to get over things like that." It wasn't entirely the truth, but that was all she was going to say for now. He squeezed her hand gently and she knew that he understood. It was funny, how so much could be said with such a small gesture.

"It's not my intention to hurt you. I wish I could erase your pains, Sarah, and take your fears away." He kissed the top of her head.

"You don't know much about me. My life is not exactly...perfect. What if you are disappointed?" She kicked a small stone.

"Your past is your past. I couldn't be disappointed in you." He stopped and pulled her close. "The other day, when I told you that I loved you, you told me to back off. A few hours later, you kissed me. Why did you do that?" He examined her face keenly.

Her mind spun, trying to think of something to cover her action the other night. Nothing came to mind. He looked at her, obviously waiting for an answer. "Do I have to answer that one?"

"Yes. Multiple choice will be okay. Let me see..."

She gently removed his arms from around her and started walking. She had no intention of telling him that she kissed him because desire got the better of her. He grabbed her hand.

"You don't have to give me an answer. "He held her chin between his thumb and index finger, and turned her face toward him. "I'm sorry if I pushed you for an answer."

"No more funny questions," she said, smiling.

They sat on the warm sand and Brandon pulled Sarah close to him. "Maybe you are worried about getting involved with me because I just broke up with Stacey. I don't blame you. What Stacey and I had, has been over for a long time. We have known each other all our lives and we started dating about nine years ago."

She wondered if he ever really loved Stacey. They had been seeing each other for nine years and never got married. Sarah looked up at his perfect profile and wondered what this man had seen in her. Why did he choose her?

Brandon took her hands in his and looked at the rings on her fingers. "This one is new, so is the one with the two hearts because I've never seen them before. Here is the pink ring, your favorite because you never take it off."

"I love the pink ring." The face of a tiny baby floated across her mind. A child who would forever live in her heart and hopefully, one day she would be able to meet.

Once Brandon found out that she had given her baby up for adoption, would he still love her? Brandon had never told her that he was adopted but she suspected it. From what he had said, Brandon disliked women who gave their children up for adoption. Would his love for her change his mind and heart? She had a strange feeling that the answer was, no. The love that they shared for each other was like a fragile blossom, it would bear no fruit, instead it would just fall to the ground and that would be the end.

"Look," Brandon pointed to the tiny lights in the distance, floating slowly through the darkness. "Tourist season has began. The ferry must be loaded. Have you ever visited any of the islands?"

The islands were just dark peaks, barely visible. "Yes. That was a long time ago."

"I used to go there every summer with my parents. There are some great places to visit. We still have a cottage there. Would you like to go there for a few days?"

Sarah lay down on the warm sand and stared up at the starry skies. "Sounds great."

He stretched out beside her, propped himself up with his arm and looked down at Sarah.

She reached up and traced his lips with her thumb. She loved him. No amount of fighting could stifle what she felt for Brandon.

He changed positon, bent his head and kissed her. "I can't help it," he whispered.

She closed her eyes and her mouth opened under his. She wanted this as badly as he did. She had told herself a thousand times during the evening that she wasn't going to encourage him in any way, yet she was the one who had initated this. He was keeping his hands to himself, like he had promised. Desire burned within her, weakening her mind and giving control to her heart. She kissed him back, her fingers running through his hair.

His breathing roughened and he pulled her closer. She slipped her thigh between his legs and pressed her body closer. His lips slid to her throat, kissing the throbbing pulse. Her hands slid under his sweater, she loved the feel of his skin beneath her hands and the smell of his cologne.

His mouth slid from her throat to the neckline of her shirt. She gasped as tiny spikes of pleasures washed over her. She didn't want him to stop. Her emotions had gone wild. The barriers she had built around them had finally cracked and there was no stopping them from running wild and free.

He caressed her thigh, his palm hot against her skin. His lips moved back to hers. "I don't want you to regret this," he murmured.

"Stop, Brandon. It's gone too far already."

He rolled aside, his breathing, ragged. He stared at the skies in silence.

Chapter 7

Sarah studied Brandon from the open window as he walked around the backyard with his walker. Over the past two weeks he had walked a lot and his legs were continually gaining strength. Emotionally, he was definitely doing better and continued seeing his psychologist. She'd have to leave soon. Her job here was almost at an end. Something painful caught at her heart.

He turned around, caught sight of Sarah, smiled and motioned her to join him. She slipped on her sandals and went out. Once she was back at the nursing home with it's crazy schedule, she wouldn't have much time to see him. Sarah tried to ignore everyone and everything that went against her and Brandon's relationship. She wanted to be with him and he wanted to be with her.

She made her way past the rose bushes and into the backyard. She knew that it was crazy to even think that she and Brandon had a chance together. Once again, she had hung her heart out there knowing that it could be shattered again. She pushed the thought aside.

Brandon looked a lot healthier than when she had first arrived. His face had a nice tan from the early summer sun and the dark circles under his eyes had completely disappeared.

His smile was genuine, happy. His eyes were full of laughter.

"Why were you hiding," he asked as she walked towards him.

"I wasn't"

"Why were you spying on me?"

"I was not spying. Simply looking. Admiring."

"Don't make me blush."

They looked at each other and laughed. When they finally stopped laughing, Sarah asked Brandon to let go of the walker and to walk on his own.

He looked uncertain at first, took a few shaky steps, then his steps became steadier. He turned to face her. "Maybe in a few days I'll be running!"

"Not in a few days but you will surely run again."

He walked toward her, his eyes never leaving hers. There was a certain urgency on his face, in his steps. He stopped a few inches away from her. "I don't want you to leave Sarah. If you leave I'm afraid that I will lose you. You've filled an emptiness inside of me that I thought would never go away. I know that you have to go back to your life and work. Promise me something. Please."

"What is it?" She was touched by his love, his sincerity. Was it possible that a man loved her this much? Was she dreaming, imagining? Love or whatever it was, it felt so good, so right. She didn't want to lose it.

"Please don't walk away from me. Sometimes I can see how scared you are and I can feel the walls that you put between us. It's so nice when those walls are not there." His voice was heavy with emotion and Sarah automatically moved towards him, her arms circling his waist. She knew that she could never to walk away from him, even if she wanted to.

"Promise."

"I promise to do my best not to hurt you."

She drew in a deep breath. Her legs felt wobbly. Brandon had won her heart, soul and mind. He had taught her to love, to laugh and to trust again. She had been avoiding relationships for so many years and was convinced that she was tough enough to keep the bargain that she had made with herself. Brandon's tenderness and love had erased her resolve, but she loved every moment of it. The future held a beautiful promise except for the one dark cloud that hung above them. Was there some way out of this situation?

His hands slid down her arms. "If you ever run away, I promise to catch you."

Standing on the tip of her toes, she kissed him lightly on the mouth. "Promise, I'm not going to run away." It seemed so naural that a promise should be sealed with a kiss." She fought back the urge to laugh at the surprised look on his face. He had kept his word faithfully. Since that night at the beach house, he hadn't touched her.

"Don't do that too often," he said softly.

She smiled up at him. "Why not?"

"Don't give me that innocent look."

The sound of the phone reached her ears and she saw the anger that briefly rolled across Brandon's face. She wondered if it was Austin finally returning Brandon's call. Austin had refused to talk to Brandon, to see him and she knew that it was tearing him to bits.

The phone stopped ringing. "We will have to face Austin and nothing is going to be easy for us. I thought he would have already shown up, like a raging bull. I don't understand what is going on. Every time I phone, he refuses to talk to me." There were haunting shadows in his eyes and the pain seeped into his voice.

"His silence is more frightening than his angry outbursts. Mom does not call and that is not like her."

"Would you like to drive me to your parents place?" Her heart was already doing a strange rythm to the fear she felt. She was comforted that Austin knew nothing about their relationship.

"No," Brandon finally said.

They started to walk back to the house, she picked up the walker, offered it to Brandon and and he shook his head.

When they reached the patio, he slumped down on a chair, stretched his legs out in front of him ansd closed his eyes.

"I can give you a ride to your parents place. Since Austin refuses to come to you, you should go to him." She moved forward to the edge of her chair.

"You don't know Austin," he said, straightening up.

"Go over and see your mom."

"I'm sure she knows what's going on. She just has to play by his rules. I wish that dad would come by. We'd have a nasty quarrel, but it would be the beginning of a new and better relationship for us or the end. At one time I longed for his silence and now I can't stand it. Do you have a good relationship with your dad?"

For a moment, Sarah felt extremely embarassed to even talk about Edward. What would Brandon think if she told him about Edward? Sarah knew that she was being irrational. It wasn't her fault that Edward was an alcoholic or that he hated her.

He sat foward on his chair, arms resting on his thighs, a questioning look in his eyes.

"Well, it's okay." She hated herself for being a liar. One day he was going to know the truth. What would she tell him then? Whatever image he had formed of her, certainly felt good and she wanted it to stay that way, at least for now.

Brandon smiled, reached out and took her hands in his. "Nothing is going to change the way I feel about you. There are lots of people who don't get along with their fathers. Just look at me, I'm a good example."

Her smile was stiff. "It's really bad between dad and me. Sometimes I wonder why he didn't give me up for adoption. Anyway, mom would have never let him."

He let go of her hands suddenly, as though he was hit by electricity. He opened his mouth, as though to say someting, then stopped and looked away. He stood up. "I don't want to go to my parents place today. Maybe tomorrow." He pulled off his T- shirt. "So humid. Want to go down by the beach?"

He stumbled. Sarah's arm shot out and steadied him.

He let out a long breath, half turned and said, "It should be the other way around. You do the stumbling and I do the catching. By the way, is it okay for my nurse to go swimming with me?" He gave her braided hair a gentle tug.

"You can't go swimming, too hard for your legs and the water is icy."

"Then you swim and I'll watch."

"Not a good deal. We'll walk at the edge of the water."

By the time they got down to the beach, Brandon was wincing with pain. He sat down on a rock. "Wow. It hurts but I did it."

"Do you want me to get the wheelchair and help you back to the house?"

He looked at her, his eyebrows raised. "You must be joking. You can't push me up that slope. I wouldn't let you!"

She laughed. "Of course I can push you up that slope!"

"In your dreams Sarah." He stood up and gently tugged her arm. "Coming in the icy water?"

"Does not scare me."

"I bet you're all talk." He winked at her. "Let's see who will stay longer in the water."

"Liquid ice," Sarah said as they stepped in ankle deep.

They stole glances at each other and continued walking. Her feet were frozen, but she continued. She wanted Brandon to be the first one to give up. She was waiting for him to crack, to say that he was getting out the water, but he continued and the cold didn't seem to bother him.

"Lets get out," he finally said. "Aren't you frozen? I am. Up to my nose."

"Told you I was going to win."

He smiled down at her. "I don't remember you saying that."

They walked back to the rocky edge and sat down. His arms circled her waist, she moved closer and rested her head on his shoulder. If only this moment could last forever.

Austin would never accept her. That was a fact carved in stone. There was no way she would get past him unless Brandon gave up his family for her. Questions began storming her mind. She had given up on many of the ridgid rules she had made for herself, and the 'tough Sarah', who she had worked so hard to create, had faded. If she got hurt again, what would that do to her? A tiny voice floated at the back of her mind, saying that it was not too late to turn back.

"Sarah."

She lifted her head and turned to face him.

"I guess Austin is giving you the jitters too."

She nodded. Another lie. Why couldn't she be totally honest with him?

He took her face in his hands. "It's not going to be easy. Austin will never accept my splitting up with Stacey. When he finds out about us, he'll go crazy. He is going to do everything in his power to break us up."

"We will survive Austin." She tried to ignore the cold, steel fingers of fear grabbing at her heart right now.

"We will." His eyes were bright, hopeful.

"We just have to be strong."

A thought, sharp as a new dagger poked at her heart, injecting fear. If Brandon knew that she had given a child up for adoption, would he still love her? She knew that he was harsh towards women who gave their children up for adoption and she suspected that he was Austin's adoptive son. Would his love for her soften his heart?

"Sarah."

What? Well….I was lost for a minute." She gently removed his hands from her face. She had to tell him

119

about her child before their relationship went any farther. She loved him and didn't want to lose him but this secret was probably a potential bomb, that could one day destroy everything. She didn't have the courage to tell him that right now.

"Where were you?"

"Thinking about Austin." The lie slid off her tongue so easily, she was surprised at herself. It was as though, subconsciously, she had prepared herself to lie.

"We are going to keep our relationship quiet for a while." Brandon's eyes swam with guilt when he saw the disappointment in her eyes.

She knew what he said made sense, but couldn't stop the fear and confusion from bombarding her mind.

"I know that it sounds bad Sarah. It's just that I want to face Austin with one thing at a time. Please, trust me."

"You're right. Why don't we go sit in the shade," she said, getting to her feet.

"Good idea." Brandon followed her to the place were low branches offered some shade from the midday sun.

Sarah spoke on and on about her job, the weather, summer plans, anything that popped into her mind. She didn't want to talk about Austin, didn't want to think about her baby for now. They were the people who stood between her and Brandon. She disliked Austin, but she loved her child with all her heart.

"Stop it Sarah. I suggested that we keep our relationship a secret for now, but nothing is going to change between us. I love you. Don't try to steer away from the conversation we were having."

She looked away from his intense blue eyes. "I'm not steering away from anything."

"There is nothing to be worried about when it comes to my feelings for you. It's not my intention to hurt you."

She traced a circle in the sand. Someone had once told her that life was a viscious circle and you could get trapped in it if you're not careful. She looked up at him, her eyes held his. "I've never felt this way about anyone in my life. It's so intense, so powerful. It scares me. I don't even recognise the Sarah I have become."

He caressed her lip with his thumb. "From the moment I saw you, I knew that I didn't want to let go of you. What I feel for you is so strong, I can never let go." He pulled her close to him. "I want to hold you like this forever, love you and protect you."

He removed his arms, tilted her head up. They moved foward at the same time, their lips met in a hungry, passionate kiss. Sarah closed her eyes and felt herself being drawn into that beautiful, forbidden world.

The sound of someone clappping their hands made Sarah and Brandon pull apart abruptly. Sarah saw the fear in Brandon's eyes, turned around slowly, her heart drumming wildly.

"No," she mumbled.

Austin was walking towards them, still clapping his hands. He stopped a few feet away from Brandon and Sarah, and studied them in silence, as though trying to make up his mind about what punishment was just. When Sarah's eyes met his, only one word existed in the dictionary, 'hatred'. Did he actually see them kiss? They were partially hidden by the trees. How long had he been spying on them?

"You!" Austin pointed a finger at Sarah, "Get the hell out of here! Now!"

Sarah felt embarassed before her mind went blank and she couldn't find one word to say to him. She stared at him with a detached awareness.

"You heard me!" He yelled moving towards her.

"Sarah is not going anywhere, Dad," he said with a surprising calmness. He got to his feet and helped Sarah up.

Austin looked at Brandon and laughed. "Why? Fun time isn't over yet? I see." He pulled out a pack of cigarettes and lit one. "Is she a lot of fun, Brandon? More than Stacey?"

He turned his attention to Sarah, studied her for a few seconds, then said, "She has no class!"

"Stop it Austin," Brandon yelled. "You have no right to say things like that."

"Get rid of that...thing! We have to talk!"

"I told you, dad. Sarah isn't going anywhere!"

"Why?" He scratched his head. "I wonder why?" He looked at Sarah and started to laugh. "That's right. You are only at the kissing part. You should have done all those positions in the Kama Sutra by now."

He turned to Brandon. "Take five minutes and do your stuff behind the trees. I'm not going to watch. Then she can go. While you're at it, do it like a dog. It goes faster."

Sarah fought hard to control her tears. Austin was so cruel, so damn nasty. She felt like an insect that should be hiding somewhere.

Brandon was still holding her hands. He slumped down on a nearby rock, looking embarassed and angry.

Austin laughed. There was a ring of evil to it. "Go ahead Brandon. Take five minutes and get it over with! Then we'll talk about fixing things between you and Stacey."

"You are so horrible! I hate you!" Sarah yelled.

"I hate you too, honey," Austin answered, grounded out his cigarette in the sand and lit another one.

"Sarah felt hot tears on her face and she brushed them away. If only she could disappear. Like Jinny, in the T.V show. Why didn't Brandon say something? He just stared at his father, like a kid who was afraid of a whipping.

Brandon's arm shot out and he yanked off a branch from the tree beside him. "Stop it Austin," he bellowed. You owe Sarah an apology!"

"That's the joke of the century! How could you do that to Stacey? Tell me! How dare you insult my dearest friend by dumping his daughter!" Austin waved his hands in the air as though chasing away insects, his voice echoing in the silence.

"I refuse to marry someone I don't love! Is that so hard to understand?"

"If you don't marry Stacey part of the company will go to a stranger. I've worked my butt off to build it and there's no way I'm going to let go. Do you hear me?" He kicked at a small rock and it flew among the trees.

Sarah took a step backward wanting to put more distance between herself and Austin. He looked like he was about to hit someone.

"You marry Stacey and the company stays in the family! That's an order!"

"Or what!" He stood up and moved towards his father. This is not about me! It's all about you! Don't you have enough money? Just buy Conrad's part of the company!"

Austin moved closer to Brandon and pointed a finger in his face. "Do as I say or you'll never believe what I have in store for you! Conrad has already given his part to Stacey. Do you think that she is going to sell it to me?" He pointed to Sarah and asked, "Are you planning to marry that thing, Brandon?"

Brandon did not answer. Sarah held her breath, wondering what he would say.

"Her name is Sarah, not 'that thing'." And what if it's, yes."

"You are crazy! Really crazy! You really bumped your head in that accident," Austin yelled.

"I am not crazy!" Brandon took Sarah's hand and started to walk away. Austin followed them. "Don't follow me, Austin! Go home."

Sarah walked alongside Brandon, her heart pounding with fear as they made their way up the slope. When they reached the top, Brandon sat down on a wooden bench.

"You want to marry her?" Austin continued, panting for breath. "Have you lost your mind?" He slammed his fist into a tree and if it was painful, he showed no signs.

Sarah was terrified. Memories of Edward's violence whizzed through her mind. Her legs were shaky and she felt like she had sand in her mouth.

"If you don't marry Stacey, you lose your job, your part of the company and the house. It's all mine and I will take it away!" He paced agitatedly, his eyes red with fury.

"I really don't care. You can take it all." His voice sounded empty. "Eversince I was a child you controlled me. You made all the decisions for me until the other day. I'm making my own decisions now."

Austin was panting for breath and looking rather pale. For one moment, Sarah wished that he would faint. That would put an end to this ugly quarrel.

"You know what is my biggest regret, Brandon?"

He went pale, all traces of anger disappeared from his face. He looked like a man expecting the worst. "Please, go home Dad." His voice sounded like there was no fight left in him.

"The day I led you out that stinking hole," Austin continued. I should have left you there. You were nothing but skin and bones. Scared of your own shadow and full of lice!"

"Stop it." Brandon's voice shook.

"I regret the day I adopted you! Look at all I have done for you and this is how you repay me. What do you think this is doing to Elizabeth? She's ashamed to face Stacey's parents. How could you do that to her?

Sarah was stunned, horrified. How could Austin be so cruel?

Austin lit up another cigarette and silence fell upon the threesome.

Brandon got up, walked towards Austin and said, "I'm sorry if I have messed things up for you. I'm sorry if I've hurt you. I can't do the things you are asking me to do. Please, try to understand me." He placed a hand on Austin's shoulder.

Austin flung Brandon's arm away. Brandon lost his balance and fell. Austin just glared down at him and didn't even make a move to help him get up. His face did not lose it's icy mask. "You have two weeks to get rid of that woman and fix things with Stacey or you lose everything and I never want to see you again!" He spun around and started to walk away, then stopped and did a half turn. He pointed to sarah. "This will cost you your job," he screamed.

Chapter 8

Brandon placed the last of the photos in an empty box. His heart felt sore, like someone had rubbed it with a stone. Never in his darkest thought had he imagined that one day he would be walking away from his family. He couldn't have Sarah and his family, too. A choice had to be made, and he had chosen Sarah. Christian would always be there for him. Elizabeth would be under Austin's ridgid control and Brandon knew that he would hardly see his mother.

He glanced up at Sarah as she walked into the living room dressed in jeans and a cotton shirt. His mind slipped back to the first night when she had come dashing into his room and hadn't even realised that she was wearing a transparent nightdress. He had never seen her with it again and wondered what she had done with it. He clamped his lips together, trying not to smile as he remembered the horrified look on her face when she had realised what she was wearing.

He continued packing in silence, feeling Sarah's eyes on him and sensing how worried she was for him. He didn't know what to say to her. How many times had she seen him bounce between happy and sad? She must be calling him a yo-yo, by now. He had burdened her too many times with his problems. If only things were different. He pushed down gently on the contents of the box, closed it, pushed it aside and pulled another empty box toward him.

Sarah walked over to Brandon, knelt beside him and took his hands in hers. Their eyes met and held and the only thing he saw in those eyes was love. He drew in a deep breath, letting the love penetrate his soul. It felt so good, like liquid silk on all his emotional bruises. They looked at each other in silence for a long time, the only sounds came from the crackling fire and the grandfather clock.

"Sarah, I feel like I have suddenly been dropped on a strange and frightening planet and I don't know which direction to take. The only father I know will definitely abandon me. I know that I'm a grown man and maybe should not be acting like this at all, but no one likes to be abandoned, especially not a second time. Everyone likes to belong somewhere, to be loved."

"Give Austin some time. When he is less angry, talk to him. Try to make him understand how you feel. Talk with your mom. Maybe she will be able to knock some sense into him."

Brandon stood up, walked over to the fireplace and threw another log into it. No matter what happened, he didn't want to lose Sarah. She was so gentle, so kind and he loved the simplicity about her. He sensed that she had secrets that she didn't want to talk about, or wasn't ready to share with him, but he knew that her love was genuine.

She stood quietly beside him, her eyes full of pain. He averted his eyes, feeling guilty that his personal problems was doing this to her.

He continued to stare into the fire for a few moments then walked across the room to the large window. The full moon still sat high in the sky, bathing the earth in it's silky white light.

He loved this old house with all the fond childhood memories. He had spent so much time here with his maternal grandparents. He had even been daydreaming about him and Sarah having kids and raising them in this house. That was not going to happen. He could no longer live under Austin's control, neither could he live without Sarah.

Brandon wasn't afraid to start over, to work for someone else or to have less financially. He knew that he could build a good life for himself and most important, he would have Sarah. Elizabeth and Christian would certainly not give up on him.

He turned around and looked at Sarah sitting on the rocking chair, where his grandmother had sat so often. He could not read the expression on her face in the dim glow of the fire. If Austin hadn't caught them kissing yesterday, maybe he wouldn't be having this many problems right now. Austin would not have been so mad with him and probably wouldn't have said half of the nasty things he had said. Brandon felt anger rising within him as he clearly recalled how his dad had humiliated Sarah. She didn't deserve that. Had it been someone other than Austin saying those things, he would have gladly smashed that person's mouth in. He felt like a wimp for not having defending Sarah more than that.

Sarah pulled open the door and stepped outside. Brandon felt the chilly air on his legs, picked up a blanket and joined her outside. The moon spilled it's milky light upon Casco Bay, creating a magical, peaceful world. If only he could drift into that world with Sarah and stay there forever.

He finally gave way to the insistent, nagging thought that he had been trying to ignore since the scene with Austin. If Sarah wasn't in the picture, would he have reacted differently to Austin's threats? Would he have given it all up? Was she the catalyst in his decision?

He stood behind Sarah and draped the blanket around her. He was about to move his ams when she caught hold of his hands and whispered, "Hold me."

He held her tightly, inhaling deeply. Something about her perfume reminded him of vanilla. He closed his eyes, enjoying the feel of her warm body within his arms. "I don't want you running away because of Austin," he whispered." I'm ready to give it all up. I have you and one day we'll have a little family of our own. I've been daydreaming about that."

Sarah turned around, still in the circle of his arms. The blanket slid from her shoulders and he felt the swell of her breast against his chest. His heart drummed frantically, desire surged through him. If she felt his hardness, she did not move away. He had promised not to touch her again and he wanted to keep that promise but it was so damn hard. Her eyes mirrored the desire he was feeling. His desire for her had been tormenting him for so long. He wished to put an end to the sweet torment.

He smiled down at her. "You know that song by 'Air Supply', where the singer said, 'my heart is a drum and it's lost and it's looking for a rythm like you'?"

She nodded.

"That's how I feel. You give the rythm to my heart." Here he was repeating words from a song and meaning it. What had she done to him?

She stood on her toes, pulled his head lower until their lips were touching. He felt her body trembling against his. His mouth crushed hers in a passionate kiss and he felt her responding just as passionately. They clung to each other, as though they were sharing the same source of life. He tilted her her head back, his mouth slid to the base of her throat, kissing the throbbing pulse, then the swell of her breast, a soft moan escape her lips. He moved lower, his mouth touching a taut nipple through the shirt. He sucked gently on her nipples throught the thin fabric.

Her hands found their way up his back, caressing him somewhat hesitantly.

He slid his hands up her back, caressing it softly before he moved them to her sides and up until he was touching the sides of her breast. He heard her sharp intake of breath. Brandon covered her breast with both hands, kneading them softly. He couldn't believe this was happening. Was she going to stop him? He pushed the unwanted thought aside.

"You are driving me crazy," she whispered.

"You have been doing that to me for far too long," he murmured. "It's my turn." Brandon's mouth clamped down on one of the nipples and sucked it gently, enjoying the way her body twisted with pleasure within his arms.

She whispered something that he did not quite understand. He moved lower, kissing her stomach. He felt her fingers running through his hair and as his mouth went lower, she held on to his head as though

131

trying to stop him. Had she changed her mind? He stopped for a few seconds, she didn't say anything so he continued. He didn't want to stop, didn't want Sarah to change her mind. He couldn't help wondering if she would look back on this and regret it. He forced the thought out of his mind. He had waited so long for this moment, he didn't want it spoilt and he wanted Sarah to enjoy every moment of it as well.

He pulled her down beside him on the blanket, his breath coming in gasps, as though he couldn't remember how to breathe. He had wondered what it would be like to touch her and this was nothing compared to what he had imagined. For Brandon, this wasn't just sex, this was making love to the woman he loved.

Their eyes held as he fumbled with her shirt buttons. He saw the fear and uncertainity in her eyes and lowered his lips to hers, hoping that he could kiss those emotions away. She sat up and slipped the shirt off exposing her perfectly rounded breast to Brandon.

"You're beautiful, Sarah." He wanted this moment to go on forever.

She reached up, unbuttoned his shirt and slipped it off. "Don't stop," she whispered, her voice urgent.

Brandon sucked in a deep breath, pulled her close, her back touching his chest. His arm circled her body, reached for her breasts and massaged them as he kissed the side and nape of her neck, her shoulders, her ears. He noticed that the tenseness had gone and she was relaxed against him. He ran his hands up her legs, on the inside of her thighs.

Sarah grasped the edges of the blanket, moaned softly and turned toward him.

Brandon unbuttoned her pants and started to slide it off, his eyes on her face all the while. She wanted him as badly as he wanted her and for a moment he was tempted just to bury himself inside of her and feel that sweet estacy. "No," he whispered. His hardness was becoming painful, he unzipped his pants slipped out of it and flung it aside.

Sarah reached out and took his part in her hands. He groaned with pleasure at her shy touch. He could tell that she didn't have much experience and it only made him crazier. Though his back ached, he leaned forward and started kissing her thighs in a slow, upward movement.

"Brandon," her whisper sounded loud in the quietness.

His mouth found her breast again, Sarah gasped, her fingers pressing into his shoulders.

She took his hand and brought it between her legs. He touched her, his finger dipping into her warmth. She arched her hips and whispered, "Don't stop."

"I want to do this everyday for the rest of my life," he whispered against her ear.

"That's exactly what we will do," she murmured as her lips found his. "I want you, now."

"Not yet, my lady."

"Now"

"I said, no," he whispered.

He was surprised at her small, commanding voice. He ran his hand along her abdomen and then he felt a slight raise of the skin. In the moon light, he saw a pencil thin line that ran from her navel to the bottom of her belly. She had some kind of surgery before. He pulled her body close to his until his hardness touched her womanly softness. He nudged her legs apart and started to thrust into her warmth. He stopped as she winced. Brandon realized that Sarah hadn't done this much in her life. He moved in and out of her slowly and carefully, not wanting to hurt her.

She raised her hips to meet his thrusts that grew faster and faster. Brandon stopped, rolled aside, stood up and helped her to her feet. "I will make you pay for all the time you made me wait." He saw the fear in her eyes and felt her body stiffen. "I didn't mean to scare you and I'm not going to hurt you. I just want to drive you crazy."

"How much crazier?"

He held her against the wall, his mouth found her breast, then moved lower to her stomach. He listened to her moans of pleasure and knew that he couldn't hold on any longer. He wanted to take her to that point of release. He stood up and eased his part into her. She held on to his hips and moved one of her legs up, he grabbed on to itand thrusted into her wildly. For a moment, he was lost in a world gone mad with desire.

She suddenly stiffened and he stopped. "What's wrong Sarah?"

"I have to get something from my purse."

"I have some." He led her inside, stopped beside the desk and took something from the drawer. "Talking about this?" He held up a condom.

She nodded and moved close to him, her hands grabbing his buttocks.

"I love you Sarah," he said and they lay down in front of the fire place. Brandon slipped on the condom, held Sarah's hands above her head and said, "This is a game. Pretend you can't touch me, but I can touch you as long as I want."

His mouth moved from her neck, to her breasts, then slowly trailed down. He loved the passion he arose in her, loved the feel of her twisting compact body and the sweet sounds that escaped her lips.

He could no longer wait, his body covered hers and he thrusted into her and the rythm grew faster and faster.

"Brandon,"she moaned .

"I love you, Sarah" He felt himself exploding as Sarah moved her body wildly against him in estacy. He showered her with kisses, rolled aside and pulled her close to him.

They were both quiet beside the crackling fire.

"I want to wake up beside you in the mornings for the rest of my life. We could stay like this forever," he whispered, his eyes searching hers.

"Don't you think that the floor will become a bit hard," she teased.

"Who cares?" His eyes roamed the length of her small compact body and he felt desire stir within him again. Stacey had never done that to him. He felt like starting all over again. "You're mine, Sarah"

She pulled up her legs, placed one arm across her breast and looked away from him. Brandon propped himself up on one elbow and leaned over her. "Where are you going to look now? There's nothing to be shy about."

She looked into his eyes. "I hope you don't think that I am...well...easy."

"Sarah, I don't think so. I know you didn't have many boyfriends." He lowered his head and kissed her.

135

"Do you know how long I've been waiting for this moment?"

"No." She smiled up at him.

"Since the first day you walked through my door. By the way, why are you carrying condoms around in your purse?"

"I knew that this was going to happen. I wanted to be ready. What's your excuse? No, wrong question. I didn't ask that."

Brandon didn't want to lie to her. "You know I was dating Stacey and…" He felt uncomfortable telling her the truth, but he hated lies.

"I understand," she whispered and kissed him.

"We had better get up before someone walks in."

"I'm going to take a shower and you're going to get the clothes from the patio."

"Yes boss. On one condition though," he kissed her on the forehead.

"What? Want to come shower with me?" She asked, smiling mischievously.

"Exactly what I had in mind." He studied her for a moment. "You're suddenly brave."

Sarah smiled, headed for her room and Brandon got dressed before going outside. He picked up their clothes and went back in. He was tempted to join Sarah in the shower but decided not to. She might just think that he was only interested in sex. The scar on her abdomen bothered him. It made him think of a c-section. Did she have a child and she didn't feel ready to tell him? "No way," he said into the quiet room, feeling certain that if it was so, she would have told him. She certainly wouldn't keep something that important from him.

When he went to her room, the water was still running He looked at Sarah through the glass shower door and was tempted to join her, instead he placed her clothes on the bed and left. He hoped that she wouldn't look back on this night and regret it.

The next morning, over breakfast, Brandon asked, "What's that scar on your belly?" He did not look her in the eyes, afraid of what he would see, afraid of her answer. The thought of Sarah having a child scared him. It was quite irrational, he told himself. Even if she had a child, that wouldn't change things between them. But then, he didn't want Sarah to be tied to another man. He looked at her, she was playing with the rings on her fingers.

"I had surgery a few years ago. Nothing serious. I hate that scar. Don't you think it's disgusting?"

"No. I love every inch of you. I wouldn't change a thing, not even the scar.

She got up, went to the counter and poured herself some coffee. Without turning to face him, she asked, "Are you sorry about what happened between us?"

He stood up and closed the distance between them, placed his arms around her waist and said, "No. Are you sorry Sarah?"

"I'm not." She smiled up at him.

The fear and uncertainity in her eyes did not go unnoticed. He'd seen it several times while they were making love. If only she would stop being so secretive and talk to him.

"You look like something is bothering you. Please, I don't want you to regret what happened between us. Sarah, I have no intention of hurting you."

"I have no regrets, Brandon," she said softly.

He let out a pent up breath. "I was scared for a minute."

"Don't do that to yourself." She gave him a small quick kiss.

"That's not enough." He covered her mouth with his, in a deep, slow kiss. "We better behave ourselves." He stepped aside and looked at her with frank admiration

****

She sank down on the kitchen chair, let out a deep breath and closed her eyes. Frustration and anger unfolded within her. What on earth had she done? Why had she given in to her dangerous emotions? This wasn't part of the deal she had made with herself! "This has to be a bad dream," she muttered.

What had he done to her? She couldn't figure out what she wanted, and what she did not want anymore. She used to be so sure of herself, so in control, now everything had changed.

Slowly, he had led her away from the path she had paved for herself. Where was the Sarah who was so determined not to become involved with anyone? She felt an increasing sense of frustration with herself as mind and emotions warred, one trying to gain control over the other.

She watched Brandon through the open window. He stood in silence, sipping coffee and looking out at Casco bay. She had come alive in his arms, became aware of her own feminity and enjoyed every moment of their love making. Now, she regretted it. The thought struck her that there was still time to walk away, call this night a mistake and go back to her plans but somewhere deep within, she knew that she could not walk away from him. She loved him.

She unconsciously touched the scar on her belly and wondered if he knew what a c-section scar looked like. She buried her face in the palm of her hands and blew out a deep breath. She had gone about everything the wrong way. She should have told Brandon about her baby before things went this far. She had made a fine mess all by herself. How long did she think that she could hide it from Brandon? Why did she deliberately hold such a thing back from him? She thought long and hard about her actions, trying to understand herself. She came to one conclusion. She acted that way, because for once, she wanted someone to see her without the mistakes she had made. To love her without those mistakes. It felt so good. If only it could stay that way.

When he had asked her about the scar, she had become really nervous but somehow managed to control her nervousness and lie her way out. How was she supposed to explain this to him now? Brandon had asked no further questions. He trusted her completely. She felt like a some slimy insect lying to him after the way they had just made love. He had made her feel so special, so loved, so wanted. She never imagined that she could ever feel that way.

She got up and went to her room. There was a tight feeling in her chest and she had difficulty breathing. She had to tell Brandon about the child she had given up for adoption.

Hilda St. James

How was he going to react? He had been given up for adoption and had told her about the horrors of being in an orphanage. He had told her about the Christmas days when he'd sit by the window, hoping for the best Christmas present in the world. For him, that was his mother showing up and telling him that she was going to take him home. It never happened.

The day Elizabeth and Austin had taken him home, he had pretended that they were his real parents. He had gone on to tell her that he had made a promise that no matter what, he would never hurt them. Would he one day abandon her for his parents?

They had both suffered in life and here she was, leading him along a path that would certainly bring them both pain.

She went to the bathroom, turned on the cold water and washed her face. She patted it dry with a towel as she tried to stop the flow of questions and doubts gushing through her mind. What had she gotten herself into again? She had obviously fallen in love with the wrong man? Again. She shook her head. She should have stopped herself from going that far with Brandon. Families had a way of coming between people, so did secrets. There were too many things against them.

She closed her eyes and took a deep breath. She had to tell Brandon this secret that was lying between them, like a hidden time-bomb that could suddenly go off and destroy them.

A new wave of guilt swept over Sarah. She felt like she was abandoning her child a second time by not admitting that she existed. "I know you are there, Lydia, and I love you. I always will." She had secretly named her baby girl Lydia. Sarah had first heard that name when she went to church with her Aunt Jenny and somehow it always stayed with her.

Today Lydia would be ten years old. Was she doing fine? Did her parents love her? Did she know that she was adopted? Sarah shook her head as though to bring order to those uneasy thoughts floating around in her mind.

Sarah sat on the bed, closed her eyes and told herself to stop it. She had gone over her child's adoption so many times with Anna and Tim and they had told her that she did what was best for Lydia. Where were all these questions coming from again?

She looked at the painting on the wall of a little girl sitting on a rock by the sea. It was stormy, but her face had such a serene look, it seemed like she was at peace even in the face of storms. Was Lydia facing storms or was she happy?

Sarah felt like someone had filled her chest with lead. Not so long ago, she was soaring with joy in Brandon's arms and now she felt so weighed down by her past. If only she had a squeaky clean life like Stacey, things would be less complicated.

She walked over to the painting to have a closer look at the child's face and heard a soft knock on the door. She turned towards the door as Brandon walked in.

"I love this painting. Who is the little girl?"

"My favorite painting," Brandon said. "It's Lisa, from the orphanage. She was always in her peaceful little world. She was sick very often. I wonder where she is now."

Sarah smiled. "You paint so well. Do you want to teach me to paint?"

Hilda St. James

"I'd love to." He studied her in silence and his eyes immediately changed. He looked rather uneasy, then embarassed. "Sarah, I know that you didn't want me touching you. Maybe I pushed you too far. I should have stopped."

"You didn't force me into anything. There is just one thing…well…my life is not squeaky clean like Stacey's." She looked at his puzzled face.

"Stop doing that to yourself. I love you just the way you are."

If only Brandon knew the real Sarah, would he still love her? She looked at him, speechless. Should she tell him the same? Finally her senses unfroze and she felt warm tears filled up her eyes. "I love you Brandon."

"You don't know how much those words mean to me." He kissed her on the lips.

Chapter 9

Sarah couldn't believe that she was this happy, never dreamt that such hapiness existed. It was like living in a dream world, a place reserved only for special people. She knew that her world was as fragile as a bubble floating on the wind, it could burst any moment and be all over. For now, she wanted to float, be happy, enjoy every moment of it and completely ignore reality.

There was Austin on one side and her secret on the other. Would these two things close in on her fragile bubble world and bring it to an end.

Brandon had made up his mind to give up everything and walk away from Austin though he still clung to the hope that his father would one day understand and all would be well. "What is life without hope?" He had asked Sarah as they talked over breakfast this morning. She had to agree with him. Life without hope was rather gloomy and frightening. She admired his courage, strength and positive attitude.

She didn't realise that Brandon was standing beside her. He gave her hair a gentle tug. "Where were you?" he whispered.

"Thinking about you." She smiled up at his curious face.

"I'm all ears." He brought her hands to his mouth and kissed them. "Are you going to tell me?"

"Let me think about that." His eyes were full of desire and Sarah felt her emotions awakening, as though to answer the need she was seeing in his eyes.

"You are so strong, so positive. How do you do it?" She was surprised at the sincerity of her words and the emotions that brought them to life.

"You just have to force yourself to stay strong and positive. Everytime you feel like wallowing in self pity, you give yourself a kick in the rear end and tell yourself to stop it."

"You make that sound so easy."

Brandon's hands slid up her arm in a gentle caress, leaving a trail of warmth that was fast spreading through her body. Their eyes locked and the raw hunger she read in his made her heart beat at a startling rate. Images of the first time they made love swam in her mind, tempting her, lulling her to feel his touch again.

He let go of her abruptly, as blaring music interupted their intimate world. They both headed for the door and stepped outside in the bright sunshine.

Christian sprang out the car, waved at them and asked, "Like my new C.D? It's cool. Don't you think so?"

"Sounds like they don't know to sing and they're not good with the musical instruments either," Brandon said.

Christian reached into the car and turned down the music. "What did you say?"

"I said they can't sing or play musical instruments," he answered.

"I'll buy you slippers and a rocking chair for Christmas. I'll even throw in one of those magic bags that you warm up in the microwave. Christian grinned. "Are you going to invite me or not?" He took off his black, cowboy hat.

"Come on Christian. Have a seat."

He bounded up the short flight of steps and sat down beside Sarah. "How are you?" He asked, his eyes eyes settling on her face.

"Doing great. It's been a long time since you came by. Busy?" she asked.

"Kind of. I can see my brother is doing better. Can't wait to hit the bars with him." He jingled his car keys in an annoying way, his eyes moved from Brandon to Sarah and back to Brandon.

"Right. Hit the bars with you." Brandon shook his head. "You know I hate your kind of bars."

Sarah listened to them joking around and teasing each other. Her eyes met Brandon's and they looked at each other for too long.

"What's going on here," Christian asked, eyeing them keenly. "There is something. I just know it," he jingled his keys louder and faster.

Sarah and Brandon were quiet and she was anxious to hear what he was going to say. Was he going to tell his little brother about them?

Christian suddenly started sniffing the air. "I can smell love." He looked from Brandon to Sarah. "You two are glowing. You are glowing so much, you can't keep me in the dark." He sprang to his feet, did an imitation of a rock star playing a guitar, and said, "This is sweet music. My brother is no longer Mr. Perfect. He is bad now, so very bad."

Sarah laughed and Brandon joined in. Christian was just what they needed. A good dose of laughter.

"I'll get the Bible and make you two swear that something isn't going on." He turned to Brandon, "Where is it?"

Sarah saw the questioning look in Brandon's eyes. She got the feeling that he wanted to know if it was okay to tell his brother.

Christian sprang out of the chair. "Okay. Keep me in the dark." He started towards the door.

"It's Saturday. How come you're not out with your girlfriend?" Brandon asked.

Christian half turned, his eyes lowered. "She's on page five of the history book," he answered before going into the house.

Sarah laughed. "Is he always like that?"

Yes. He'll never grow up. That drives Austin crazy. Mom got calls from school at least once a week. He was always clowning around and disturbing the class. I hope he'll grow up soon."

Elizabeth was lucky to be getting calls only from school and about something not serious. Her mom, Anna, kept getting calls from the police. Tim was always getting into trouble. At fifteen, he was picked up several times by the police because he was drunk and couldn't even remember where he lived. The following year, he started doing drugs and the police was constantly looking for him.

Christian came back out wearing a puzzled look. "Why are you packing up your stuff?"

"It's a long story," Brandon answered

"I'd like to know what's going on," he said, his face serious.

Brandon told Christian what had happened and about his decision to leave it all behind and to start over.

Christian looked like someone had unsuspectingly punched him in the stomach. He stood rooted to the spot, his mouth hanging open. He shook his head, blinked a few times and sat down.

"Where are you going to live? You can come stay at my place if you want. There's not a lot of space but it's better than nothing."

"If I don't find something soon, I'll come at your place for a while."

"I can't believe Austin said such horrible things to you." There was a hard edge to his voice. "If I were you, I wouldn't leave this house Brandon. It belongs to mom, not dad."

"No. Dad bought the house from grand-ma. It belongs to him."

"No matter what happens Brandon, I'll always be your brother. Don't ever forget that!

Sarah was touched by Christian's words. They were so sincere, so full of love. His face had lost it's jovial expression and she could tell that he was hurting. When Brandon had told him about their relationship, Christian hadn't shown any reaction at all.

Christian stood up, walked over to Sarah and said, "I'm happy for you and Brandon."

She looked at the brothers, they were silent, lost in their own thoughts. If only Austin would accept Brandon's decisions, accept Christian's choices, they would be a happy family. It was sad to see him desstroy their hapiness. Austin made his own choices. Why wouldn't he let his sons do the same? Where was Elizabeth in all this?

"No wonder mom hasn't called," Christian said. "It's not like her. I suspected something was wrong, somewhere in Austin's kingdom but, I didn't know it was that serious. I respect your decisions Brandon and

I'm glad you are finally standing up to Dad." He stood up, brushed off the back of his pants and walked from one end of the patio to the other, like an animal in captivity. "I have to talk to mom. No use calling now. Dad is home. He'll be the first one to jump at the phone."

"One day, dad will wake up and realize his mistake and things are going to change." Brandon walked over to his brother and placed an arm on his shoulder.

"Let's hope he does it before he gets Alzeihmer's." He turned to Sarah. "Don't let dad scare you away. When he met mom, she wasn't rich but she was educated, like you. He married her so I don't see why Brandon can't marry you. Mom wouldn't have a problem with that. Austin is the…" He flung his hands in the air. "I won't say it."

The weather was beautiful and Sarah spied the gas grill through the half open shed door. "Why don't we have a barbecue?" she asked. Without waiting for an answer, she walked down the steps and headed for the shed. The stiff door creaked open as she pulled on it. She turned towards the patio, "Come on guys. Pull this thing out."

Brandon and Christian came over to her. Sarah noticed how steady Brandon was on his feet and the thought struck her like a hammer on her forehead. It was time to leave. Brandon didn't need her anymore, at least not as a nurse. She was taking his money for nothing. She felt horrible. She decided to return that week's paycheck and to leave very soon. Later, when Christian left, she would talk to him about it. With all that was going on, Sarah hadn't given much thought to her job and she felt rather uncomfortable that she didn't call the nursing agency to tell them that Brandon was fine and that he didn't need her anymore.

"Where do you want it?" Christian called out.

"Beside the patio."

The phone rang and Christian dashed inside to answer it. "Sarah, it's for you," he called from the open window.

Sarah was surprised. It had to be Tim or her mom. Was something wrong? She picked up the phone. "This is Sarah," she said twirling the cord around her finger.

"Gertrude here." Her voice held a hint of anger. "I had a call from Austin Chase, a rather disturbing one. He said that you are having an affair with his son, who is quite emotionally disturbed at this time. I don't believe him but he told me that he has very intimate photos of you two. What's going on? Why didn't you let us know that Brandon was fine and didn't need your help anymore?"

Sarah bit down on her lip, searching for the right words to say. She felt like she was suddenly caught up in a storm. She could get into real trouble.

"Sarah," she said impatiently.

"Gertrude, you know me better than that. Do you think that I would have an affair with one of my patients?"

"You never know when love will jump out at you from nowhere. I don't make the rules here. But it is an agency policy. You can't have an affair with your patient!"

"There is nothing going on between us. I don't know where Austin got his information, but it is all wrong!"

"If you say so. Does Brandon still need your help?"

"No. But he asked me to stay a few more days just to keep his company."

"Austin wants your job so you had better get out of there. You are not being paid to keep Brandon's company. If there is something going on between you and Brandon, tell me and I'll try my best to help you.""

"There is nothing going on. You know me better than that.

They talked for a few more minutes before the call ended.

Sarah hung up the phone and dashed to her room. She went straight to the bathroom, opened the cold water and splased it on her face. Austin was trying to make her lose her job. She couldn't afford that. He had told Gertrude that he had intimate photos of her and Brandon. When were they taken? The night they had made love outside? She covered her face with her hands. She hoped desperately that Austin was just bluffing. But what if he wasn't bluffing at all? She felt dizzy, nauseated. She held on to the side of the sink and took a deep breath. Surely she couldn't lose her licences to practice because she and Brandon had a relationship. But if the agency fired her, what was she going to tell future employers? If Austin really had such photos, she didn't want him to show them to anyone. She would die of shame. She clenched and unclenched her fists. If Austin was standing before her, she would gladly claw at his face. Angry tears blurred her vision and hatred surged through her. Austin was horrible,disgusting, a beast! Sarah had faced enough shame in her life, she wanted no more.

"Stop it. Maybe Austin is just bluffing," she said into the empty room, her mind going down the twisted roads that he would probably take. Gertrude had said that Austin had spoken to a few girls working for the agency. She wondered what he had asked them and what they had told him. Would he show them such photos if he really had them? "This can't be happening to me," she murmured.

She took a few deep breaths until the nauseated feeling subsided and she felt a bit in control again. It took every ounce of strength she could draw from within to go back outside. She had to tell Brandon about this.

When she went outside, the two brothers were deep in conversation as Brandon ripped the plastic off of a package of steak. They hadn't even noticed that she was there. She went back inside, grabbed a table cloth and some plates and started setting the table. The clattering noise of the plates drew their attention. Brandon gave the package to Christian and walked over to her.

"Is everything okay? I went inside and you were in your room. Is something wrong with your family?"

"No. They are fine." She glanced over at Christian who was putting more steak on the grill. She spoke in a whisper, "I got a call from the agency and my supervisor is not very happy. Austin went to see Gertrude and he told her that we are having an affair and you are emotionally unstable. He wants them to fire me. My supervisor said that, seeing you don't need my help anymore I must leave now. I know that I had to leave soon and I was planning to talk to you about that."

All the while she spoke, Brandon just stared at her open mouthed. Then she saw the anger in his eyes. "There's no way he is going to make you lose your job! I'll see to that! This shouldn't surprise me, but it still does. If the agency asks, I'll deny it. To protect you and your job."

Sarah wondered whether or not she should tell him about the photos and decided it was best to do so. "There is something else. Austin told my supervisor that he had photos to prove that."

"What?" He sucked in a deep breath and in a split second his arm shot out and he punched the wall. He leaned against it, breathing hard, his eyes cold. Blood covered his fist that was still clenched.

"What's going on?" Christian asked hurrying toward them, his eyes wide and questioning.

Sarah was mad at herself for not waiting until Christian left before telling Brandon. That's what she had wanted to do, but it was so overwhelming. She just had to get it out. She looked at Christian, who was looking at her impatiently. Sarah didn't know whether or not she should tell him. There were already lots between him and his father and she didn't want to be the one to add more.

Brandon turned to face Christian. "Austin went to see Sarah's supervisor and he told them about us. He wants them to fire Sarah."

Christian looked confused. "But they can't fire you because you're in love with Brandon," he said.

"The agency has their rules and they could fire me for that." She sounded calm but her chest was tight with fear. 'Please, dear God, I don't want to lose my job', she prayed silently. She would never be able to handle a situation like that.

"I'm ashamed to admit he is my father," Christian said. "What weird pleasure does he get from making other people's life miserable. Mom is such a wonderful person. I can't understand how she could live with such an insect." He looked at Brandon's bleeding hand. "You should go clean that up." He turned and walked back to the barbecue.

Brandon took Sarah by the arm and led her inside. He washed the blood from his hand. "Soon Austin will not bother us anymore," he said. "I will be moving out and he certainly won't know where to find me. He does not know where you live, so we will have some peace. At least for a while." His voice was hard, full of anger and embarassment was printed on his face. "I wonder if he really has photos of us. When were they taken?" He dried his hands and pulled Sarah close to him. "I'm sorry for all you are going through."

"It's not your fault. You haven't done anything wrong."

He kissed her on the lips. "I promise you that things will be better. I'll go see Austin. If he really has photos of us, he will have to give them to me! He has gone too far! I will turn his office up-side-down if I have to!" His fingers were clamped onto the edge of the counter and his knuckles turned white. The cuts on his right hand started to bleed again. He let go of the counter, turned on the tap and washed his hand again.

Sarah took his right hand and pressed a small towel against the bleeding cuts. She looked away from his intense stare, wondering what was going through his mind. She didn't want the gap between him and his father to widen. Sarah knew that despite the differences, Brandon loved Austin and hoped desperatelty that their relationship would mend. He dreamt of one happy family and she wished that his dream would come true. She removed the towel, examined the small cuts. The bleeding had stopped and she let go of his hand.

Christian looked through the half open door. "Everything is getting cold. Except the salad. And I'm hungry."

Over dinner, no one mentioned Austin and they barely touched their food. Christian talked about his plans for the summer and he rambled on and on about a pretty girl, he had named Tina, because she wouldn't tell him her name.

"Why did you break up with the girl in Saco?" Brandon asked.

"She told me to grow up. Said she couldn't continue seeing me because I wasn't serious. I want to have fun. I'm too young to get into anything serious. I'm not old like you, Brandon." He folded and unfolded his napkin. "Maybe I should grow up." He looked up at Brandon. "Don't say a word."

Brandon laughed. "You said it for me. What about school? Are you planning to go back?"

"Austin refused to pay my school expenses. Remember?"

"Then you'll just have to work and pay it yourself. I'm here if you need help."

Christian looked at his watch. "Do I have to wash dishes? Please say no. I'm going out with the guys."

"There's a dishwaser," Brandon said.

Christian stood up, pushed back his chair and for a minute he looked quite serious. "Phone me. If you don't find a suitable apartment, come over to my place for a while."

"I will let you know. Thanks Christian."

"Bye guys." He walked over to his car, slid inside and waved good-bye before leaving.

Sarah couldn't help laughing. She wondered why he had painted his car that colour and if girls his age wanted to be seen in it. Christian was good-looking and had a good sense of humour and she liked him a lot. "There's only one Christian in this world," she said.

"I have to agree with you. I can't see myself living at Christian's place. He told me that he was going to do some cleaning tomorrow because his place was a mess and he didn't want me to see it like that. It will probably take him a week to clean his bedroom."

Brandon fell silent and Sarah could see that he was lost in his own world again. She knew he loved this house, the magnificent view of Casco Bay, the sprawling lawn with the tiny beach at the end. It must be so hard to let go of it all. She loved this place too and was going to miss it. But most of all, she was going to miss being around Brandon so often. She could hardly believe it. Brandon was walking away from all this because he loved her! Even though she didn't want to, she was going to end up hurting him. Her heart felt like an open sore, throbbing with pain. Would he be able to forgive her?

Sarah stood up and looked out at the bay. Dusk was slowly giving way to night and the moon had begun it's climb into the sky. There's so much that she didn't think about. She would have to give her phone number to Brandon. What if Edward answered the phone when he was drunk? What if he insulted Brandon? She hadn't told Brandon the entire truth about her dad and Sarah realized that her little white lies were slowly weaving a web around her. She had told Brandon that sometimes Edward took a drink but didn't tell him that her father was a hopeless drunk. She gulped in fresh air, feeling like she couldn't get enough. What if Edward told Brandon about her child? She held on to the railing, her heart pounding. She had to tell Brandon before someone else did. Questions crowded her mind until she felt like her head was going to explode. There has to be a way out she told herself, fighting back the panic that was threatening to engulf her. She would have to manipulate things to her advantage. The thought of holding her secrets for as long as possible crossed her mind. She pushed the thought away. That would only make things worse. Maybe that path would lead to ultimate destruction.

Brandon came to stand beside her. She glanced at his silent profile as he stared out at the bay. This was her last night in this house with him. Tomorrow she would have to leave. Her heart swelled with sadness. Were they going to survive all those issuses that threatened to destroy them? 'Love conquers all', Sarah reminded herself and clung to that phrase desperately, hoping that it was true.

He moved closer and whispered against her ear, "Lets go for a walk. We can go down by the beach."

She placed an arm around his waist. "Sounds good."

As they walked along the stone path towards the garden, Brandon stopped and looked down. "I remember the day my grandmother was making this grey stone path. Back then, the garden was so beautiful. Grand-ma was very good with her plants. Now it's so neglected. I'm not good with plants and a bit lazy when it comes to the garden. She would be horrified if she could see her garden now."

Sarah smiled up at him. "I'm not good with flowers either. Everything I touch die. Like your african violet."

He laughed. "You didn't just touch that poor plant. You yanked the leaves off in rage. It seem like so long ago and it isn't. By the way, what did I say to make you that upset?"

"Maybe the psychologist in me." Another lie, she thought. This was absurd. Was it ever going to stop?

They walked around the garden in silence. If their relationship ended, Brandon would be one of those people who walked into her life and left footprints forever. She would never be able to forget him. Never in her wildest dreams, had she thought that she would fall so deeply in love, or that it was possible.

"I'm going to miss having you around. Stop."

She stopped walking and looked up at him. "What is it?"

"Why didn't I think about it before. I should have pretended not to be able to walk and then you would have stayed." He fell silent for a minute then said, "Remember the first time you helped me to shower? I would kill to see that look on your face again."

"You don't have to kill to see that look! Want to go for a shower?"

"Don't tempt me!" He took her hand and started to walk. "Want to go down to the beach?"

"I'm going to misss you," she said as they made their way down the gentle slope and onto the sandy strip of beach.

The sand was cool in contrast to the warm evening air. Brandon pulled her close as they sat down. Darkness was slowly setting in. Stars were scattered abundantly in the night sky.

"Too bad we can't live here," he said and turned to look at the house. "I'm sure we can find another place like this with a tiny beach at the back of the house." His arms tightened around her.

She felt the drumming of his heart and his warm breath. She was already missing him. "I will phone you everyday."

"Not good enough."

"I'll come to see you everday." She didn't want him coming to her parents place. Images of what it would be like stormed her mind. She took a deep breath and stopped her thoughts from going down that gloomy path. For now, she didn't want to think of their future and the problems that awaited them. She wanted to enjoy this moment, the present. The future will take care of itself, she mused. It always did.

"I will…"

She moved aside and placed a finger on his lip. "Let's just enjoy the present and forget what we have to deal with. Let's just pretend that we are living in a magical world and that reality dosen't exist.

He pulled her down gently beside him, their eyes held and Sarah saw desire in his eyes. It taunted her, tempted her and finally took her in its grip.

Their lips met and Brandon kissed her slowly, awakening every fibre in her body. She wanted to walk the streets of naked desire, like lovers before them had done and those of the future will do. She had never loved anyone this way in all her life and was sure that there wouldn't be a second time. This happened only once in a lifetime and she was determined to keep it all. Even if she had to lie about certain things!

When Brandon started to unbutton her shirt, warm tears filled her eyes. Tears of love, of genuine hapiness.

He kissed her again-soft, slow kisses, kisses that drew her into a world where unharnessed emotions ran wild and free. His mouth trailed along her neck and dipped lower. She gave in to his roaming hands and warm mouth leaving trails of havoc wherever it touched. No matter what the future held, these precious moments belonged to them and was not spoilt by what he didn't know.

Waves of pleasure washed through her, ripples of desire and the urge to give him as much pleasure as he was giving her. She pushed gently against him and he rolled onto his back. Sarah covered his mouth with hers, kissing him hungrily. Her mouth found his neck, his chest, his entire body.

Sarah drifted through a world of passion and desire, of emotions unleashed and wild. Her entire being was tuned into their needs, their hunger and she floated in that world where nothing else mattered and reality hung suspended in time. Then came the blinding flash of estacy, satisfaction. They clung to each other, their ragged breathing interupting the silence.

He showered her with kisses and rolled aside.

Brandon propped himself up on one arm and looked down at her. "Are you crying?"

The emotion in his voice made her heart contract. "Yes. But I'm not sad," she lied, hating herself for doing that again. She wished that she had told him the truth from the beginning. Now her lies were like poison at the root of their love. "I'm happy."

He brushed her tears away. "I have something for you." He reached for his shirt, took out a small wood box and opened the lid. "This is my grandmother's engagement ring. She gave it to me and told me to give it to the woman I love."

Sarah sat up, unaware of her nakedness. Brandon stripped her fingers of all the artificial rings she was wearing.

"Wait. Not this one," she said, taking back the one with a pink stone. This one was a reminder of Lydia. He asked no questions as she slipped it back on, feeling guilty. He was surely wondering why that ring. What was she going to tell him? Another lie?

He looked at her in silence as though waiting for some kind of explanation. Sarah's thoughts went around in circles. She had to tell him something. It wasn't fair to leave him wondering. He had always been so honest with her. Why couldn't she do the same with him?

"Sarah. Please tell me why that ring is so special. I know that there are things that you don't want to talk about and I have never forced you. I know that you will eventually tell me. She got the impression that Bandon was jealous and that he wanted to be sure that the ring did not remind her of another man. She couldn't tell him that she had bought it as a reminder of the daughter she had given up for adoption! She had never even told him about her child! Yet denying that she had a child made her feel guilty. It was like abandoning her daughter all over again.

"It's kind of a silly reason," she said, still not sure what that reason would be. She hoped that Brandon would not see through her fake smile.

"What is it?" He insisted.

"My brother gave it to me after I graduated from nursing school. It was meant as a joke but I always kept it on. I love Tim very much." She turned her attention to the ring Brandon was holding between two fingers, diamonds glittering in the dark. She didn't deserve it and even if she accepted, for how long would she wear it?

He took her ring finger and slid the ring on. "This is a token of my love."

Sarah felt special, loved, wanted. She couldn't ask for more. "Are you sure… Well.. You want to give me this."

He answered her with a kiss on the lips.

She wondered if Stacey had ever worn it but did not ask. As though reading her thoughts, he said. "Stacey never wore it. I never gave it to her. You're the one I love."

"I love you Brandon." She moved closer to him, their naked bodies touching. For a few moments, they just sat quietly, holding each other.

"I wish it was my mother's ring instead of my grandmother's. I mean my natural mother. It would be so much more special. Sometimes I wonder why she gave me up for adoption. My mother brought me into this world and then abandoned me. I detest her and all women like her. I would never have anything to do with a woman like that!"

Sarah's mind, heart and soul froze over for a few seconds. His last sentence crushed her and her throat tightened painfully with the tears she desperately fought back. She was one of those women! She stared at him, trying to think of something to say. She felt grateful that he hadn't been looking at her as he spoke or he would have certainly seen that something was wrong. There has to be a way out she told herself. There has to be a way to make him change his mind.

In the deep quietness of the night, she heard the faint chiming of the grandfather clock. It was like fate was saying that this was the end. Sarah felt her soul slipping out, like marbles from a broken bag. Her fragile bubble world had just popped. It died within seconds, and all it took was a few sentences. Tears rolled down her cheeks. This was the end.

Brandon pulled her into his arms.

"I'm so happy with you, Brandon," she said, resting her head on his shoulder.

Chapter 10

Life suddenly seemed so different. She flung her small suitcase onto the bed. When she had gone to work for Brandon, her life was in order, everything well planned and in a certain way, she was happy, secure. Now she felt like a tornado had passed through that well organised, perfect world leaving choas behind. Her emotions had gone haywire and she felt like a part of her was slowly dying. Brandon's words echoed in her mind, 'I detest her and all women like her'. She closed her eyes, leaned against the cool window pane, a strange numbness settling upon her heart and mind, like an emotional blanket, protecting her from reality. If only she had told him the truth from the beginning, walk away while she still could. Too late now.

She looked at the diamond ring on her finger, it winked at her as a ray of sunlight caught it from the open curtains. She shouldn't be wearing this ring. She had let Brandon fall in love with an image and not the real Sarah. Once he found out the truth, would his love turn to hate? She closed her eyes tightly as though to shut out some violent image. She had given her heart to a man who would now refuse her love, refuse to have anything to do with her. Another heartbreak. A heaviness filled her chest, and though she felt like crying, no tears came.

Edward's swearing drifted through the closed door. She heard the floorboards creaking under his weight, then his heavy footfalls as he stomped downstairs. She sighed and relief washed over her. He didn't know that she was home.

Why did Brandon's mom given him up for adoption, she wondered. If only he hadn't been, he would understand her choice of the past. But that's not the way things were. He'd been given up for adoption, he had faced hard times. Times of lonliness, feeling unwanted, unloved. He had waited fervently for a mother who never came back to get him. Her heart swelled with sadness for Brandon and herself. Their past was now going to destroy their future. Life had thrown them on two different paths, paths that were not suppose to cross.

She picked up her car keys and headed downstairs, wincing as Edward's loud swearing reached her ears. He was in the kitchen, his back towards her as he searched through the cupboards. She pulled open the door and slipped out, grateful that there was no confrontation with him. She dashed down the stairs and climbed into her car and started the engine. Edward's loud swearing caught her attention. He was standing by the open window, his face was puffy and pale, his hard eyes bore into her. She felt like an unwelcome stranger, dropping by when it was forbidden to do so. He laughed, it was cold and cruel. If hatred made a sound, that would be it.

She rested her head on the steering wheel and silent tears rolled down her cheeks. This man was her father, a father that she needed and longed for all her life but would never have. Didn't children, no matter what their age, run to their parents in times of distress? She couldn't run to her father.

There he was, laughing at her, cursing her and she was already in so much pain. Couldn't he see what she needed was comforting?

"What the hell is wrong with you?" he yelled. "Go cry somewhere else! That man patient of yours kicked you out?" She continued crying and did not raise her head to look up at him. She did not care if the neighbors were looking. She couldn't hurt more than she already was. His words seemed to come from a distance and suddenly stopped.

Her tears stopped and the heaviness of pain and grief settled in her chest like a ton of bricks. He started hurling insults at her again. She straightened up, dabbed at her eyes with the back of her hands, started her car and headed down the street. She needed to talk to someone, someone who could give her sound advice. Farther down the quiet tree lined street, she stopped beside the phone booth and got out the car.

She popped some quarters in, dialled a number and after a few rings, Tim answered. "Yeah."

"Tim, it's Sarah. What time are you getting off from work?"

"In a couple of hours. What's wrong?"

He sounded worried. He knew her better than either of her parents.

"Sarah."

"I need to talk to you." She tried to keep her voice steady.

"I'll meet you down at the beach around five."

"Thanks Tim."

She took some quarters from her purse, slid a few into the slot and started to dial Brandon's number, stopped halfway and hung up the phone. It was barely two hours since she had last seen him. She had told him that she was going to phone him because her dad wasn't the nicest person to deal with.

She started to dial his number again, wanting to hear his voice and deep within, she wanted to be sure that he still loved her. Sarah twirled the phone cord around her finger and moved around the tiny space restlessly.

"Hello," he answered.

"Just calling to see how you're doing." She took a deep breath, not trusting herself to say another word. He would know that she was on the verge of tears.

"It's lonley out here. I miss you."

"Already?"

"Yes. Too bad we couldn't finish that kissing stuff this morning."

She didn't answer, tears rolled down her cheeks.

"Sarah. Are you still there?"

"Yes," she answered, her voice unsteady.

"You don't sound okay. What's going on?"

"I just miss you." The lie slid off her tongue and she felt frustration rising within her.

"Come back to the house. No one will know."

She was tempted to say yes. She wanted to feel his protective arms around her, to see the love in his eyes. Sarah wanted him to promise her that he would never stop loving her.

"I can't. I have so much to do today. Just hearing your voice makes me feel better. I'll come by this evening."

"You know what. Just hearing your voice isn't enough. I want you here with me."

"I'll see you around seven."

"Hurry up."

Sarah reluctantly hung up, got into her car and joined the steady flow of traffic. She had to go to the Nursing Agency but didn't feel like.

She played around with questions and answers in her mind. Questions that Gertrude may ask concerning Austin's accusations and how she was going to answer. Glancing up at the rearview mirror, she caught sight of her puffy eyes and windblown hair. She had to clean herself up before meeting her supervisor.

Further down the road, she pulled into the parking lot of, 'Big Jim's Restaurant'. She grabbed her purse and hurried inside. The washroom was smelly but at least it was empty. She turned on the tap, splashed cold water on her face, patted it dry and started to apply powder, then mascara and a bit of lip gloss. She combed her hair and headed back to the car.

What if Austin really had those photos he claimed to have? What if he had shown them to Gertrude or to other staff? Sarah pressed a cold clammy hand over her mouth and whispered, "This can't be true. This can't be happening." She sat back on the seat, breathed deeply and tried to pull herself together. She had faced numerous embarassing situations in her life, but this was by far, the worst.

She pulled out the parking lot and into the flow of traffic, her mind working like a clock. Sarah forced herself to concentrate on the traffic. The three storey building housing the nursing office drew into sight.

Her heart pounded like someone hammering frantically as she knocked on Gertrude's door.

"Come in," came the soft answer.

Sarah entered. "Good-morning. How are you?"

"Hi Sarah. So nice to see you. Sit." She pointed to the leather chair across from her. "You should wear make-up more often. It enhances those beautiful eyes of yours."

Sarah sat down, a half smile on her face, despite her nervousness and listened as Gertrude talked non stop.

"I can't wait to go back to work at St. Joseph's." Her eyes roamed the tastefully decorated office so she wouldn't have to look at the woman in front of her.

"I take it that you didn't like working for the Chases' family." Gertrude eyed her keenly.

"Some days were good, some bad." Brandon's image sprang to mind. She glanced at her watch, it was already two-thirty. In a few hours she would be seeing him.

"Austin came in here like a mad man, called you all sorts of names and said that he wanted you out of there. What's going on between you and Brandon?" Gertrude studied her intently as she waited for an answer.

Sarah saw the hint of anger in those normally kind, blue eyes and it surprised her. "There is nothing going on between Brandon and me." She had the impression that Gertrude was seeing right through her, was looking into her mind and knew that her answer was nothing but a lie.

"I saw his photo and he is a looker. Handsome. I'm sure you noticed that."

"Yes, he is good looking. You know the rules I live by."

"You should stop living by such harsh, ridgid rules. Why would Austin accuse you of having an affair with his son?" She looked at her watch and turned her attention back to Sarah.

"I don't know." She had forgotten the diamond ring on her finger and quickly removed her hand from the desk. The older woman's eyes followed her movement.

"He showed me a certain photo with the two of you," Gertrude said, her eyes angry again.

Sarah fought to stay calm or at least to look calm. "With me and Brandon Chase?" She tried to look surprised, but didn't know if that was working, afterall she was no actress.

"Yes. It looked pretty harmless. Looks like he was putting a blanket on your shoulder. And it was pretty dark."

Sarah realized she was shaking her legs and stopped. "Austin is very unpleasant to deal with."

Gertrude looked at her expectantly, obviously waiting to hear more. After a moment of silence, she asked, "Why are you so nervous."

"I have lots of things on my mind," she answered.

Gertrude nodded.

Sarah wanted to ask if there were other photos but dared not. Her supervisor would only become suspicious or was it the opposite? For a moment, she was confused, not knowing if she should ask or not, but she wanted to be certain.

"Did he show you any other photos?" she heard herself asking.

"Yes. Don't lie to me Sarah. I will do my best to help you. I saw a photo of you and Brandon kissing. This agency has rules and you just broke one. I suggest you get those photos from Austin before he does you real harm."

It took her a few minutes for reality to sink in and Sarah stared at Gertrude in shock, not knowing what to say or how to react. She felt terribly embarassed that her supervisor had not only seen the photo, but caught her lying as well. Why had Gertrude deliberately lay a trap for her? Sarah's eyes darted around the room, never settling on her supervisor.

"There's nothing wrong about falling in love. Just be careful," Gertrude said, her voice was surprisingly soft.

"What about the agency's policy? Are you going to fire me?" Without realizing it, Sarah started chewing on a finger nail as she waited for an answer.

The older woman looked at the pen she was holding in her hands, she blinked several times then looked up. "Sarah I didn't make the rules for this agency and I'm willing to break some to help you. If Austin comes looking to stir up some trouble, we will find a way out." Gertrude looked at her with motherly concern. "I know that you didn't choose to fall in love with Brandon Chase but you should have known better." She shook her head, as though she couldn't believe it. "I'll try my best to help you."

"Thank you Gertrude. I can't afford to lose my job. I'm supposed to start my phsycology course in one year."

"Are you ready to go back to work?"

"Yes. Monday would be great."

"Why don't you take a few extra days. Go out and have some fun."

"No. I'd rather go back to work." She picked up her purse from the desk.

"I understand. I have a temporary position for you."

"Thank you very much for everything."

"You are welcome, dear."

Sarah got into her car, closed her eyes and took a deep breath. She felt so embarassed. Gertrude had seen photos of her and Brandon on the night they had made love. Luckily it was just a photo of them kissing. Did he have other photos, she wondered, and if he did, was he going to show it around the office? How was she supposed to face those people again?

Alone on the beach, she welcomed the embrace of quietness and peace, just what she needed to sort out the jumble in her head. How was she going to deal with this? She had had many years of practice at denying things, pushing them in some remote corner of her mind and continuing with life. It was the only way she knew how to deal with painful situations. In this case, she couldn't do that. She had to get those photos. But how?

She passed beside the lop-sided cabin half hidden by trees. It had been there eversince she could remember. She stopped beside it, remembering her teenage years, when she went there after her fights with Edward. It seemed so long ago. So much time had passed and Sarah realized what a long way she had come since then. She continued walking, occasionally glancing behind her to see if Tim had arrived.

She was in a hurry to see Brandon. Tonight, she would just do what she had done so many times before, pretend that everything was okay. That would give her

171

more time to think, to find solutions, more time to enjoy his love for her.

She debated whether or not to tell Tim about her dilema. He had gone through so much with her already. She could have never survived without him or made it this far. Anna was always working and for the first time Sarah suspected that she and Anna had one thing in common- Anna hid from the truth, denied things to make life bearable. Had Sarah learnt this from her mother over the yeras without really realizing it?

She looked at the trail of footprints following her, stopping at nothing, like her past. If only Edward had been a different person, if only her life had been better, if only she hadn't made so many bad choices. She could go on and on, but that wouldn't change a thing. Today, the woman she had become was inevitably formed from the past and nothing could change that. Thank God it wasn't all bad.

Brandon's love was overwhelming, it slipped into all those painful wounds in her soul, soothed them, gave her hope and hapiness. Yet, this same love could destroy her. How could something so sweet, so pure and beautiful result in destruction?

She had changed so much. It was hard to recognise the person she had become. Once upon a time, her mind had controlled her, now, her heart and emotions had taken over.

She glanced at her watch, then behind her, still no sign of Tim. She decided to leave. He probably had plans with Allana anyway. She had just started back to her car when he came down the beach towards her.

172

"I'm late," he said, giving her a quick kiss on the cheek. "Had to finish fixing up a car before I left." Though he smiled, a flicker of fear lingered in his eyes.

Tears sprang to her eyes and she felt Tim's protective arms around her. He was her brother, her best friend, the person she could tell her secrets and fears. Somehow, he always helped to make things right.

"Tell me what's wrong," he said softly, letting go of her and putting some space between them. He brushed away the dark hair that feel over his eyes.

"I let myself fall in love with him. I slept with him," she blurted out.

Tim opened his mouth to say something, shut it and stared at her in shock. He shook his head, then fixed her with a serious look. "You're talking about Brandon?"

"Yes."

He stuck his hands in his pants pockets, looked up at the sky and asked, "Are you pregnant?"

"No!" She glared at him angrily. "How stupid do you think I am?"

The relief on his face was as clear as day. "Sorry I asked that."

"What's so wrong with falling in love," Tim asked. "What's making you so sad?" He sat down and she joined him.

"I was not supposed to fall in love. Remember? What's wrong with me Timmy?"

"You can be in love and still persue your goals in life." He looked at her with sad eyes. "Does he love you?"

"He loves me, but there are too many things wrong," she whispered.

Sarah filled him in on everything. Tim listened, staring out in the distance. When she had stopped talking, she waited for him to say something. He remained quiet, a deafening silence settled upon them.

"I don't know what to say or how to help." He fell silent again. "Why did you have to fall in love with the wrong man?" He picked up a stone and flung it as far as he could.

She deliberately avoided his question. She didn't choose to fall in love with Brandon. It just happened. "I have to tell him about the baby."

"You should. It's no fun living a lie and it's not fair to him."

"I know. If I tell him, it's over. I don't want to lose him."

"Tell him the truth. If he really loves you, he'll forgive you." Tim hugged his knees and looked from one place to the other, as though looking for the perfect solution.

"I want to but I'm scared. It used to be so easy to pretend, to go on with my daily life and now it has become a burden. He does not know about my past and I felt so clean, so perfect in his eyes. I wanted it to stay that way. Tim, it felt so good. I can't go on lying to Brandon and I can't tell him the truth. Maybe I should just walk away. Tell him it's over. I don't want him to hate me." She slipped off the diamond ring and placed it in the palm of her hand.

"If he truly loves you, he will forgive you. Sarah, if anyone deserves to be happy, it's you." His eyes shone with unshed tears. "Did you ever suspect that he was adopted?"

"Yes."

"Why didn't you ask him about it?"

"I wanted him to tell me when he was ready." She slipped the ring on her finger.

"So, are you going to tell him," Tim asked.

After a few minutes of silence, she said, "I want to but I'm scared." She rolled around a perfectly smooth stone between her fingers. "Sometimes I just think about living a lie and never telling him the truth."

"It's not a good idea. Besides, if you don't tell him the truth, you will never know how he really feels. By the way, the house is overflowing with flowers. They are from him I guess." He turned to her and smiled. "Dad was just walking around and glaring at the flowers and mom warned him not to touch them."

"I didn't give him my address."

Tim shook his head in disbelief. "You didn't. What do you expect him to think?"

"I don't want him showing up and running into dad. I told him a bit about my situation. I wonder where he got my address."

They looked at each other, she could see the worry in Tim's eyes. He picked up a twig and drew a stick figure in the sand. "I can't believe it. You fell in love with someone. The runner finally gets stopped in her tracks." He took her hands in his, looked her in the eyes and said, "Everything is going to be fine. All you have to do is tell the truth." He touched the diamond ring on her finger, "It's beautiful."

They fell silent. Sarah was examining the ring, while Tim concentrated on the stick figure he had drawn in the sand. A few sea gulls swooped down on the sand and started fighting over a piece of bread. Darkness was quickly approaching. Sarah glanced at her watch. It was after six. Brandon would be waiting for her. The thought made her heart soar and at the same time made it sad. She had to see him. She had already made up her mind to pretend, just a while longer. She didn't want her fragile world to burst and be over in the blink of an eye, like a soap bubble floating on the wind. She shook her head, blinked and brought her attention back to Tim.

"You're seeing him today. Right? Don't lie to me." There was something hard in his voice.

"Yes."

"You've come a long way little sister. You should be proud of yourself. I don't want anyone destroying you and your dreams. If he can't accept that you have given a child up for adoption, then he doesn't deserve you. Look at all the guys you've chased away. Brandon is not the only man out there." He traced an 'x' over the stick figure he had drawn in the sand.

"I will see him later."

"Tell him the truth."

"I can't. I don't have the courage." She looked away from Tim's angry face.

"Stop pretending that reality isn't standing in your face." He fell silent then let out a long breath. "If you don't have the courage to tell him, then write him a letter."

She nodded but knew in her heart that she wasn't going to do it. At least not today.

Tim stood up. "Let's go. Allana is waiting for me. I'll see you tomorrow."

"Thank you for coming. Please, don't tell mom about this.

Chapter 11

Brandon walked through the automatic doors as they slid open before him. He made his way into the store, stopped and quickly scanned the new lines of clothing and new decoration. He wondered who was preparing the catalogues and buying for the store now that he was no longer in the picture. Austin had certainly hired someone to replace him. He headed towards the back of the store, his head bent, hoping that no one would recognise him. He felt like an intruder and it hurt him. He was no longer welcome here, no longer Austin's son. His throat felt tight. Brandon never imagined that a day like this was written in his future.

The store was busy as usual and a small crowd waited outside the dressing rooms with clothing hung over their arms. He saw the familiar faces of Cindy and Jane and was grateful that they were busy with clients and did not see him.

The light in Conrad's office was on. Brandon stopped, momentarily scared of running into Stacey's dad. If he did, what was he supposed to say? 'Sorry it did not work out with your daughter'? He made his way silently down the corridor, stopped in front of what used to be his office and looked in the small window. All his things had been moved out. Austin certainly did not believe in wasting time. He quickly covered the short distance to his dad's office, knocked on the door, then entered.

Austin looked up from the paper work spread out in front of him. His face quickly changed into an angry mask. "What the hell do you want?" He yanked off his glasses and flung it on the cherrywood desk.

Brandon ignored the pain he felt, pulled out a chair and sat down. If he said that his father's actions were not hurting him, he would be lying. "We have to talk."

"Austin stood up and glared down at him. "Get out!"

"I'm not going anywhere. You will listen to me," he said firmly.

Austin leaned foward until his face was close to Brandon's, let out a string of nasty words and moved back, his eyes dark with fury.

Brandon was taken by surprise. He had never heard his father swear like that before.

"Where is that dumb nurse? How much of your savings did you give her for the good times?" His face twisted into a wicked smile.

"Listen Austin, she's not dumb and she's not after my money. She has left. The contract is over and…"

"Gone as in gone for good?" he quickly asked.

"No. We plan on seeing each other."

Austin walked around the spacious office, his hands behind his back and silence filled the room. Brandon looked up at the family photo hanging on the wall. He and Christian were just kids when it was taken and it suddenly hit him. He bore no resemblance to any of them. He stood out. Surely even strangers could see he was not Elizabeth and Austin's son.

"I want those photos you told Gertrude about," he said, turning his attention back to Austin.

Austin ignored him and continued pacing the room.

179

Brandon's patience slipped away. "I want those damn photos! Give them to me now!" He met Austin's cold, challenging eyes.

Austin stopped in front of the desk, placed his hands on the edge and stared at Brandon. "If you don't stop seeing the nurse, I'll use the photos against her. I've already given one to her supervisor but it showed only a kiss. There's more Brandon."

Brandon sprang to his feet and slammed his fist down on the table. Austin moved back. "Go ahead Austin. I'll marry her in a flash to protect her."

"Marry her? Are you out of your mind? How could you choose a little piece of crap over a classy woman like Stacey? Sarah is the daughter of a drunk! The sister of a drug addict and pusher! She has a nasty past. And the best, I shall not tell. You will find out for yourself and you will hate her." He smiled, obviously enjoying himself. "You're going to really hate her."

"What nasty accusations! You're so mean!" How did Austin know that Sarah's father had an alcohol problem? Was he just making wild accusations and happened to stumble on a fact?

Austin laughed. "She didn't tell you? What a fool you are! Poor Brandon. There's so much she didn't tell you."

"Of course I know about Sarah's family and there's no drunkard or druggie included. I met them. They are really nice people." When Austin wanted to find out something, he always did and his sources were usually right. What on earth was going on? Sarah owed him some answers. He laughed. "Your sources are so wrong. Find yourself some new detectives and I want those photos."

Brandon stood up, walked around to the other side of the desk and started pulling open the drawers and going through the contents.

"What the hell do you think you're doing? This is invasion of privacy!" Austin grabbed his upper arm. "This is not your office! Get out!"

Brandon yanked his arm free and moved over to the filing cabinet, determined to find the photos.

"I said get the hell out of here!" Austin pushed him aside and closed the drawer.

"Give me the damn photos!" He felt frustrated.

"Why should I?" Austin challenged.

"You don't have any photos."

"So it is true." He started to laugh again. "I caught you."

Brandon held back his anger, reminding himself that this was his father. He couldn't recall ever being this angry in his life.

"You remember what went on out there on the patio. She was wearing a red shirt. I mean, 'was wearing', until someone pulled it off."

He did have photos. Brandon remembered clearly how the buttons on that red shirt got on his nerves. "You're sick! Give me the damn photos!"

"How dare you call me sick! How dare you talk to me like that! No son of...." He stopped for a moment and stared at Brandon. "I forgot. You're not my son."

Brandon swallowed. Those words were said with the intention to hurt and like hell they did. No matter how hard he tried, he couldn't get used to not being part of this family anymore.

"Good-bye and good luck," Austin said. You're bent on doing things your way. Fine. But somebody is going to get hurt and I just have a feeling it's the nurse."

Brandon strode towards the door.

"Wait." His loud voice filled the small room.

He stopped, his hand on the door knob and half turned to face his father. Austin picked up an envelope from his desk.

"You want the photos. Here they are."

Brandon felt bitter anger rising within him. He walked towards his father, snatched the envelope and ripped it open. There were photos of him and Sarah when they had made love the first time. His body and mind felt numb, frozen. How far would his father go?

"You get to keep the photos and I get to keep the negatives. I might just have them developed and show them to her supervisor. Too bad her knight can't do anything about it."

Humiliation, anger, frustration, all surged through him in a single minute. If the man standing in front of him wasn't his father, he would have punched him in the face. He glared at Austin, not knowing what to say.

"Lost your tongue," Austin asked mockingly.

"Does mom know about this?"

"Don't you dare go to Elizabeth! You've hurt her enough! She has been crying herself to sleep at nights! She can't face Stacey's parents! How could you do that to her? You've no feeling. You're cruel! Ungrateful!" He raised his arms and made a half circle in the air. "Who knows? Maybe your real mother was psychic. She saw who you were and decided to dump you. Too bad Elizabeth and I are not psychic."

Those brutal words made him sink into a chair. He had spent most of his life hating his natural mother, now, with Austin's words, he hated her even more.

He hadn't given much thought to Elizabeth in all this. Maybe it was because she was such an understanding person and he felt like she would accept his decisions. Maybe he was wrong. He had gone to the house five times today and no one had answered the door. Was she there and refused to answer the door because it was him? As for her not returning the phone calls, he had assumed that she was playing by Austin's rules for a while. Did he really hurt her like Austin had said?

He climbed into his car, feeling angry and confused. He was late and hoped that Sarah had not left. He grabbed the cell phone and dialled his home number as he pulled out the parking lot. The phone rang on and on. Of course Sarah wouldn't answer his phone. She wasn't even supposed to be there. He flung the phone on the passenger seat and turned his attention to the road in front of him. What Austin had said about Sarah's family and what he did not say about her, weighed heavily on his mind. He decided not to question Sarah about Austin's accusations.

Maybe Sarah's family didn't have a good reputation, but that was not Sarah's fault. He slammed hard on the brakes. Another red light. The driver of the other car in front of Brandon, rolled down his window and showed Brandon his middle finger.

When he got home, Sarah dashed out the house, down the stairs and circled his waist with her arms. She smiled up at him and he got the impression that something about her was different. She seemed so happy. No, too happy. It was like there was something false about her.

He forced a smile, telling himself that he was feeling that way because of what Austin had said to him.

"Something is wrong? What is it?"

"Just had a fight with Austin." He took her hand and they walked into the house.

"I'm sorry about that."

Brandon went to the cabinet, took out a bottle of wine and popped it open. He filled two glasses and offered one to Sarah. She took it and they sat at the counter and sipped their wine in silence.

"I was afraid that you would leave before I get here."

"I'd wait for you forever." She turned towards him and smiled.

Her words flowed over him like warm honey, sweet and soothing. He leaned foward and kissed her on the lips, savoring the moment. Did she even realize how much she meant to him.

"Thank you for all the flowers. It makes me feel so special."

"Wondering how I got your address?" Anger rose up within him, seeped into his voice.

She pulled back and looked at him. "Well…yes."

"You left your text book here and that's where I found it." He looked into her eyes, studying her keenly. "Why didn't you want me to have your address?"

"I was going to leave it with you. It just slipped my mind…you know …with all that's going on."

184

She looked so sincere, there was no way she could be lying and he felt relieved.

She looked around the house. "It looks so empty. I'm sorry you have to leave this house. I know it means so much to you." Her hand covered his.

Memories of childhood crept into his mind. All those Christmas and Thanksgiving dinners with his grandparents. His grandfather would let him and Christian turn the house up-side-down if that was what made them happy.

"Did you find a place?"

"The two apartments I visited were not nice so I'll go at Christian's for a while. How did it go with your supervisor?"

She took a sip of wine, stared into her glass and said, "There was some good and some bad."

"And?" He asked impatiently.

"Austin has photos of us...that night on the patio. He showed two photos to Gertrude."

Brandon finished his glass of wine in one gulp and refilled it. "I can't believe it. No, bad choice of words. It shouldn't be a surprise to me." He stood up.

"I'm not going to lose my job. Gertrude is willing to help me but it was so embarassing. I wished that by some sort of magic that I could have disappeared."

Brandon closed the distance between them and took her in his arms. "I'm so sorry, Sarah," he whispered in her ears. He felt the slight tremor of her small body within his arms. He knew that she was scared, nervous and all he wanted to do right now was protect her. "Austin gave me some of those photos tonight."

"Where are they? Let's destroy them!"

He picked up the envelope from the counter and handed her. She pulled them out, looked at them over and over, shaking her head. Tears fell on the photos. They were so revealing. There was no doubt that she and Brandon were making love.

Brandon took them from her. "Even if we destroy the photos, he still has the negatives. He wouldn't give them to me."

"This can't be happening to me. Of all the embarassing things, I..."

Brandon finished the glass of wine. He was hurting for her. She was so shy, so reserved. Surely she wouldn't want anyone seeing those photos.

"I hope he will not show any more photos to Gertrude," her voice was barely a whisper. She just stood there, like she had just witnessed something that traumatized her. He held her in his arms for a long time, feeling her warm tears soak through his shirt. If only he could change things for her, take away her pain, he would gladly do it.

She looked up at him. "Here you are comforting me and I didn't ask how you feel. I know Austin is capable of ripping you to pieces."

He looked into her eyes. "He was nasty as usual," he said without going into details. Sarah was going through enough and he had to be strong for her. He could always deal with his pain after.

"I envy your strength, your courage, your conviction that everything could be worked out."

"Maybe we should go out. Have some fun, think about other things for a while," he said.

"Sounds good. Forget reality for a while." She smiled up at him.

He felt his facial muscles tense, anger churning within him and he saw the fear in her eyes. Her words, 'forget reality for a while', disturbed him. Was she trying to forget reality for a while and that was why she didn't want to tell him certain things? Austin's accusations snaked through his mind. She 'forgot reality for a while' a bit too often.

"What's wrong?"

He kissed the top of her head. "Tell me, is that how you deal with things? Forget them for a while?"

Her body stiffened against his. She looked up at him and softly said, "It gives me time to think. Time to find solutions."

He looked into her eyes, not wanting to miss anything, wishing he could see into her mind.

Her eyes held a guarded expression and whatever hopes he had of her opening up to him, disappeared. She was so sweet, so sensitive, but when it came to her personal life, she guarded it like a sentinel.

He let go of her and walked over to the widow. Just earlier today, he could hardly wait for her to show up. He had wanted to make love to her so badly and he had dragged that desire around with him all day. Now she was here and all he could think about was what her secrets were. He had asked her several times to write her address and she hadn't. She was certainly lying about things. He couldn't keep it to himself anymore. He turned to face her, she was sitting on the sofa.

"Tell me the real reason you didn't want to give me your address? I asked you about it several times this morning. I even left my address book open on the counter."

187

She looked down at the floor. "I was afraid that you would come to my place and my dad would be nasty to you. It's the only reason."

Their gaze locked. "Why didn't you tell me so earlier."

She looked like an animal who was suddenly cornered and looking for a way out. The sadness in her eyes changed to anger.

"How can you start to understand how embarassing it is to even talk about a father like mine! What did you want me to say? Here's my address but don't come. My dad is horrible. Makes a person feel real good."

He knew she had lied to him a few times because there were certain things that she was too embarassed to talk about. He got the impression that this was just another one.

"Sometimes I feel like I'm standing at a half open door and you just refuse to let me in. That hurts, Sarah."

She walked over to him and opened the window. A gentle wind blew in bringing with it the smell of flowers, the gentle rustling of leaves and insects in the night.

"I don't mean to hurt you. If I tell you everything, will you still love me?"

"Of course I will. I have never loved anyone the way I love you and never will. This is a once in a life time thing."

"I would love to be perfect for you. Like Stacey. She grew up with money, she is classy, part of your world. My world is so completely different. We grew up in two different worlds."

"I don't want you to be like Stacey. I love you just the way you are. I don't care if you are from Mars, I still love you."

She looked away from him but he saw that her eyes were bright with tears and he felt guilty. Guilty for drilling her this way instead of waiting for her to talk to him.

"I never thought that one day I'd be this happy. That I'd fall so deeply in love. I don't want this happiness to end," she continued.

"Come here," he said taking her into his arms. "This will not end. I'm sorry if I pressured you. I love you Sarah." He cupped her face in his hands and brought her lips down on hers in a long passionate kiss. The anger he had felt towards her earlier, had completely disappeared. Maybe when you grew up in a world like hers, you learned to lie because some things were just too painful to be said. The scar on her belly, for some reason flashed through his mind. The only answer she had given him was very vague and he always wondered if that was a c-section.

"Lets go somewhere. It will do us the world of good," he said, smiling.

Sarah went to the washroom, splashed cold water on her face and applied light make-up. Brandon stood beside her and shaved.

"When we have our own place, remind me to put a huge mirror in the bathroom. You're taking three quartes of this mirror."

"You're supposed to wait until I'm finished."

"Says who?" He looked at her, an eyebrow raised and they both laughed.

"Oh no. Look at his." There was a large stain at the side of her dress. "I have to run home and get changed or we stay here."

"Or we could just stop off at the store and get you a new dress." He looked at her for a while and all he could think about was making love to her. "Or we could just stay here and you don't have to wear a dress." The hunger and desire in her eyes did not go unnoticed. "What do you say?" After a moment of silence, he said, "We're going out."

"I'd better hide my car," she said, climbing in. "I'm not supposed to be here." She looked around.

"Park it by the apple trees at the back. No one will see it there."

She nodded, slammed the door and drove towards the back of the lawn. When she came back, Brandon was sitting in the driver's seat, patiently waiting for her. She climbed in beside him.

They chatted about music, movies and the news. Brandon slipped in a CD and soft piano music filled the small space.

"Like that kind of music? I guess not. You like Phil Collins. I bought a CD for you." He pressed on a small button, took out the CD and slipped in the Phil Collins. Here you go my lady," he said.

"That's so sweet. When did you get that?"

"Yesterday." After a few minutes he said, "Did you hear those words? 'She'll take your heart and you won't feel it. She's like no other'. That's you Sarah. That's what you did to me." He took her hand in his and squeezed it gently. "I will always love you, Sarah."

They turned onto the store lined street. There was not much traffic and Brandon drove slowly scanning the stores. "That's where we will go." He stopped in front of a small boutique. "I'm shopping and you don't say a word."

"This place looks expensive."

He kissed her on the lips. "Be quiet. What do you want? A dress? Yes. You look real good in dresses. I get to see all those curves."

They looked through racks of dresses and Sarah said, "Too expensive Brandon."

"No." He picked up a black dress. Like this one?"

She tried it on and came out. Brandon was standing there with a pair of shoes. "Wow lady. You look great. Turn."

She turned around. The back of the dress was opened almost down to the waist in a V shape.

She turned to face him.

"You look great Sarah." He gave her the pair of shoes and she slipped them on. "Perfect."

When they were back in the car, he asked, "Where do you want to go?" He pushed a small button and the sound of Phil Collin's voice rang through the car.

"Let's see. You know that little restaurant by the beach where we went once. You ran into some of your friends there."

"The Marina. Okay."

They stood at the edge of the beach and stared out at the small dark shapes of boats and in the distance a bright light swept around in a circle from the lighthouse. A lone gull roamed the beach and not too far away, a couple was walking hand in hand.

191

Hilda St. James

As the evening wore on, he felt more relaxed . A crazy idea went through his mind and he wanted to tell her but he didn't know how she would take it. He wanted to ask her to go away with him and get married. Must be too much wine, he mused. Sarah deserved more than that. He finished his paêlla and moved the plate aside. He noticed that Sarah had hardly touched her lasagna. She was busy twisting the paper napkin with her fingers. She glanced up at him, then at the shreds of paper in front of her.

"What's going on in that head of yours? There's a strange little smile on your face," she said.

"Thinking about you, trying to figure out what you have done to me." He smiled at her. She looked so shy and he loved it. "What could I say to keep that shy look on your face all night?"

"Or what can you do?" she teased.

"That's interesting. I think of only one thing." She smiled shyly, yet her eyes were flirtatious. Their gaze held. It was funny the way she got to him, the special world that she drew him into.

Half an hour later, they were passing outside a diso when Brandon stopped. "Feel like dancing?"

"Why not." She unfastened her seat belt as he brought the car to a stop.

"Great."

As he stepped out the car, he felt sharp pains in his legs again. He had to go see the doctor. He took her hand and they walked into the disco with it's flashing, blinding light and loud music. There was a small crowd on the dance floor and he could hear their screams over the blaring music. They sat down at the bar and Brandon couldn't help noticing the way some men were eyeing Sarah. A pang of jealousy shot up inside him and he moved closer to her.

"Is this one of your favorite places?"

"Not exactly. I've been here a few times with Christian." He kissed her hand.

They found vacant chairs at the bar, sat there and continued talking.

"You guys want something to drink?" The bartender asked. Over his left eye, he wore two rings and his ear was lined with tiny earrings. Must have been painful, all that piercing, Brandon thought as he ordered drinks.

He turned his attention back to Sarah. "Why did you decide to go back to work so soon? We could have taken a little vacation somewhere."

"Sounds tempting but it's not possible." She opened her purse, pulled out an envelope and gave it to Brandon.

"What is this?" He wore a puzzled expression.

"I don't want you to feel bad. I'm returning the last paycheck. I didn't work...you know...I just hung around your place."

"You must be joking. I'm not taking this back." He took her purse, opened it and stuffed the envelope in it.

"Brandon, I can't take it."

He stood up. "Let's go dance. I don't want to ever hear about that paycheck again."

The waiter slapped the drinks down in front of them and Brandon paid him. He looked at Sarah's legs and he was tempted to touch them. One glance at the nearby tables told him that he was not the only one admiring her.

He placed a possessive arm around her and they walked to the dance floor. As they danced, she tilted her head and looked up at him. "I'm going to miss being around you all the time." After a moment of silence, she said, "I have to work tomorrow. I guess it's time to go home."

"Home as in 'your place'?" He asked, his lips brushing her ear. "I don't want you to go."

"I have to."

"I know. I just don't want you to go." Sometimes he had a rather disturbing feeling that Sarah would walk out of his life and he would never see her again

When they got back to his place, he walked to the back of the lawn with her where the car was parked. She looked up at him, kissed him on the mouth, "Good-night. I'll see you tomorrow."

Grinning, he braced her against a tree, his hands running up and down her bare arms. He kissed the throbbing pulse at the base of her throat, listening to her rapid breathing. She started to touch him but he brought her arms to her side. His lips moved up the side of her neck and came to rest on her ear.

"Remember, you can't touch."

His mouth moved back to the base of her throat, lingered there for a while and moved lower.

His mouth found a nipple through the thin dress. He slipped the dress from her shoulder and heard her gasp as his mouth covered a nipple.

"We'd better go inside," he said, gently pulling the dress strap in place.

"I have to go."

He gently pulled her down on the grass beside him. The ground was full of flowers that had fallen off the trees and the smell of apple blossom filled the air. He slipped the dress off her shoulders and his mouth found her breast. He teased it, nibbling gently and he enjoyed Sarah's soft moans. He covered her body with his, kissing her neck, her mouth .

He stopped, rolled aside, propped his head up with an arm and looked at Sarah. Her hair was full of apple blossoms, her eyes were closed.

"I'm being selfish. You have to get some sleep."

She opened her eyes, looked at him tenderly and moved closer.

Their love making was short and passionate.

They lay side by side and looked up at the starry sky while Brandon kept dropping apple blossoms on her.

"That tickles," she said, rubbing her abdomen.

"Let me do that for you." His hand caressed her abdomen, he loved the smooth, velvet texture. He ran his finger along the scar. "When are you going to tell me about this?" He waited patiently for her to say something.

She looked thoughtful, as though she had to come up with an answer and at that moment he felt certain that she was going to lie.

"I had a cyst on my ovary," she answered, turned to him and smiled.

He knew Sarah well enough to know that it was a fake smile, one meant to mask something and Brandon felt anger and impatience simmering within. Austin's words slammed into his mind. He lay down, his thoughts taking a different direction. If Sarah had a child and did not tell him he would be very angry. He didn't mind her having a child, but it would be the lie that would make him mad.

"I love you Sarah." He kept a firm hand on his anger. After what they just shared together, how could she lie to him!

Chapter12

Sarah glanced up at the clock. Twenty minutes to three. Thank God she had only twenty five more minutes at work. For the past few nights, she had lain awake for hours trying to figure out how she was going to tell Brandon about her child. She hadn't seen him in two days, mainly because she could no longer face him, no longer pretend that there were not important things that she had to tell him and that the end of their relationship was just a breath away.

She walked into the nursing station, pulled out a chair and finished charting on one of the residents. Call bells kept ringing and it got on her nerves. Jenny, the other nurse joined her.

"It's so busy today," she said, pulling out a chair. She eyed Sarah curiously. "Something is not right. You are not the same Sarah." She winked and asked, "Did you fall for that guy you were working for?"

"Where on earth did you get such an idea?" Sarah snapped.

Jenny got up. "No need to get mad."

"Sorry, Jenny. I'm just so tired. That's all."

Jenny nodded.

Sarah gave the days' report to the evening shift nurse and left. The afternoon was hot and the streets were busy with people strolling by, and sports cars that had spent the winter locked away in garages. She unlocked her car and got in. The questions and fears that she had managed to ward off all day by throwing herself into her work came back with an amazing speed.

Anna and Tim were sitting on the patio when she arrived home. She took one look at Anna's worried face and knew that Tim had told her what was going on. Sarah felt guilty. She had caused Anna so much pain already.

When she got up the short flight of stairs, Anna pulled out a chair, "Sit down."

Sarah threw Tim an irritated glance and sat down. Why did he have to tell Anna about Brandon! What was going on? He usually kept her secrets.

"Want some ice tea?" he asked and without waiting for an answer went into the house.

"Tim told me," Anna said, her face tense. "Did you have a chance to tell him about the baby?"

Sarah looked at her mom, the older version of herself. "No. I can't tell him."

"Why?"

"What do I say? Brandon, it kind of slipped my mind to tell you something. I had a kid when I was sixteen and gave her up for adoption. Can you forgive me for not telling you?"

Anna's eyes brightened with tears and Sarah regretted those words. How she wished that she could take them back.

"I just don't know how to tell him," Sarah whispered.

"You can do it. You have to tell him everything. If he can't accept your past and forgive you, then he dosen't deserve you."

Sarah remembered as a child, Anna was hardly ever there because she had been working two jobs to make ends meet. Tim was the one who took care of her. When Sarah had problems and went to her mother, Anna was so tired, she would always say that they would talk about it another time. Eventually, Sarah had stopped talking to Anna about her problems. When Sarah had become pregnant, for the first few months, Anna had avoided her, as though she couldn't handle the problem.

Tim came back, placed a glass of ice tea in front of Sarah and left.

"Sarah, if Brandon really loves you, he will forgive you," Anna said gently.

She nodded and stood up. The word, 'if', standing strong and tall in her mind. "I'm going for a shower."

Anna stood up. "Don't do like me."

Sarah looked at her mother, feeling somewhat confused. "What are you talking about?"

"Years ago, I should have told Edward it was over. I never had the strength to do it. I just held my head high and pretended that everything was fine and I learned to live a life apart from him, though we still live in the same house. But I robbed you and Tim of a real life. I should have left with the two of you. Maybe neither of you would have suffered this much if I had walked away from Edward. I kept sweeping things under the rug, putting it off for another time and look who is paying for it. You and Tim. You especially Sarah and all because I was such a coward. I didn't want to go to my family for help. My parents had warned me not to marry Edward and I did it anyway. Then I was too proud to say I had made a mistake. Don't be afraid of the mistakes you have made Sarah. Learn from them and move on. Don't pretend your problems are not there, be brave, face them. How long are you going to live a lie? I see so much of myself in you. I was afraid that If I left Edward that people would have shun me. Everyone makes mistakes, Sarah, but you have learned from yours and should be proud of yourself. The longer you keep putting things off, the worse it gets. Tell him the truth. Living a lie brings tremendous pain."

Sarah looked at Anna, surprised that her mother had said this much. She had never even imagined that Anna had thought about leaving Edward. Anna was so dedicated. She was one of those, "until death do us part", kind of people.

Anna cried. Sarah made her way around the table and and hugged her mother. A hug should have been a normal thing between them, but it wasn't. Sarah couldn't remember the last time they had hugged each other, it felt so uncomfortable, so false. Hugging Tim was much more normal. Afterall, he had been a father and mother to her. The woman in her arms felt like a stranger and Sarah realised how much was missing in that mother and daughter relationship.

"Don't cry, mom. And don't blame yourself. You did the best you could." She let go of her mother and stepped away, putting some distance between them.

"I didn't do the best I could. I was never there when you needed me. I always thought that your problems could wait. Today you are suffering because I was never the mother I should have been." She dried her tears and looked at her daughter. "Stop covering things up, Sarah. Deal with them." She broke down in tears again. "I don't want to see you get hurt again."

"Stop it mom." Sarah took Anna's hands in hers. The last thing she wanted to see was her mother crying.

"I hope you can see why I adviced you to give the baby up for adoption. I didn't want your child growing up in misery. I wanted her to have a better life than you did."

Sarah legs were suddenly trembling. She sat down and looked at her mother. Eversince the baby was born, this was the third time Anna had ever mentioned her.

"If your father was a different man, we would have kept the child. It broke my heart to send her away. I know you were looking for love. Don't we all? We never gave you the love you deserved and you just tried to find it elsewhere and I don't blame you. I want things to work for you and Brandon. I know you love him."

Tears were still streaming down Anna's face and Sarah looked at her, feeling lost and confused. Her mother had never been so open with her before.

"Go see Brandon. Tell him."

"Please mom, stop crying and don't blame yourself for what has happened to me. At sixteen, I should have known better."

"When someone does not get the love they need, they try to find it. It is so important."

The pain in Anna's voice was blatant and Sarah wondered if it was pain for her daughter or Anna's own bad marriage and wrong choices. If only people were allowed to go back in time and change their choices and course of future, the world would be one happy place.

"Mom, please stop crying. I can't stand it."

"All that you are facing now, I am to be blamed for it. Why didn't I have the courage to walk away, to make a better life for you and Tim? Reality was staring me in the face and I kept ignoring it or putting things off for another time."

"It's not too late mom. You can still find hapiness."

She shook her head. "It's too late for me but not for you. Go see Brandon and tell him everything. Today. You can't continue living like that."

She looked away from her mother and to the diamond ring winking at her in the sun. She slid it off and put it in her pocket. Time to give it back, she thought.

"I'm going for a shower," she said, stood up and walked to the doorway. Half turning, she looked at Anna who was still looking at her.

She locked the bathroom door, stripped off her uniform and let the hot water run over her tense muscles. Closing her eyes, she tried to relax, to get rid of the tension that had made it's home within her.

Brandon was staying at Christian's place for a while. It would be kind of hard to talk to him with Christian around. She needed a quiet place, with no one around to talk to him. Things would probably get ugly. She had witnessed his quarrel with Stacey and it was not nice.

She stepped out the shower, dried herself quickly and slipped on a pale, blue summer dress. She picked up her uniform, took out the ring and slid it back on her finger. That way she was sure not to lose it.

She dried her hair and applied light make up. Taking a deep breath, she said to herself, "Well Sarah, the time has come. You have to do it."

She went back to her room, emptied the contents of her purse on the bed and pulled out an envelope. There was one photo of her and Brandon. She walked over to the closet, took out a small box and opened it. Sarah placed the photo on the tiny pink dress she had bought for Lydia. This would be another precious memory. She closed the box.

She slipped out the house, got into her car and pulled out the driveway. She tried to think of a way to tell Brandon the truth and lots of words and sentences flowed through her mind but none were right. Were there any right words to undo all the lies she had told him? To tell him the truth that she had deliberately witheld? Was there a way to spare him the pain that the truth would bring?

She turned the corner where a sign read, 'Jim's Antiques', and despite her pain, she couldn't help but smile. She had gone in there once with Brandon. He had fallen in love with an old clock but thought that the price was too high. He had tried and tried to bargain with the owner, but it didn't work. Brandon had said, "See there is a scratch and here is another one."

The owner had said, "It's over a hundred years old. What do you expect?"

For a few seconds, Brandon had looked embarassed, then smiling, he had paid for it.

Sarah had wanted to laugh so badly but had held back. She couldn't understand why he'd pay so much money for such an ugly clock.

She continued on a few more streets and turned left. She passed the Ocean View Restaurant, where she and Brandon had gone for supper and she had ended up flirting with him and later that evening he had kissed her for the first time.

She shook her head. So much had happened in such a short time. Unbelievable how life or destiny, or whatever you call it, could feed you with such hapiness and suddenly take it away. She caught sight of Christian's pink car and pulled into the empty space beside it. Brandon's car wasn't there. She went up the short flight of stairs and pushed on the buzzer. There was no answer. A note was stuck to the door, "Go in. Will be back soon."

Christian's apartment was small and Brandon's boxes stacked against the walls, made it look even smaller. On a small table in the corner, there was a collection of cars, a stack of Asterix and Obelix books and a photo of Christian standing beside his pink car. On the sofa there was a pile of Times Magazine, no doubt belonging to Brandon. She sat down, picked up one and started flipping through the pages. She tried to read but her mind seemed unwilling to understand anything, acknowledging only the problem at hand. How was Brandon going to take this revelation of hers?

She closed her eyes and said a silent prayer. It seemed so strange. When was the last time she had prayed? She couldn't remember. For a moment she wondered if God would answer her prayers. She paced the apartment, peeking out the window quite often. Where was Brandon? Nervousness and fear was slowly invading her being, pushing aside courage.

She touched the ring on her finger. She had felt so special the night that Brandon had slipped it on her finger and it was clearly the happiest moment of her life. If only it didn't have to end. Just minutes after he had slipped on the ring, he had told her that he despised his natural mother and women like her, who gave their children up for adoption. He had gone on to tell her that such women were not worth much and he would never spend his life with such a woman. She had been too shocked to say anything.

She went to the kitchen, took a glass from the cupboard and filled it with cold tap water. She sipped it and continued pacing the apartment. Her palms were becoming sweaty and her heart was beating a few paces too fast.

She heard footsteps, excited voices and then the door swung open. Brandon covered the distance between them and kissed her on the lips. He looked happy, like he had just won the lottery.

"You look great," he said.

"You look happy. What's all the excitement about?"

"Tell you later. I have some great plans." He kissed her again, his arms circling her waist. "It seem like I haven't seen you for ages," he murmured.

Christian cleared his throat loudly, then said, "Break it up guys. You're not alone and you don't have to remind me that I'm single. Unattatched. A bachelor for life."

Christian stood there, trying to look sad but he started laughing.

"What about that girl? Nina was her name, right?" Sarah asked. "Don't tell me it's over already."

205

"Never started. What's wrong with me?" He scratched his head and looked Sarah in the eyes. "You are a girl. Tell me something. Am I ugly? Repulsive? A bad guy?"

"No you're none of those things. Maybe it's your car," she teased.

"No way. Chicks love that car. No, they adore it. You're not helping Sarah. Forgive my manners. Would you like something to drink? Coffee, tea, water, milk, beer. You choose."

"Water," she answered, smiling at Christian. She adored him. He could always make her laugh.

"You, Brandon. Something to drink? I can't afford expensive wines. Sir, will you accept my humble offering? A beer." He bowed.

"Give me a beer Christian. You should take up acting. I think you would do a better job than, what's his name." Brandon scratched his head. "You know the guy who does not talk a lot."

"That's Mr. Bean," Christian called from the kitchen. "Am I allowed to pick my nose while I pour your beer into a glass."

"Stop it, Christian. That's disgusting."

Christian came back with a glass of beer and a glass of water. "Why don't we go sit outside? Take advantage of the sun while it is there." He slipped open the patio door. "This is heaven," he said, looking at the sky. "I wish there was no dumb winter."

Sarah and Brandon followed him to the small balcony. A soft refreshing wind played in the trees and on her bare skin.

She sat down beside Brandon and listened to him and Christian talking on and on about cars.

Glancing up at Brandon, she noticed that he was looking at her, his eyes were questioning. He smiled and covered her hand with his.

"You are rather quiet," Brandon said. "Is something wrong?"

She started to put her glass on the table, it slipped from her hand spilling water on the plastic table cloth.

"I'm fine," she answered without looking at Brandon. "I'd better clean this up." She tried to sound as normal as possible.

"It's only water. I'll wipe it up later," Christian said.

"No. I'll do it." She stood up, wanting to escape Brandon's probing looks, even if it was just for a few minutes. He was no fool and could certainly tell that something was wrong.

"Sit down," Christian said. He went into the apartment and came back with a roll of paper towel. He pulled off a few pieces and wiped up the water.

An uncomfortable silence fell upon the threesome and Sarah thought desperately of some excuse to leave. Panic was crawling around her insides and she knew that it was starting to show.

"I'm going out with the guys for pizza," Christian said. "Have fun guys."

"I'm going over to the beach house. Robert is away for a few weeks," Brandon said.

"See you guys," Christian said and winked at Sarah.

Her mouth was dry, she picked up the glass of water and started to drink what was left in it. The phone rang and before she knew what was happening, she had dropped the glass a second time.

Brandon went to answer the phone. From the tone of his voice and his words, Sarah suspected that he was talking to Austin.

Brandon came back out. "That was Austin. I guess mom gave him Christian's number." His eyes rested on her face for a while then he reached out and caressed her face. "Why are you so nervous, Sarah? What's wrong."

"We have to talk." Sarah was surprised at her words.

"You remember the beach house where we went, with the tiny beach at the back?"

She nodded.

"My friend is away so I thought we would just go over there. It's nice and quiet. We can talk there. There is a man who is building a house just close by. I'm not crazy about it but he is a nice guy."

She felt like blurting it all out right now. Why change place to tell him the bad news when she could do it right here. "He is going to build really close to your place?"

"Yes. I have news for you too. I'm so excited but I'm going to tell you over a bottle of wine on the beach."

She felt like screaming, not just crying. Here was the man she loved, who obviously had something exciting to tell her, a man who was thinking that she was his life partner, but he didn't know that all was about to crumble.

She walked over to him, placed her arms around his waist. "I love you Brandon."

"I love you, Sarah." His lips found hers in a long passionate kiss and she had to fight her tears back.

A few minutes later, they climbed into Brandon's car and headed for the beach house. He slipped in the Phil collins CD and said, "He is good."

"Yes."

For most of the trip, they were silent, glancing at each other. When they arrived outside the beach house, a blue Sedan was parked in front. A man hurried towards Brandon's car, busy talking on a cell phone.

"It's Ralph," Brandon said, opened the car door and got out.

Sarah heard the name, looked up and her heart stopped. This couldn't be happening. Ralph and Brandon knew each other. Impossible! What on earth was going on? For a minute, she had seen the shock on Ralph's face, then he smiled.

She closed her eyes for an instant, needing to block out that image. She fought to control her thoughts and feelings. How she hated this man! She leaned forward, fumbled with her sandals as their voices grew closer. 'Brandon must not suspect anything'' she told herself sternly.

Sarah took a deep breath and got out of the car, her smile felt stiff as Brandon introduced them. Ralph reached out to shake hands, she turned away, pretending that she didn't notice. Sarah didn't want to feel his touch. "So, you're building next door," she said, angry at herself, because she sounded so nervous.

"Yes. For a moment, I thought you were someone I know," Ralph said, smiling, his eyes probing hers, lingering on her face.

Anger and humiliation stirred deep within Sarah, she masked it with a smile. She excused herself, went into the beach house and locked herself in the washroom. Memories of her relationship with Ralph whipped through her mind. He had taken advantage of her, seduced her, made promises that he had no intention of keeping. He had gotten her hopes up then cruelly ripped her apart. He had promised to take care of her and Lydia when all the while he was married to another woman and she did not know. The first time she had slept with Ralph, she had done so with a heavy heart. She had cried, it was not what she wanted. But, if she wanted to keep her baby, she had to. The sound of music drew her attention, she took a deep breath, opened the door and joined Brandon in the living room. Did Ralp mention the baby to him?

"I'm starting to become worried," he said, taking her in his arms. "You look so sad, so scared. I'm afraid of what you have to say." Their eyes held and she saw a hint of sadness.

If only he knew that a part of her was dying, dying a slow and painful death.

He smiled at her. "We are going to cook and we can talk about that stuff later."

She didn't answer, instead she walked over to the window and pushed it open. From below, Ralph looked up at her, smiled and walked away. She felt nauseated.

Brandon walked over to her, circled her waist with his arms, his chin resting lightly on top of her head.

"Something is really bothering you. Maybe we should talk about it now. What's going on Sarah?" His voice was so soft, so full of love.

"I told you that I grew up in poverty and that my dad is an alcoholic. There are other things that I didn't tell you. Our families are so different. Tim was arrested for selling drugs and he did some time in prison and…"

"Sarah, what does this have to do with you? With us? I don't see you any different because your brother messed up."

She moved away from the circle of his arms.

"You don't know the real me. I've made so many mistakes that I'm so ashamed of. Tim tried to protect me as much as possible but I still messed up." She sat down and looked up at Brandon. "Please don't hate me for what I am about to tell you. When I was sixteen, I had a baby and…" She couldn't say the rest. She was crying so hard that she couldn't say another word.

Brandon sat down opposite her. "And?" he asked impatiently.

"I was too young. I had dropped out of school. The baby's father denied that it was his child. I had no other choice. I gave her up for adoption."

"What!" There was blatant anger in his eyes, then it turned to raw pain.

Her heart pounded so loudly, it felt like her chest could no longer contain it and she couldn't get enough air. Sarah couldn't stand the looks of anger, pain and even hate, that she had seen in his eyes over the past few seconds.

"How could you lie to me like that! Who are you, Sarah? Is there anything else you forgot to tell me? How could you give away an innocent child, like some piece of clothing that couldn't fit you any more!"

"It's not like that."

"Then tell me what it's like because I'd really love to know." He held her gaze, shook his head and laughed, a low sarcastic laugh. "Liar! What a liar you are. I'm curious. Did it just slip your mind to tell me about the baby or were you forgetting reality for a while!"

"By the time you told me that you were given up for adoption, I had already fallen in love with you. I didn't know what to do anymore. And... I don't want to lose you."

She hated the hard, cold light in his eyes, like sunlight on an icicle. His voice dripped with anger and hatred. "Who the hell are you?"

She dried her eyes and stood up. This was the end. She couldn't stand the hatred and anger in his eyes. This wasn't the man she knew. But, how could she blame him for reacting this way?

"I hate my own mother for what she did to me! Do you think I could continue loving you? Do you know if your child is happy?" He stood up, picked up the bag of grocery and emptied it in the garbage can and flung the bottle of wine out the window.

"Maybe your mother was a fifteen year old child when she had you. Do you know how confusing and frightening it is to suddenly find out that you're pregnant!"

"My mother gave me away because she didn't want the responsibility and I hate her for that. You gave your child away, for the same reason. It's heartless, cold, cruel, nasty." He spun back and faced her. "You are a cold, heartless woman! It doesn't matter how poor you were, where you've come from, it's all about being human. And you're not human!"

"I did what was best for my baby! Why can't you understand that?"

"It's over Sarah. I can't have anything to do with you."

"Please. Try to understand."

"Try to understand what? That you lied to me all this time? That you let me fall in love with you when you know that this would be the end of us? I curse the day I met you." With an outstretched arm, he said, "Give me the ring."

She took it off, placed it in the palm of his hand and watched his fingers clamped over it.

"Brandon I was so young when I had the baby and….."

"Shut up!"

They looked at each other and Sarah hated the new man who was standing in front of her.

"Get out! I never want to see you again! You are by far worse than Stacey!."

She grabbed her purse, opened the door and ran down the stairs. It was dark and the dirt road was deserted. She hurried along, going towards a house where the lights were on. She needed to get a taxi. The house was farther away than she thought. Sarah stopped at the side of the road, sat on a tree stump and stared into the darkness. It was over. An unforgettable chapter of her life had closed. How could something she had done, in the best interest of her child, now destroy her life? She sat there and stared into space. She could no longer cry, instead a silet grief settled upon her soul and she knew that it would be there for a long time.

A bug landed on her arm, she sprang to her feet, hitting wildly to knock the creature away. She started walking towards the house with the lights on.

The noise of a car caught her attention, she stopped and turned around. It was Brandon. For a crazy instant she hoped that he was coming after her. Instead, he slowed down, looked at her and drove away. She felt numb as she watched the tail lights disappear in the distance. This had to be a nightmare. This couldn't be happening.

She continued on the dirt road, past the house ablaze with lights. She was going to find a main steet with a pay phone. It was not the time to face people and besides she wanted to be alone with her misery for a while longer.

When she got to the main street, she walked into a small convenience store and used the phone. The taxi showed up twenty minutes later. She climbed in and gave him her home address.

"Are you okay," The elderly man asked.

"Yes." She suddenly remembered that her car was at Christian's place. "I have to go to another address," she said, fumbling in her bag. She pulled out the address and in the dim light read it to him.

He nodded and didn't ask further questions.

When they got to Christian's apartment, she payed him and got out the taxi. Brandon's car was in the parking lot and lights were on in the apartment. She looked up at the widow, it was wide open and she wanted to go talk to Brandon. Just one more time. Try to make him understand.

He appeared at the window, a surprised look on his face. He looked from Sarah to her car.

She wondered if he had forgotten her car was here. They looked at each other. No one spoke. Sarah climbed into her car and left a numbness slowly crawling over her heart, mind and soul. Brandon's words were lodged in her mind. He had told her to get out and that he didn't want to ever see her again. Back at the beach house, it had hurt so much and now she felt nothing. It was too much to handle, to accept.

Chapter 13

"How long are you going to do this to yourself?" Christian yelled

"Do what?" Brandon looked at him out of red, tired eyes. "I'm just getting rid of what's bugging me. Eliminating the liar from my heart and mind."

"By drinking? It's all you have done for the past two weeks. Why don't you swallow your pride and go get Sarah?" He picked up the dirty wine glasses from the coffee table.

"Are you out of your mind! She's one of those cold, heartless women!"

"Because she gave her child up for adoption? I hate to tell you this. You are being an idiot! We both grew up with money."

"See, that's where you're wrong. You grew up with money. I spent six years in an orphanage. Do you know what that's like? You wait for a mother who never shows up. You go to bed hungry and scared and nobody cares. I saw couples coming and going and they only wanted the babies not the older ones like me. I missed my chance because I was sickly. Nobody wanted a sick baby. My mother made me suffer and didn't give a damn! I hate her!" Do you think I can love a woman who is as mean as my mother!"

Christian glanced at the clock on the wall. It was ten-thirty in the morning. He took the bottle of wine from Brandon's hand, took it to the kitchen and came back.

Brandon buried his face in his hands, elbows resting on his knees. Eversince he could remember, it always haunted him as to why his mother had abandoned him. He wondered if she ever thought of him, if she loved him. Why didn't she ever try to find him? "Why did Sarah have to be one of those hateful women! Cold, horrible creatures who cared only for themselves! She had hurt him deeply.

His mind went back to those years in the orphanage. The children cried during the night and were told sternly, "Shut up and sleep!" When they didn't stop crying, some of the staff would hit them, threaten them. What mother would want to leave her child in such misery? Sometimes, as punishment, they got no food. And Lisa, she cried almost everynight and the day he had left with Elizabeth and Austin, she was standing by the window, her small body shaking as she had sobbed. Was she still alive now?

Sarah was no better than his mother. How could he love her! He fought desperately against the feelings he had for her, wanting them to die, to disappear, maybe even wanting them to turn to hatred.

He looked up, the palms of his hands still pressed against his cheeks. "Tell me Christian, why did it take me so long to discover that Sarah is a liar and a woman carved from stone?"

"She may be a liar but she isn't carved from stone. Why can't you forgive her? She did what she thought was best for her child." He scratched his head, then slowly said, "Your mom...your natural mom, maybe she did what was best for you, too."

"You just don't abandon children or give them away to strangers!" He pounded on the table.

217

"You fell into the arms of a gentle stranger. Elizabeth. Why are you so bitter? Did Mom ever treat you badly?" Christian's voice was heavy with pain.

"My pain has nothing to do with our mother. It's just that I can't forget all those years of suffering."

"In Sarah's case, it's not the same. Her baby didn't go into an orphanage. She went to a couple. Well, I think so. Orphanages don't exist anymore."

"What's the difference! She gave her child away! And that's so horrible!" He stood up, went to the kitchen and came back with a bottle of wine.

"I should have thrown it out the window!"

"I know where to buy more!"

"I'm going to see mom. She's got to come talk to you." Christian eyed him in silence for a few moments, then said, "Or I'll just go get Sarah."

Brandon laughed. His feelings were so mixed up. He didn't want to see Sarah, yet he missed her. If only she hadn't given a child up for adoption, none of this would have happened. If the child was still living with her, he would have gladly accepted the child.

"Bad idea. There is nothing more between us." He filled his glass with wine and raised it to his lips.

Christian walked over to the bookshelf, came back with a dictionary and flung it beside his brother. "Search for the word, 'forgive'."

Brandon laughed. "Even when you want to be serious, you're funny. I know the meaning. I can forgive other people but not women like them."

"When you broke up with Stacey, it seemed like that didn't bother you at all. You must really love Sarah."

"Correction. Used to love her." He finished the glass of wine and poured himself another. "She is worse than Stacey. By far. Definitely. Stacey is a saint compared to her!" He drummed his fingers on the table and looked into Christian's eyes.

"You think Stacey is a saint. Just before you had that accident, she met another man and that's why she wasn't coming to see you. I saw them many times."

Brandon was surprised. He had suspected it, but was not really certain.

"Why didn't you tell me?"

"I didn't want to be the news carrier." He grabbed his car keys and looked at Brandon's suspicious eyes. "Stop looking at me as though I'm lying!"

"I can't drive now. Go buy me some wine."

"If you can't drive, then walk! I'm not buying you any wine! Go shave and take a shower. You look like hell. It's full moon tonight. Someone might mistake you for a werewolf."

"Right. And I'm supposed to listen to you? Leave me alone."

Christian slipped on his shoes and left.

Christian was right. No problems were ever solved this way. He went to the kitchen, the bottle of wine in one hand the glass in the other. He started to pour the wine down the sink, then stopped. Instead he filled his glass, took a sip and stared out the window. A group of children were playing soccer in the street, yelling as loud as they could. He envied them. Their lives were so simple.

He could still picture Sarah walking down the dirt road that night. Her movements were slow, almost painful and a sense of gloom had settled upon him. It was so hard to drive away and leave her there. "Sarah, what have you done to us?" he muttered. One hour later, she had showed up for her car and he had gone to the window. When she had looked up at it him, it was a look of someone lost, lonely and really scared. He closed his eyes, wanting to forget that look on her face.

For a moment he wondered how she was dealing with their break-up. Was she still working and still planning on going back to school? He stopped that train of thought. "What the hell do you care Brandon? It's over!" He finished the glass of wine, went back to the living room, slumped down on the couch and switched on the television. He scanned channel after channel, hoping to find something interesting, something to take his mind off of his problems. It wasn't working.

He fell into a restless sleep and a place of disturbing dreams. He saw the 'faceless woman' and Sarah walking side by side, both holding the hands of young children. The children were then abandoned on a quiet road in a wooded area. He tried to scream, to tell them it was wrong, but no sound came out. The women were running away, and the children were crying. He tried to go towards the children but his legs won't move. The women looked at him and laughed.

He was awakened to someone sitting beside him on the couch. His eyes flew open and for a while he looked at his mother, confused.

"Brandon what's going on?" Elizabeth asked softly.

He didn't answer, wondering if she was part of the dream. He looked around, shook his head and realized that he was fully awake.

"Are you okay?" she asked gently, her hand resting on his upper arm.

"I'm fine." He sat up and turned to face her. "What are you doing here?"

"Christian came to see me. He told me that you broke up with Sarah."

He nodded.

"I was afraid that you'd end up getting hurt. She looked like a nice girl but there was something about her eyes. Something that made me think of a woman who were keeping secrets."

Brandon told her everything.

Elizabeth listened in silence.

"I never thought that I'd ever see you hurting this way." She pushed aside the wine bottle as he reached for it. "You must really love her."

"Used to"

"You still do."

"Do you think that it is wrong that I'm not able to accept that she gave her baby away?"

"People make mistakes but it does not mean that they should pay for it all their lives. From what you told me, she has come a long way and she is ambitious. Austin told me about her family and I certainly don't want to see you around such people. I don't mean to be cruel but I think it's a good thing you broke up with her."

Somewhere deep within, he suspected that he wanted to hear something different. Maybe he wanted Elizabeth to tell him to pardon Sarah and go after her.

"Stacey is such a nice girl. It's not too late for you two. She misses you."

"Stacey is seeing someone else. Has been since before my accident."

The surprise on Elizabeth's face was genuine. "Who told you that?"

"Christian. I'm sure dad knew but he just wanted to protect her, as usual."

Anger settled on her face. "How could she?" Elizabeth was silent, her eyes held a distant look, as though trying to remember something. "I had heard something about her seeing a strange man but I had thought that they were just ugly rumors. Anyway, Christian wouldn't lie to you."

"Enough about her. Why did you stop coming to see me? Why didn't you return my calls? I didn't want to go to the house because of Austin."

"Because I was so angry that you called off the wedding. When Christian came to see me, I knew that something was really wrong and here I am. I'm sorry, son, for the way I treated you. I have no right to force you into something that you don't want. You are going through a lot right now, but things will change, with time. You'll meet someone nice, when the time is right."

"I just can't forget Sarah." He had to say it, couldn't keep it to himself anylonger. What did he feel towards her? Definitely anger, but beneath it, his love for her was still very much alive. "She is one of those women like my biological mother. I can't accept that! Why did I have to fall in love with her?"

"Brandon. I don't want you to hate your biological mother. She gave me what I thought I could never have. A child. For years I had thought that I could never have a child and I was so sad and depressed.

You became the light in my darkness. I couldn't hate her. Please, don't hate her. She gave me so much joy, a meaning to life that only a child could have given me.

He squeezed her hand gently. "I didn't mean to make you feel bad in all this. You're such a good mother to me. I love you."

He didn't tell her about the questions that went through his mind, the suffering at the orphanage or the bitterness of being abandoned. She had done so much for him. A sudden thought struck his mind and he just had to ask. "Mom, do you know anything at all about my birth mother?"

Elizabeth stood up and walked around the living room, a hint of sadness in her eyes.

"Mom. Do you know something and don't want to tell me."

"When we started thinking of adoption, Father Martin told us about the orphanage where he worked several times a week. He told us about you. And a bit about your mother."

"Father Martin?" Brandon had known this priest for many years. He was a close family friend but Brandon couldn't remember seeing him around the orphanage.

"Yes. Father Martin. He was worried about you. About you never getting adopted. We went to see you and I fell in love with you instantly. After the adoption was final, we moved to Maine because we didn't want people questioning us. In a new place, no one would know and that's when Austin and Conrad became business partners.

"Does he know my mother?"

"Yes."

223

"Did he tell you anything?"

Elizabeth sat down opposite him, her gaze averted. "I know that she was very young. A child making a child. That's all I know."

Disturbing thoughts wandered through his mind. Who was his father? Why did she have a baby so young? He didn't ask. A feeling of sadness settled upon his heart. "Did he tell you anything else?"

"No." She looked him directly in the eyes. "I couldn't love you more if you were my own child and I'm grateful to your mother for all the joy and fulfillment I got by having you."

He covered the distance between them, and hugged her. "I love you mom and I didn't mean to hurt you."

She kissed him on the forehead. "I love you son. I only want you to be happy. How old was Sarah when she had her baby?"

Brandon let go of her and went to sit on the couch. "Sixteen"

"Sixteen is way too young. She wasn't ready for a child. Raising a child is a big responsibility. Where is the baby's father in all this?"

"I didn't ask. I was so shocked and angry."

"I see. Do you still love her?"

He looked away. His emotions were all tangled, he had difficulties figuring out how he really felt. Sometimes he missed her and his heart felt like a throbbing, open wound. At other times, he was angry with Sarah, even felt like he hated her. "I can't love a woman like that. There was a time when I loved her."

"You can't switch on and off your emotions, son. You just don't stop loving someone in the blink of an eye."

"I've had two whole weeks to think about it."

"You were always drunk. How could you think clearly?"

"I know that it is over and it will stay that way."

"Because of the child. How can you blame her for wanting to give her child a better life. You know what I admire about Sarah?"

Brandon's head shot up. Did he hear right? "What are you talking about?"

"Some women choose to have abortions and that's not fair to any unborn child. Sarah had her baby, and then did what she thought was best for the child. In your mother's days, abortions existed too, but she choose to have you. She's a woman of courage. They are two courageous women."

Her words were like a slap in his face. He had been too angry at his birth mother and at Sarah to see further than that. What if they had chosen abortions? He wouldn't be around.

"If I had become pregnant at fifteen or sixteen and was unwed, I don't know how I would have handled it." She fell silent for a long time. "My parents would have never let me keep the baby," she finally said.

"Where is Father Martin now?"

"Still living at the presbytary a block away from church."

After Elizabeth had left, Brandon took a shower, shaved and decided to go see father Martin. For the first time in his life he was desperate to know about the girl who had brought him into this world. Maybe if he understood his natural mother's actions, he would in some way understand Sarah and be able to forgive her.

He rolled down the car window, the wind sweeping through his hair. It had been such a long time since he went to Church. As a child, he went with Elizabeth and Christian every Sunday. Austin rarely went with them. Father Martin was a frequent visitor at the Chases' home and Elizabeth did a lot of work for the church.

A dark cloud drifted in front of the sun, hiding its light. Raindrops spattered on the widshield. He glanced up at the sky. Not a lot of dark clouds, he thought. This was going to pass soon. He finally found the presbytary, parked on the side of the street and got out the car. He pushed against the iron gate and it swung open. The cloud had drifted away and the sun was shining brightly again, but a soft drizzle still fell. He hurried to the side entrance and knocked on the door. An elderly woman answered.

"I'm here to see Father Martin."

"Is he expecting you?" she asked suspiciously.

"No. I am Elizabeth Chase's son."

The woman pushed her glasses up and squinted her eyes. "You are the older son. I remember you."

Brandon smiled. He couldn't remember ever seeing her. She was probably one of those women who pinched his cheeks after church.

She held the door wide open, pointed to a wooden, highback chair in the corner and said, "Sit down."

Despite the heat outside, the building was cool. He looked around the large, quiet room and listened to the echoes of her shoe heels on the wooden floor. Suddenly there was only silence. His thoughts drifted back to Sarah. Had it not been for her, he wouldn't be here trying to find out about his natural mother. After a few minutes, sounds of shoe heels interupted the silence and she was back.

"He will see you. Go to the end of the corridor, you will find his office."

"Thank you." He got up and headed down the cold, quiet passageway.

Father Martin had aged quite a lot and was much thinner than the last time Brandon had seen him. He still found it hard to believe that Father Martin had known his mother and had never said a word to him.

"You look well Brandon. What can I do for you?"

"Mom told me that you are the one who told them about me when they wanted to adopt a child. I was wondering if you know my mother."

"Certain things are confidental and I can't tell you son." He placed his thin arms on the desk and continued to stare at Brandon.

His words sounded so final and Brandon felt frustration mounting within. It's not like he wanted this information to go hunt her down or anything like that. "I spent all my life detesting my birth mother for giving me away. Today I learnt that she was very young when she gave birth to me. Please, I don't want her name and address. I'm just trying to make sense of her decision."

He hesitated, as though trying to make up his mind what to say. "So many years have gone by. I can't possibly remember them all."

Brandon nodded as he looked into the priest's reluctant eyes.

"Elizabeth and Austin gave you a good home and a good life."

"Yes. I couldn't ask for a better mother than Elizabeth. My birth mother, did she have family who could take care of me?"

"In those days, life was so different for women. They had a child out of wedlock and they were considered lepers. No one respected them anymore. There are so many young girls who lost their lives when they went for abortions. I've seen so much suffering and loss of life. That's why when young girls in trouble came to me I always tried to help them." He stared at the photos on the wall, at the book shelves and finaly out of the widow.

"Please, try to remember." Brandon pleaded.

"Does Elizabeth know that you are here?"

"No."

"This will probably hurt her deeply."

"I love her and I'm sure she will understand why I came here." He stood up and thanked father Martin for his time. Brandon could tell that the priest wasn't about to give him any information. Was he doing this because of Elizabeth? Or, he probably didn't remember Brandon's mother at all.

"I'm sorry that I couldn't tell you anything." He rubbed his tired eyes.

Brandon nodded, feeling a profound sense of disappointment. He hurried down the silent hallway and out the door. It had stopped raining and the wet grass looked greener and vibrant with life. He opened the car door, an uneasy feeling fell upon him and he looked up at the presbytary window. Father Martin was looking at him. They looked at each other for a while and Brandon felt like going back to the priest and beg him for information.

He drove around aimlessly for a while and as he turned the corner, Brandon suddenly realized that he was in the area where Sarah lived. He drove slower, his eyes scanning the streets. Maybe he would get a glimpse of Sarah somewhere around. He stopped at the crosswalk, waited for an elderly woman to cross the street as his eyes continued searching. "What the hell is wrong with me?" He said. "Why am I looking for her?"

He pressed on the gas and sped away.

He felt disappointed that the priest hadn't told him more. When he had heard that his birth mother was very young, that had changed something inside of him. Why hadn't she tried to contact him before? She was now a grown woman and probably had other children. Brandon felt bitterness rose in his throat. Other children. Maybe she didn't want them to know about him.

I have to stop this, he told himself. Life goes on. The truth may forever be kept from him and there was nothing that he could do about it.

He got back to the apartment and was grateful to find it empty. He picked up the newspaper, checked the ads for houses to rent. He had to find a place of his own and a job. He made a few calls about the houses that interested him.

Father Martin's face kept springing up in his mind and Brandon had the feeling that the priest was hiding things from him. What was so wrong about wanting to know about your biological mother?

His love for Sarah was behind his quest for understanding his mother's actions. His grandfather used to say that destiny worked in strange ways. Was this the hand of destiny? If he was still with Stacey, Brandon was certain that he would have never tried to find out about his real mother.

Stacey. It was not hard to get over her. He had felt no pain, just a bit of sadness and he hadn't missed her at all. With Sarah, it was so different. Sarah with her gentle smile, eyes that were shy and flirtatious at the same time. She had made him so happy. At one time he had felt like their destiny was sealed in some other mysterious world, before they came on earth and they were meant to be together. How foolish, he thought.

Christian opened the door and stepped in. He pulled off his overalls, flung them in the corner and said, "Be ready. We're going out right after my shower. I know the coolest place to get lobster rolls. Your favorite."

"Going out sounds good."

Twenty minutes later, he was sitting in Christian's car, the loud music hurting his ears. He turned it down and Christian turned it up.

"Mom came by. Thanks tell tale." Brandon turned down the music.

"I must say, you look clean. Did mom give you a bath and shave you?"

"Yes." Brandon looked at the street sign and back to his brother. "Where is this place?"

"Not so far away. Sarah lives around here. We might just bump into her." He looked pretty pleased about himself.

"What do you think you're doing?"

"Nothing." He turned the corner, pointed to a house and said. "Sarah lives there. Memorize the address if you ever want to go visit." He stopped the car.

"What the hell is wrong with you! Drive! I'm not interested in her! By the way, how did you get her address?"

"From your address book. She should be home soon." He looked at his watch.

"Are you out of your mind! Drive!" He didn't want Sarah to see him sitting outside of her house. The sooner he forgot her, the better. He had given up on that idea that if he knew why his mother gave him up then he would probably understand the situation with Sarah. In the days of his mother, so much was different. The situation with Sarah wasn't the same.

"Listen Christian, if she sees me here, it will just get her hopes up and that's not fair since I want nothing more to do with her."

"You're right."

As his brother drove away, he looked back and caught sight of her car. She certainly recognised Christian's pink car. He turned around and stared at the grey road unfolding in front of him.

She has lost a lot of weight. I saw her at the restaurant the other night."

"I see she is out and having fun." His voice sounded bitter.

"She was not having a good time. She's was working. Accompanying some patient there."

"Good for her. More work, more money and she can go back to school faster."

"Maybe the extra work is her way of trying to forget you," Christian threw him an irritated glance.

Those words were like a dagger in his heart. Sarah wanting to forget him. What the hell is going on with me, he thought. He wanted to get her out of his mind too and get on with his life. Why shouldn't she do the same?

"Give her a break, Brandon. She did what was best for her child."

"She could have found a job and taken care of her child!"

"Welcome to the real world, rich boy. Do you know how hard it is to live on minium wage? How can you survive on that and take care of a child, too? Wake up Brandon. Oh let me see, she could have probably become an exotic dancer. Somehow I can't picture her doing that. Or, she could have found one of those jobs or.... never mind. You are damn stubborn, judgemental and self righteous! People has to be a certain way to have your respect. Some of Austin sure rubbed off on you."

Brandon laughed. "What the hell is wrong with you?"

Christian's fingers curled over the steering wheel and he was obviously angry. Brandon was surprised at his reaction.

"What's going on, Christian?"

Christian turned to face him. "I've seen her pass outside the apartment several times. Who is she looking for? Certainly not me. I had a chat with her at the restaurant and she is in nasty shape. She's a good girl, Brandon. She loves you. I would give my life to have someone love me like that."

'She loves you'. Those words were lodged in his mind and it hurt him to think how much she was

232

suffering. Sarah, the woman he dreamt of waking up beside every morning, the woman he thought would bear his children, the woman who just stuck herself permanently in his heart. Would he ever be able to forgive her?

Chapter 14

Sarah finished her second cup of coffee, grabbed a Kleenex, wiped her sweaty palms and continued preparing her medicine cart as residents shuffled into the main dining room. There was a note attatched to the chart open in front her, concerning the changes in dosage of Mrs. Jacobs and Mr. Smith's insulin. She took bottles of insulin from the medicine cabinet, examined them over and over before starting to fill up syringes, scared of making mistakes.

"Are you okay?" Kelly, the other nurse asked.

"I'm fine." She wanted to say, 'mind your own business', but refrained from saying so. She was tired of people asking if she was okay and her nerves were haywire, she just wanted to be left alone.

She wheeled out her cart and came to stop beside a long table where eight residents were seated and being fed by the nursing assistants. She took her time placing the small cups of medication beside each patient, forcing herself to smile at her co-workers.

"Sarah," one of the nursing assistants called out. "This doesn't look like Mr. Chin's medication. I don't remember him having so many pills."

Sarah turned towards her and took the small cup from her outstretched hand. "Maria, pass me the other cups, please." She picked them up as Maria pushed them towards her.

Taking a deep breath, she checked the medications against the packages that had been prepared for each patient and realized that she had made a mistake. The last thing she wanted was to give the wrong medicine to the wrong people. She took back the medication to the table and thanked Maria. Thank God, Maria had picked up on her mistake.

Sarah concentrated extra hard as she continued to give out medicine. Unwanted thoughts buzzed around her like unwanted mosquitoes on a summer night in the woods. Some days hard work was her fortress from pain and on other days it didn't work. Like today. Yesterday she had seen Brandon sitting in Christian's car and for a second, hope had washed over her and then it was gone, like a wave lapping the shore and moving away almost instantly. Why was he waiting in front of the house and as soon as she approached, he was gone?

She took back the medicine cart to the med room, relieved that she hadn't made any more mistakes. After breakfast, she had insulin to administer and made a mental note to double check the doses and patients.

She went to the dining room and sat down beside Jane, one of the residents. "I hope you will eat something this morning," she said gently. Jane had become a skeleton over the past few months, constantly refusing to eat and lately hardly responding to anyone. Sarah held out a spoon of porridge. "Jane, open your mouth, dear."

The woman just stared at her blankly and refused to open her mouth.

"You should eat something." A rush of frustration rose within Sarah and tears rushed to her eyes. She just could not handle all that was happening.

"No!" Jane's arm shot out, grabbed the bowl and flung it on the floor.

Sarah sighed, got up and picked up the bowl. She turned to Kelly, "I'm off on my break."

Sarah poured a cup of coffee and headed outside. She looked up and down the street, somewhere within, she hoped that Bandon might just pass by to get a glimpse of her. She slumped down on a small vacant chair in the shade of a tree. She had been trying so hard to go back to her ways before she had met Brandon, but just couldn't. Too much had changed. Not so long ago, she didn't want a man in her life and now she felt like she could not live without Brandon.

It was more than two weeks now since she and Brandon had broken up. She had known even before it happened that it was inevitable, but she never imagined that it would be so painful, that it would affect her so deeply. It was as heart wrenching as the day she had given Lydia away. These days, she walked around with a heavy weight in her chest and went about her duties like a robot. And after work, she always felt like she was walking into a huge void, where nothing existed.

She had taken two contracts to take care of patients in their homes and that kept her busy, but she had to stop and rest and that was when she couldn't run from reality, from heartbreak and pain.

She went back inside and Kelly fixed her with a stern look. "You had better get your act together. Those patients insulin is still lying there on the cart," she said, before turning and walking away.

Sarah took the insulin and went off to Mrs. Jacobs room. "Hello, how are you today?"

Mrs. Jacobs smiled but said nothing, her eyes were distant.

"I'm going to give you your insulin." She raised up the patient's shirt and stuck the needle into the skin of her tummy.

"Ouch," she said, her eyes wide.

Sarah smoothed back the older woman's hair and started to walk out of the room. She stopped, fear sucking her in like a giant vaccum. That injection was meant for Mr. Smith. She ran back to the med room, hoping that she hadn't made such a mistake. She picked up the other syringe with medication and discovered it was for Mrs. Jacobs! She had made a terrible mistake!

"No," she said into the empty room as she sank down on the chair. For a few moments she couldn't think. She grabbed the patient's chart, flipped through the pages and found her doctor's number.

Dr. Kim's receptionist answered and Sarah explained the situation. A minute later, Dr. Kim was on the line and Sarah explained to him what had happened. He told her to send Mrs. Jacobs to the hospital right away. Ten minutes later, the ambulance was there and Mrs. Jacobs was sent to the hospital.

Sarah went to the washroom and splashed her face with cold water, dried it and stood there in the quiet, her heart hammering with fear. Mrs Jacobs had gotten out of hospital just yesterday. The doctors had had a hard time controlling her diabetes. "What on earth have I done?" She was afraid that something would go terribly wrong with the resident. She opened the door, walked out and headed for the supervisor's office.

Janet looked at her sternly as she took a seat. "I'm waiting for an explanation." Her tone was chilly.

"I made a mistake. There have been changes made to her dose of insulin and I looked it over several times." She shook her head.

"A terrible mistake! She got out of the hospital yesterday!" She started to write in the open book in front of her. "You look real tired and you have been making mistakes over the past two weeks. What's going on? It's not like you."

"I have some personal problems."

"Why don't you take the rest of the day off. I'll get another nurse to come in. Go home and sleep. And let's hope that Mrs. Jacobs will be fine."

Sarah nodded. She had been messing up at work. She had better go home and sleep.

"Maybe you should take a week off and get some rest," janet suggested.

"No. I can't do that. Please."

"Then get your act together!"

When Sarah got home, she changed, climbed into bed and fell into a deep sleep. She awoke to the sounds of her mother moving around upstairs. A glance at the clock told her it was four-thirty five. She got up, slipped on a dress and went downstairs.

"What time did you get off from work?" Anna asked.

"Earlier than usual." She told her mother what had happened at work.

"Maybe you should take a few weeks off. Go visit your cousins in Philadelphia."

"I can't. I want to go back to school this winter and I need the money."

Anna poured her a glass of ice-tea. "I know, dear, but there are certain things you have to deal with first.

238

You are not handling this break-up well. Before you make some major mistake, take some time off. Get rid of those two contracts that you picked up. I know that you took extra work because you don't want to think of Brandon, but maybe that's not the best solution." Anna touched Sarah's face. "You look so tired, so worried. I've seen you out on the patio all hours of the night. You can't continue like this."

"I know." She took a sip of ice tea. "What did I get myself into? How could I have been so stupid? Before I met him, my life was so stable."

Anna stopped peeling potatoes and looked up. "Did you ever try to talk to him after that night?"

"No." How could she ever face Brandon again? She was so ashamed of herself, ashamed of all the lies she had told him and the things that she had deliberately forgotten to tell him. He would still be angry with her. "He does not want to see me again. It's over."

"He is angry. Give him some time and then call him." Anna washed the potatoes and put them in the pot. "Why don't you go out with Tim and his friends tonight. It's Friday, go have some fun."

"I'll think about it."

"Don't think about it! Just go!" Sarah looked up in surprise at her mother's unusually sharp voice. Anna looked extremely worried and tired.

"What's wrong mom? Please, don't be worried about me. I'll be fine."

"You can't live like that! Work, eat and…I can't say sleep. You don't even sleep. Go out. It will do you good."

Sarah was off for the week-end and the the thought of two long days without anything to do bothered her, got on her nerves. This would only mean two days of thinking about Brandon, two days of torture. A restlessness awoke within her, as though it had started with the flip of a switch. She got up, picked up her purse and told Anna that she was going to be back later.

She drove around, then turned off the highway and headed in the direction of Christian's place. She had passed by several times over the past two weeks, hoping to see Brandon, trying to find the courage to talk to him one more time, to make him understand her choices. She could barely live with the fact that Brandon was no longer a part of her life. How she wanted him back. She wondered how he was doing. Was he taking this as hard as she was?

Christian's apartment floated into sight. Brandon's car was not there. Sarah parked at the side of the street and walked towards the building. She was not sure of what she was doing, but climbed the stairs anyway. She didn't stop to question herself, if she did, she would choose flight instead of fight. If Brandon was there, she would talk to him. Before she could even press on the buzzer, the door swung open.

Christian stood in the doorway. "Sarah, come in."

Her eyes searched the room as she entered. There were no more boxes in the living room.

"Brandon's not here. He's at the beach house, you know, where you guys went the other night. He's going to stay there for a while. Sit down."

She sat down. "How is he doing?"

"Well, he has been drinking himself stupid for almost two weeks and he is not doing great. What about you?" His eyes lingered on her face.

"Things could be better." She felt uncomfortable in Christian's presence.

"You look...tired and sad."

They sat in silence for a while. "I shouldn't even be here. I'm sorry to bother you."

"I'm happy to see you. Brandon is being an idiot."

"Why was he outside my house yesterday?"

He looked away from her gaze. "It's my fault. I took him there and he really didn't want to be there."

"I see." She stood up. "I have to go."

"Are you going out tonight?" He lifted his shoulders in a careless gesture. "With friend's. Maybe I can drag Brandon out there and then the two of you can have a chat."

"I might go out. If I do, it will be Jake's Pub."

"Be there. I'm gonna kidnap Brandon."

Back home, Sarah sat quietly in the kitchen with her mom and Edward. She looked at him out of the corner of her eyes, waiting for him to say something nasty but he remained quiet. An uncomfortable silence hung upon them. A restlessness started in her legs and found it's way into her heart and mind. She stood up and went out on the patio, thinking back to the times she had passed outside of Christian's apartment hoping to get a glimpse of Brandon. What had she become? It was almost like stalking someone, but she had wanted to see Brandon so badly, like right now. Would Christian keep his word about bringing Brandon over to the pub? She went down the stairs, jumped in her car and left. She should have done this two weeks ago.

Getting those negatives were very important and now that Austin knew that it was over with Brandon, he would probably give it to her.

She walked into the crowded store and took a quick look around. No offices were in sight so she walked among the racks of clothing and pretended to be interested. A sales girl walked over and asked if she needed help. After a few questions concerning a summer dress, Sarah said, "I was wondering if Austin is still here."

"Is it for a job?" The girl's attitude went from friendly to serious.

"No. I have been trying to get in touch with Elizabeth for a while because I have something for her. I just thought that I'd leave it with Austin." She tried to sound calm, but she heard the nervousness in her own voice. Smiling at the girl, she asked, "Is he in?"

"Yes. Just go up the steps there." She pointed to the back of the store. "His office is there."

"Thank you." As she headed down the aisle, her heart started to hammer frantically and she forced herself to go on. If she had to be insulted once more to get those negatives, she didn't mind. It was worth it.

The name 'Austin Chase' was written on the door. She stood there a few minutes before she could finally bring herself to knock.

"Come in!"

She pushed the door open slowly and a sudden urge to turn around and leave engulfed her. Austin was busy on his computer and didn't even look in her direction. She stepped in.

"Mr. Chase."

His head snapped up, he spun around to face her, anger and hatred in his eyes. "What the hell do you want!"

She stood rooted to the spot. Why on earth did she ever think that this man would give her the negatives? He could have lots of fun using it to make her life miserable.

"Have you suddenly gone dumb? There's a two fold meaning to that. You were already dumb in one sense and now I am talking about dumb as in losing your power of speech!"

She licked her dry lips and ignored his insults. "You have something that I would like to have."

"My son?" He stood up, looked her in the eyes and laughed.

"No. The negatives." She fought back her anger, trying to stay as calm as possible

"Oh that. So you don't want my son anymore. No. He does not want you anymore. Does it hurt Sarah?"

His words bit into her, she forced herself to stay strong. "It's not your problem whether or not I'm hurting. It's over between Brandon and me, so why keep the negatives?

"Maybe just to make your life a living hell." He sat down, leaned back in the chair and smiled up at her. "You made my life hell. Give me one good reason why I shouldn't do the same to you?"

Sarah rubbed her hands together, they were so cold. Did he want her to say she was sorry? No way! She wasn't going to say that! But she had to get those negatives.

"So." He smiled, obviously enjoying himself.

She walked over to the desk, placed her hands on it and said, "Do whatever the hell you want with it! You want to make my life miserable? Go ahead!" He couldn't make her more miserable than she already was.

"Let me think about it." He stood up, walked around the desk and came to stand beside her.

Sarah's body was trembling from the anger building up within her. Who the hell did he think he was? If he wanted to use them against her, he could go right ahead! "What are you expecting? You want me to fall on my knees and beg for mercy?"

Austin stuck his hands in his pockets. "Yes, I'd love that. By the way, you're photogenic. Great photos. You're doing the wrong job. You should work for a porno magazine."

Sarah's hand flew out and she slapped Austin really hard. Surprised at her reaction, she stepped back, stood rooted to the spot and watched him rubbing his cheek. His eyes burned with fury and for an instant she got the impression that he was going to slap her back.

"Get out of here before I do something I regret!"

Sarah spun around and hurried out on shaky legs. As she started down the stairs, her heart almost jolted to a stop. Brandon and Elizabeth were standing at the foot of the stairs.

He started up the stairs, raised his eyes and stopped. She saw the sadness in his eyes, then it turned to something cold, something she couldn't quite figure out. She looked at Elizabeth and the older woman gave her a gentle smile and started up the stairs.

"Hi, Sarah. It's nice to see you. I was wondering…well…you know…" She looked uncomfortable.

"Why I'm here." Sarah's eyes filled up and she was really angry with herself. She didn't want to cry here and especially not in front of Brandon who had turned his attention to the racks of clothing below him as though she didn't even exist.

"Yes, dear."

Sarah wanted so desperately to tell her, to beg her to get the negatives from Austin. She got the impression that Brandon didn't care what Austin did with it.

"Why are you crying?" Elizabeth asked.

She brushed the tears away. "I don't want to bother you with my problems." She glanced over at Brandon, his back was still turned to her. She wished that he would turn around so she could look into his eyes to see if there was any love there. Earlier all she had seen was anger but maybe she had missed something. If only he still loved her, loved her enough not to hold the past against her.

"If you're here, it has something to do with Austin, unless you were expecting to find Brandon here." Her tone was so soft, so motherly.

"I need your help."

"Don't bother her!" Brandon's voice was sharp and cold as the blade of a sword.

"Brandon! Can't you see she is upset?"

"Mom, I'll take care of Sarah."

"Maybe I could help her." She turned back to Sarah. "What is it dear?"

"I will take care of the problem," he said, hurrying towards them, his eyes dark with anger.

She looked at Brandon for a minute, wondering why he was here. Was he trying to work things out with Austin? If so, that meant she was out of the picture for good. Probably Brandon was going to work things out with Stacey, for all she knew. A pang of jealousy and anger swallowed her up and she wondered if she ever really meant anything to the man standing two steps below her.

"Elizabeth, your husband has something that I need to get from him. There are some negatives with me and your son." She ran her tongue over her dry lips and continued. "Not very... not very nice and Austin has threatened to use them against me. I want the negatives so I can destroy them. I've worked so hard. I don't want to lose all I have worked for because of a mistake I made. Please, help me."

Elizabeth's eyes were wide with shock and disbelief. "I will get it all from him and give them to you. What's your phone number?"

Sarah scribbled it on a piece of paper and handed it to Elizabeth. "Thank you," she whispered and without looking at Brandon, she dashed down the stairs. She knew he was mad with her because she had gotten Elizabeth involved in all of this.

By the time she got home, it was already dark and as she stepped into the house she heard voices and laughter. It was Allana and Paula.

"Well, you're going out with us tonight. Time for some fun. And you are not saying, no." Paula stood up, held out a bag to Sarah. "And you're dressing up, lady."

"It will do you good," Allana said. "When was the last time you went out and have some fun."

"Not so long ago," Sarah answered. Memories of her and Brandon the night he had given her the black dress swam into her mind.

"You're coming with us," Allana said, taking her by the arm. "And we are not taking no for an answer. Wait until you see what's in that bag."

Sarah eyed Paula's short, black leather skirt. She couldn't help but smile. "We're going to Jake's pub." She desperately hoped that Christian would keep his word.

"As you wish," Allana said.

When they entered the pub one hour later, Sarah squinted and waited for her eyes to adjust to the darkness before walking towards a vacant table. "Where is Tim and the others?" Her eyes swept the crowd before she sat down. There was no sign of Christian.

"Mike and Tim will be here later on," Paula answered, signalling to the waiter.

The waiter arrived at their table. "What are you ladies having?" His eyes lingered on Sarah and unconsciously she placed her arm on her crossed legs trying to cover her thighs.

"Heineken. Three," Allana said, her eyes going from Sarah to the waiter.

"You are new to the gang." he said to Sarah. "I hope you come more often."

"Maybe I will," she yelled over the loud music and looked away, not wanting further conversation with him.

Allana and Paula were teasing her about the waiter when Mike and Tim walked over to them.

"Am I dreaming or Sarah is really here?" Tim almost shouted.

"It is Sarah." Allana kissed Tim on the lips. "Told you she was going to come."

The evening rolled by slowly and Sarah found herself warding off boys who came to ask for a dance everytime the other couples went to dance. She still hadn't seen Christian or Brandon. She wondered what had happened after she left the store. Did Elizabeth confront Austin and was Brandon even angrier with her?

A tall, lean boy walked over to her and asked her to dance. Sarah accepted. As they danced, the stranger leaned foward and said, "I'm Ryan and you're a great dancer."

She did not tell him her name and when the song ended, she just walked away.

"Who's that guy you were dancing with?" Paula asked, placing another beer in front of her. "Look, he can't keep his eyes off of you."

"Here he comes again," said Allana, obviously enjoying herself.

Ryan leaned close to Sarah. "May I have another dance?"

As they danced, Sara kept turning away and looking at the crowd, hoping that Brandon would show up. He was still not in sight. Maybe Christian couldn't convince him to come.

"Waiting for someone," he asked.

"No."

As she walked back to the table, she caught sight of Brandon sitting at the bar and Christian was just a few feet away from him talking to a girl. In the dimly lit pub, they looked at each other, then Brandon turned away and Sarah went to her table.

"Sarah. There's a guy at the bar. Real good looking. He has been looking at you for the longest while," Paula said.

"How long was he there?" She asked nervously.

"I don't know exactly. Why?"

"It's Brandon."

Allana and Paula said, "Brandon?" They both turned and looked in his direction and back to Sarah.

"I have to go to the washroom," Sarah stood up and left. How long has he been sitting there? She wondered if he was waiting for someone. She locked herself in one of the washrooms and stood there for a while, trying to pluck up the courage to go over to him. She had to talk to him one more time, try to make him understand but she was afraid to make a fool out of herself. What if he just stood up and walked away or insulted her? After a few minutes, she came out the washroom, crossed the pub and went to him.

He stared at her, as though he was seeing her for the first time in his life. His eyes travelled the length of her body and came to rest on her face but he remained silent.

"I want to talk to you," she said.

"I have to talk to you too." He stood up. "Let's go outside. It's too noisy in here."

She nodded and followed him, a flicker of hope sprang up within her. Her feet were aching from the high heel shoes and her legs felt so wobbly with nervousness.

They went to a quiet corner of the parking lot and for a while they just looked at each other in silence,

Sarah playing with the rings on her fingers and Brandon running his fingers through his hair.

"This is for you," he finally said, pulling out an envelope from his shirt pocket. "The negatives you wanted. Don't go around Austin again, neither Elizabeth. I'm really mad that you got her mixed up in such a thing."

"I'm sorry to have dragged Elizabeth into my mess. I saw it as the only way out. As for Austin, why would I want to see him again? I have what I wanted. Thank you for the negatives. I appreciate it."

"I told you what I wanted to. What is it you wanted to talk to me about?" He stuck his hands in his pockets and looked at her like she was just a stranger.

"I wanted to tell you..." She stopped talking, angry at herself for the tears that rolled down her cheeks. To her surprise, he brushed them away. "I ... still love you. We can work this out."

"No we can't." His fixed her with a cold, hard look.

"Maybe if you find out the truth about your mother, then you won't hate her and you wouldn't see things the same way."

"My mother is Elizabeth! There's nothing more between us!"

Sarah followed his gaze as he stared into the darkness. She saw the wild, dark hair first and slowy the image sank into her mind. It was Stacey.

"You are back with Stacey! It sure didn't take you a long time to forget me. It makes me wonder why you don't want to see me anymore. Is it really because of the baby?" Anger and jealousy whizzed through her. "It was all about sex, wasn't it? You got what you wanted, found an excuse to break it off and go on. I should have known. We're not from the same world. I thought that you loved me and it made me crazy with hapiness but it was all a game. Brandon, you would never spend your life with a woman like me. I'm poor and not a bit classy. I sure wouldn't fit in your world. I was good enough for a fling, that's all."

He looked at her, shifting his weight form one leg to another and remained silent.

"Why did you do this to me Brandon? My life was so perfect before I met you. How I wish I had never set eyes on you. Go to your lady. She's waiting."

He walked past her and she leaned on a car for support, her shoulders shaking as she cried softly. Sarah dried her eyes. Why cry? It wasn't going to change anything. She stood in the dark, thinking of the good times they had together, regretting all the lies she had told him and was certain that he would never change his mind. She felt a pair of hands on her shoulders, her body stiffened as the person turned her around. She looked up, it was Brandon.

"I couldn't leave you out here like this," he said.

"But you could have left me on a dirt road out in nowhere the other night. What do you want? My body? Get your hands off of me!"

His hands fell to his side. "I just want you to know a few things. At one time, I really loved you. It had nothing to do with sex. The real reason we broke up, is the issue with the child."

"You're always the good guy and you had to leave Stacey to come tell me this because you don't want to be stained. You have to stay pure and clean. Go away, I don't want to soil you!"

Hilda St. James

"What the hell is wrong with you? Do you think you're the only one who got hurt in all this? Think again. You let me fall in love with a shadow, with a person who really didn't exist. You lied to me. I was ready to walk away from my family for the sake of you. And you broke my heart Sarah. I don't know how you did it. How you made me fall so deeply in love with you." As he spoke, the hardness left his voice and he sounded like a broken man.

"I'm so sorry if I've hurt you. I didn't mean to and I promise that I'll keep out of your way from now on. I saw Christian today and I told him that I was going to be here and I guess that he is the one who convinced you to come here." She started to walk away when his arm shot out and held her upper arm.

"I miss you Sarah." She shrugged off his hand and walked away. She had to get over Brandon.

He took her arm in a firm grip. "You are going to listen to me."

She turned to face him. "Say what you have to and then we can get on with our lives," she yelled.

Voices reached her ears and she noticed small groups of people walking towards them. "Go ahead," she whispered. "Stacey is waiting for you. Oh, I fogot. You guys will have the rest of you lives together so a few minutes dosen't matter."

"Why did you lie to me? Why didn't you tell me about your child at the very beginning? We could have spared ourselves a lot of pain."

"Spare ourselves a lot of pain! Your pain passed really fast. You're with Stacey!"

"You think I'm not hurting? That you're not haunting me? Let's go in the car. There are too many people around."

She went with him and climbed in the passenger seat.

"I wish that I had never met you," he said.

"Well, you have. But you never really loved me, Brandon. If you had truly loved me, my past would never stand between us."

"Never loved you! When I look at you, this is what I want to do." In an instant, he caught her face between his hands and his lips found hers in a long, passionate kiss."

Sarah pushed him aside. "That's not love! It's lust! What is it you want Brandon? Sex?"

Sarah couldn't get a hold of her emotions. It kept going back and forth between pain and fury. She reached up, unbuttoned her shirt. "Is this what you want. I can take it all off. One more time wouldn't kill me."

The next instant the car was moving and she yelled at Brandon to stop but he wouldn't. After a few minutes, he stopped on a quiet street. Her shirt was still open. He reached over and buttoned it. She watched as he buttoned her shirt, slowly, almost reluctantly and then he moved away.

Their eyes held. "Why did you do that? Had enough?" She laughed. It was a dry, cruel sound.

"Stop it, Sarah. I never saw you as a sex object." He started the car and drove towards the pub, his face hard with anger.

Outside the pub, he said, "Your friends must be looking for you. Go on."

Hilda St. James

She decided that she had made a fool out of herself tonight and that was enough. Why on earth had she unbuttoned her shirt and asked him if it was sex he wanted? She stepped out the car, slammed the door and went back inside. She went to the ladies room, washed her face and went to join the others. This was it. It was really over. She joined the others and though they looked at her curiously, they asked no questions.

Sarah watched as Brandon and Stacey walked out together.

Chapter 15

Brandon sat on the balcony, thinking of the offer his friend had made to him about working in France for a few months. It sounded tempting. It would take his mind off of Sarah and Stacey would stop running after him. The summer night was humid, he took off his shirt, went into the house and switched off the lights. The darkness felt somewhat comforting. Sarah had told him that if he understood his natural mother's reasons for giving him up, then he would probably see her differently. He felt tempted to go back to see Father Martin.

He sighed. What a night it had been. Inspite of the anger he felt towards Sarah, he couldn't help feeling sorry for all the pain she was going through. It had hurt him when she had accused him of wanting her only for sex and he was really shocked when she had unbuttoned her shirt. This was a side of Sarah he did not know.

He saw light on the darkened street, pulled the curtains aside and closed them back just as fast. It was Sarah. He moved the curtain aside and peeked out. She had brought the car to a stop and sat there, looking up at the house. She stayed there for a long time. He felt like going to her and tell her to forget him, that it wasn't going to work between the two of them.

Tonight, she had said to him, that if he had truly loved her, her past would never be a stumbling block between them. Was she right?

She wiped her eyes, rolled down the window, stuck her head out a bit and looked around. He thought that she might be looking for Stacey's car. He wanted to go tell her that he and Stacey were not back together. Stacey had come up to the beach house just as he and Christian were leaving for the pub and had said she was going to meet them there. Brandon had told her that he had no objections. He had known Stacey all his life and there was no reason why he could not at least remain civil to her.

A few weeks ago, he had been so mad with Sarah, he didn't even want to see her. Some of that anger had faded, but he could not get past that one hurdle. Sometimes he wished that he could find a way to deal with it, to make things right between him and Sarah again. But, how could he spend his life with a woman who fell into the same category as his biological mother?

Sarah started the car and drove away.

Sadness and pain tugged at his heart, he switched on the lights, went to the guest room and pulled out a box full of oil paintings. He took out the one that he called, 'the faceless woman', and examined it carefully. He had done that painting many years ago. He was still a child and though Elizabeth was a great mother, he couldn't help thinking of his biological mother. He had started that painting and couldn't imagine what his real mom looked like so he had painted a veil over her face. He had spent years despising 'the faceless woman'. Maybe it was really time to let go of the past, a past that troubled him, made him so sad, at times.

The next day, he went to see Elizabeth, determined to find out if she knew anything at all about his biological mom.

Elizabeth was in the garden, tending her rose bushes. She looked up as he walked towards her and though she smiled, he could tell that it was not genuine. Brandon felt embarassed as he remembered the events of last night. When Austin had given her the negatives, she had held the negatives up to the light for a few seconds just to be sure she had the right thing. She had given him a look that had told him she was not pleased, then hande him the negatives and told him to give them to Sarah.

"Well Brandon, did you give that thing to Sarah?" She pulled off her gloves, poured a glass of water and did not look at him.

He sat down opposite her. "I did."

"How is she?" Their eyes met and he saw shadows of sadness in hers before she lowered them and started flipping through the pages of a magazine.

Brandon didn't want to go into details and he really didn't feel like telling her how things went. "I don't really know. I gave it to her and that was it." It was so much easier to lie at this point. He wondered if Sarah had lied to him for the same reason. Who wanted to talk about embarassing situations?

"Do you still love her?" She looked at him with motherly concern.

"Yes. But we can't be together. You know why." He saw the hurt in Elizabeth's eyes and was perplexed.

"Sometimes I wonder if I have been a good mother to you. You have spent so much time despising your biological mother, as though you were so unhappy with me and you blamed her for it." She looked away.

"Mom! That's not true! I couldn't ask for a better mother than you and you've always been there for me. How could you say something like that?" He stood up. "You know mom, it hurts to be abandoned. I suffered a lot at the orphanage and no matter how hard I try I can't forget those days."

"In the days when you were born, unwed mothers were not accepted. If she had kept you, what kind of life would she have been able to offer you? Not much. If I was in her place, I probably would have been pushed to make the same decision. Stop hating her Brandon. I'm a mother and I would die of a broken heart if you or Christian hated me."

"Sarah could have kept her baby if she wanted to. The world is so different today than it was thirty years ago."

"Have you met her family?"

"No," he answered, picking off dry leaves from a small tree.

"Probably they could not help her in any way possible. Just look at it this way, Sarah made a big sacrifice, she gave her child to people who could offer that child a better life even though it was so hard."

"I get the feeling that you are taking sides with Sarah. What's going on?"

"You and Sarah love each other. Why destroy that love?"

"Mom I always thought that you wanted me to marry some society girl."

"Austin wants you to, not me. Marry the woman you love. Do you love Sarah?"

"Yes. I love her like I never thought I could love anyone. And that is why I am thinking about going to work in France for a few months. I want to forget her."

Elizabeth stood up and looked down at him angrily. "You are so set in your own stubborn ways. Over the years, you learnt that from Austin! It's not a good thing! Let's go inside. It's getting quite hot out here in the sun." She stood up and started towards the house.

Once they were seated in the living room, she told him. "I phoned Sarah this morning. She is in so much pain. I couldn't stand it. The other day when you went to see Father Martin, there are things that he did not want to tell you because he thought it would hurt me. I called him this morning and told him that it was okay to tell you whatever he knows. Go see him Brandon." She took off her glasses, wiped it with her apron and put it on again. "Maybe what he has to say will help you. Hatred is a hard emotion to deal with." She touched his shoulder lightly, "I can't stand to see you suffer this way, to know that you are letting go of a woman you love deeply."

Brandon felt like he had stepped into a rather confusing world. "You phoned Sarah?"

"I wanted to find out if she got those negatives."

"I see. Did Father Martin tell you what he knew?"

"I didn't ask him."

"Mom, I love you. You are a great mother." He leaned foward and kissed her on the cheek. "I know that I despise my biological mother but that's not your fault."

"I just want you to be happy."

An hour later, Brandon drove over to the presbytery and after a short chat with the receptionist,

259

he was shown to Father Martin's office. He hoped that whatever the priest had to say would somehow help him to understand his biological mother and Sarah. That it would help him to stop hating one and stop him from destroying the other.

"Sit Brandon." The priest fixed him with keen eyes. "Elizabeth phoned me this morning and asked me to tell you whatever I know about your mother. The first time you came here, I didn't want to tell you anything because I was afraid of hurting Elizabeth."

Brandon nodded, his eyes resting on the older man's skinny fingers toying with a sheet of paper.

"I remember your mother. Her name was Rebecca. She lived with her mom. Rebecca's father had abandoned them when Rebecca was born. They were very poor and your mother was a frail girl. When she became pregnant, she came to see me and I did my best to help her. I had seen so many young girls die because they went to people to have abortions. Rebecca didn't want to have an abortion, she wanted her baby. I helped her to find work. She was so sick that none of her employers kept her for a long time. She loved you Brandon and wanted so desperately to keep you." Shadows of pain filled his eyes.

Brandon let out a deep breath. The word, 'loved', lodged itself in his mind. He felt like she loved him once, but not anymore. He rubbed the back of his neck. "If she loved me, why didn't she ever try to find me?"

"That is impossible. She died a few months after you were born."

He ran his fingers through his hair, propped his head up with his hands and closed his eyes. Pain and guilt washed over him. He had been despising her for so long and he had no idea that she had passed away. He felt rotten.

"Tell me about her. What did she look like?" His throat tightened and he fought back the tears.

Father Martin looked at him sadly. "She was a very gentle, trusting person." He stopped, his eyes grew distant. "She trusted too easily. You have her eyes." He said nothing more.

"How did she die?" The room suddenly felt too small and he needed some air. He stood up, walked over to the open window and breathed in deeply.

Father Martin came to stand beside him. "She died a natural death. She was so frail. When you were a baby, you used to be sick all the time and that's the main reason you were not adopted earlier."

Brandon half turned and looked at the older man, their eyes level. "You remember my mother so well. Why? Is there something that you are not telling me?"

"She spent a lot of time with you. Sometimes she slept on the floor beside your crib. She was not like the other girls who just left their children and never looked back. She rocked you to sleep many nights. She came to the orphanage every day until she passed away."

Those last words hit Brandon like a fist in the face. "She really did?"

"Yes. Stop hating her. She doesn't deserve to be hated. Every time she saw me, she begged me to watch out for you, to see that you go to a good family and I promised her that much."

Tears sprang to Brandon's eyes and there was a question burning in his mind but he wasn't sure whether or not he should ask.

"Do you know about my father?"

"As for your father. I have no information. Rebecca never told me who he was."

"How old was she when I was born?"

"She was fourteen or fifteen. I don't remember. Can you see Brandon? It was a child having a child." His voice fell to a whisper. "Even though she's not here, she deserves to be loved."

"I'm sorry for all the time I spent hating her. I didn't know." Unable to hold back his tears, he wept for the girl who had brought him into this world. The girl who wasn't able to keep him, love him, watch him grow up, all the things she certainly desired. She had had a sad life and even more pain when she had left him at the orphanage. If only she could hear him, he would tell Rebecca that he love her. He was grateful that she would never know for how many years, her son, who she cherished, had spent despising her.

"Why don't we take a walk outside?" The priest touched him lightly on the shoulder.

"Sounds good." Brandon felt like a huge burden had been taken off his shoulders. He followed the priest down a long dark corridor, then through a side door and into a small sunny garden.

"Elizabeth told me a bit about your girlfriend." He looked up at the sky, obviously enjoying the heat of the sun on his face. It was chilly in that building.

Brandon told him about Sarah and how he had problems accepting her past. The priest listened intently. "Now I understand why my mother left me at the orphanage but I still can't understand Sarah. Times are so different now. She could have found a job and raised her child. Sarah is a nurse and she will go back to school. She wants to become a child psychologist."

The priest sat down on a wooden bench. "Sometimes, in life people are so confused, so scared, they make wrong decisions. That does not mean they should pay for it for the rest of their lives. Have a talk with her, find out why she really gave her child up for adoption. Some choose abortions, some adoption. I'm happy Sarah did not choose abortion."

"I think she gave up her baby because she didn't want the responsibility."

"Who are we to judge, Brandon? To cast the first stone? How old was she when she had the child?" The priest looked so calm, so at peace. Brandon envied him.

"Sixteen. There are lots of sixteen year olds who work." He stood up, moved his head from side to side, in an effort to relieve some of the stiffness in his neck.

"I agree that lots of sixteen year old kids are working but did she have a place to go with her baby? Was the baby's father willing to help her?" He stood up and they continued walking.

"Her parents are alive so she would have had a place to go with the baby. I don't know much more. I was too angry to listen to what she had to say."

"Maybe her parents didn't want her to bring the baby into their home. Where was she supposed to go with her child? What kind of life did she have? If it wasn't a good one then I think that she would want to spare her child the same fate. What do you think Brandon?" They stopped and looked at each other.

"I was too angry to really see all those points that you mentioned."

"You have to respect and accept people. Some are weak, others are strong, some make good decisions, others make bad ones. If you really love her, go work things out."

"Thank you father Martin." They shook hands and Brandon walked away.

He drove back to the beach house, still feeling angry towards Sarah. He hated to see innocent children suffer. Was her child suffering right now? His heart softened towards his biological mother and she had done the only thing possible, but it was not the same with Sarah. He compared Sarah and Rebecca's situation and could not find much in common. He suddenly remembered the pink ring that she refused to take off. Was it a reminder of her child? He pulled into the driveway and saw Stacey's car parked outside.

As he climbed the stairs, she opened the door. She was as beautiful as ever and she stood there smiling.

"Hello Brandon. I was starting to think that you were not coming home."

"What are you doing here?" He wanted to be alone, to sort out his thoughts and didn't want her around.

"What a nice way to greet your visitor."

He moved aside her arm that was stretched across the doorway and walked into the house. "I just want to be alone. I'm in no mood for talk."

She crosssed the room, stood in front of him and said, "We don't have to talk. There's other exciting stuff we could do. Remember how much fun we had together." She reached up and kissed him on the lips.

He took her by the shoulders and moved her away gently. "That's the past and it will stay that way. It's over Stacey." He looked at her wearily. "Go home."

She looked at him through narrowed eyes. "Still dying a slow death because of that little tramp?" She shook her head, laughed and said, "I'm disappointed in your choice."

The name she had called Sarah made him angry. "You are behaving like a tramp right now! Where is your lover? Maybe he will enjoy the tramp in you."

"You used to love when I behaved like a tramp." She walked to the kitchen and came back with a bottle of wine. "Care to join me." She took two glasses from the cabinet.

"I want you to leave. Since I'm here, you're always stopping by. I asked you not to come back here." He took the bottle of wine from her hand, placed it on the table and opened the door. "I need to be alone right now."

"Scared your darling will show up and see me here?"

"She will not come here." He handed Stacey her purse. "Please leave."

She did not take it. "Your darling will not come here?" She smiled at him. "I saw her sitting in her car, staring up at the house and I went outside so she could get a look at me. The woman looked like she was seeing ghost then drove away."

"Why did you do that?" He took her by the arm and led her to the door. "Why didn't you just stay out of sight?"

"My car was outside. She would have known anyway." She grabbed her purse and dashed down the stairs. "Go to hell Brandon!" she yelled.

Brandon closed the door and leaned against it. His thoughts were in a jumble, his emotions, worse. He had repeatedly asked Stacey not to come here and yet she did. Brandon knew that it shouldn't matter that

Sarah had seen her, yet, it disturbed him. It bothered him that she would think that he and Stacey was back together and she was so easily forgotten.

He exited the house through the side entrance and went down to the beach. He stripped off his clothes and plunged into the water. He swam for about five minutes and his back and legs started to hurt. He came out the water, disappointed that he couldn't swim longer. It always helped to relax him. Brandon pulled on his pants and went to lay down in the patch of shadow and let his mind go back to his conversation with the priest.

His heart flooded with joy and sadness. Joy that his mother had loved him, and sadness for the life she had had. Knowing that she loved him, released him from a burden that he didn't realize he had been carrying around for years and now he felt so free.

He started comparing Rebecca and Sarah's situations again, trying to find something in common, but he still couldn't get past his anger for Sarah. Father Martin had told him that love forgives all but it wasn't that easy. He wondered if Sarah had even tried to keep her baby, if her family had offered to help and she refused. He sat up. There was only one way to find out. Go see her.

He drove past Sarah's place several times and just didn't have the courage to face her. After all that she had gone through, she probably just wanted to forget him. He finally parked beside her car and slowly climbed the steps, his eyes stuck on the open window. He stood outside the door for a few minutes, took a deep breath and tried to think of what he would say to Sarah. He knocked on the door and waited, but there was no answer. He listened for any sounds coming from the inside and heard nothing. He knocked again, this time he heard heavy footsteps and the door swung open.

Brandon stared at the man standing in front of him, with a receding hairline, a pale almost grey colour face and sunken eyes.

"Who are you?" Edward squinted from the glare of the sun.

"I'm Brandon Chase. Sarah used to take care of me a while ago. I want to talk to her." He looked past the man and into the house hoping to see Sarah. There was no one.

"Brandon Chase." His breath smelled of alcohol and a wicked look slid into his eyes. "Come in."

"Is she at home?" Brandon didn't like the looks of this man. "Are you Sarah's father?"

"Yes. I'm Edward. Come on in," his voice was cold and unfriendly.

Brandon followed him to the living room, his eyes quickly taking in the small house. Edward pointed to the couch that had obviously been repaired a thousand times. It looked like a patchwork couch. He sat down and watched Edward pick up a bottle of vodka, examined it and put it back on the table.

"You want to see my daughter?" Edward lifted the bottle of vodka and took a drink. "She likes to play around with men. I see you fell for her acts. If you know what is good for you, you'd forget her. She is in the wrong profession. She should be on the street corner."

Brandon couldn't believe his ears. Why would a father talk like that about his daughter? His eyes slid to the bottle of vodka and Brandon realized that it was not a father talking, it was an alcoholic. "Where is Sarah?"

"You never know. Looking for a new man I guess!"

"I'll come back another time." He stood up. How many years Sarah had endured a man like Edward. No wonder she was embarassed to talk about her father.

"No. She's going to be here soon. Want a drink?"

"No. Thanks. I'll come back another time." His eyes fell upon Sarah's graduation photo. She was smiling but her eyes were so sad.

"Some nurse! Is she good in bed?"

Brandon stared at him, shocked. He refrained from asking Edward if was crazy. "Why do you talk about your daughter like that?"

"Because she is a damn disappointment! She was an unwanted kid anyway." He grabbed the bottle of booze, took another drink and slammed the bottle down on the table.

"Where does she work?"

"Sarah started messing around with men since she was fourteen," he continued, completely ignoring Brandon's question. "She said it was because she got no love at home. Then she had a baby and wanted to bring it here. I said no way. Not in this house. She cried and begged and promised she will work hard to take care of the child. I wouldn't let it happen. She even slept with a married man hoping that he would leave his wife and take care of her and the kid."

Brandon's heart softened towards Sarah. This was certainly no home to raise a child. Edward was blocking the doorway. "I'll leave now," Brandon said.

"Why? You don't want to hear about Lady Sarah?"

No wonder Sarah didn't want him to know her address or give him her phone number, he thought. It must be so embarassing to have a father like Edward. He understood now why Sarah could not keep her child and deep within he was sorry that he had treated her the way he did. He heard footsteps, saw the door knob turned. He waited, hoping that it was Sarah. Edward moved aside and the door swung open. A young man bearing a strong resemblance to Sarah stepped in, stopped and looked at him in surprise. Brandon didn't have to ask questions. He had to be Tim. The two young men looked at each other for a while.

"Who are you?" Tim asked, closing the door behind him.

"Sarah's man friend!" Edward laughed and went back to the living room.

"I'm Brandon. You must be Tim. I came by to see Sarah." He felt uncomfortable under Tim's gaze.

"I didn't recognise you. The other night it was dark at the pub anyway. Why don't we go outside and talk. My father could be a real nuisance."

Brandon gladly followed him outside. "Is Sarah at work?"

"No. She was forced to take some time off because she made too many mistakes .She went away for a while."

"I'd like to talk to her. Would you mind telling me where she is." He looked into Tim's angry eyes.

"You've hurt her enough. When I look at what she has become, I don't even know it's my sister. I liked her old style better even though she might have ended up being lonley. Why did you hurt her like that? It certainly didn't take long for you to get back with your ex. Sarah saw her at your place yesterday and that is when she decided to go away."

"I'm not back with my ex. She was there yesterday while I was out. She thinks that we can get back together. I didn't mean to hurt Sarah. Things are so complicated. Was so complicated." He stopped talking and looked away. "I'm sorry that I've hurt her so much. I need to see her."

"I will talk to her and if it is okay I will let you know. What's your phone number?" Tim shifted his weight from one leg to the other as Brandon dashed to his car and came back with a business card. Tim looked at it, then at Brandon. "I'll call you later on. Wait. I have something to tell you. I shouldn't be doing this but I will. After you hear what I have to say, you decide whether or not you can still love her."

The conversation went on for about ten minutes, Tim doing most of the talking.

Brandon waved to Tim, headed for his car and drove away. He was shocked by what Tim had told him and Brandon was desperate to find Sarah. If only Tim would tell him where she was. Was he going to take forever to phone Sarah? Would she want to see him?

He didn't feel like going to the beach house, drove around aimlessly for a while, then decided to see what Christian was up to.

When he got there, his brother was stretched out in the sun, a cold beer sitting beside him. Brandon stood in a corner on the small balcony. "You're going to get skin cancer," he said.

Shadows of the Past

"We all have to die from something." He sat up and looked at his older brother. "Stacey giving you problems?" he asked mockingly. "I went by your place and she was there. How fast you forgot Sarah!"

"Stacey and I are not together. She hopes we could work things out but for me it's over. I'm curious. Why are you pushing so hard for me and Sarah to be together?"

"Well, she is a nice girl and ..." He stopped talking and looked down at his toes.

"And?"

"It would kill Austin to see you marry her. That's the biggest reason. You are my brother and I don't want to see you unhappy. I know that I'm out to get my father in all this but I just know that you would be happy with Sarah. Before you met Sarah, you were becoming just like Austin and I hated that. She was making you human."

Brandon nodded. "You're still after Austin. Forget it, you will end up getting hurt."

"Me? Get hurt? I'm immune to that." Christian smiled up at him. "Have a seat. What's going on? You look like you have the world upon your shoulders."

Brandon told him all about his biological mother and the incident at Sarah's place.

"Well, what are you waiting for? Go find Sarah," Christian said. He sprang to his feet. "I can think of a thousand ways to find her." His eyes levelled with Brandon's. "Call up the radio stations and ask them to play special songs for her. Put an article in the newspaper asking her to forgive you, tell her how much you love her. It's better than sitting and waiting for her brother to tell you whether or not she wants to see you. You have to be aggressive…and loving."

Brandon couldn't help but smile. "Anymore ideas, little brother? You have a knack for making everything sound so simple."

"If you hadn't been so pigheaded, non of this would have happened."

Chapter 16

Sarah stood beside the kitchen window, watching the dark clouds floating in. The trees swayed restlessly in the wind, as though anxious about what was coming their way. A dark cloud slipped beneath the sun, robbing the earth below of it's light. The first streak of lightening crossed the sky and half a minute later came a low, menacing rumble of thunder. The bay was turbulent, the waves crashing against rocks. The first raindrops spattered against the window pane and a soothing sound filled the air. She opened the window a crack, breathing in the fresh air and forcing herself to relax.

Peaks Island was the perfect place to relax and she needed to. There was not much traffic and everything was so peaceful, so quiet. It was a completely different world and Brandon would never be able to find her here, unless someone told him where she was.

She missed him, but she just had to get used to living without him. It seemed like ages since she had last seen him and the heaviness in her heart became heavier. Unconsciously, she lifted her head, looking quite confident and told herself that she was strong enough to live without Brandon.

He was probably with Stacey right now. It certainly didn't take him long to make up with his ex girlfriend. How could he have forgotten me so easily, she wondered. All those words of love were nothing but lies. All along, they had been two liars, lying to each other. She laughed, a dry sound without any emotion.

Life could be hilarious, sweet, bitter, anything it wanted to be.

Another flash of lightening ripped across the sky, a low growl of thunder followed and the rain came down harder. She wished the storm would pass soon so she could walk along the beach.

The phone rang, it's sound filling the small cottage. Tim had insisted that she bring his cell phone with her. Sarah picked it up, pushed on the button, "Hello."

"Hi Sarah. Is everything okay?" Tim asked.

"Yes. I feel a lot better. It's really nice and quiet here. Just the thing I need."

"I'm glad to hear that. Randy's parents said that you can use the cottage for as long as you want."

"They are so kind." The connection was bad. "You might just lose me. There's a storm here."

"I saw Brandon…quite a few times."

It seemed like her heart swelled and shrunk back to it's normal size in a split second. She drew in a long deep breath.

"What did you say?" she asked loudly. For a moment she wondered if she had heard correctly.

"Brandon came by the house several times. He wants to talk to you."

She did not answer for a full minute. Finally realization spreaded through her mind.

"Sarah. Are you there?"

"Yes. When did you see him?"

"He came to the house a few times yesterday and very early this morning, almost begging to see you. I felt so sorry for the poor guy."

"What should I do, Tim?" The surprise of it all still held her captive.

"What you think is right."

"Don't tell him where I am. Let me think about this some more." Over the past few weeks, she had been hoping that Brandon would have a change of heart and was terribly hurt when he didn't. Since she had been here at the cottage, she had been trying to forget him, to convince herself that it was the best thing to do.

"As you wish…but never mind."

"Tim…" The phone cut off.

The rain came down harder, there was another flash of lightening, momentarily lighting up the cottage. She put the phone down, went to the door and opened it. Looking up at the sky, she noticed that most of the storm clouds had dispersed and the sun was peeping out from behind a dark cloud. If only the storm would pass, she would be able to walk on the beach, even make a fire. That would help her to relax.

Brandon's face floated across her mind, tugged at her heart. It was hard to believe he had gone to her home, had talked with Tim. Did he have a change of heart? Certainly. If not, he would never try to find her. She should have been happy with the news, it was what she had hoped for, now she felt nothing.

Walking around the tiny cottage, her mind went back to the last time she had seen him, he was with Stacey and that had torn her to pieces. Had they gotten back together for a while?

She opened the door and examined the sky again. The storm would pass soon. She contemplated whether or not to see Brandon. Part of her longed to see him, while another part was telling her it was not wise.

"What should I do?" She asked herself, a mixture of fear and a spark of joy mingled within.

Brandon had loved her, made her feel special, like no one had ever done. He had made her lose that feeling that she wasn't worth loving. Then he had turn his back on her, undoing all the beautiful things he had done for her and had thrown her back to the starting line. Yet, how could she blame him? She was the one who lied to him and betrayed his trust. He had a right to be angry. If they got back together, would he ever really trust her?

She shook her head. It would be better to leave Brandon out of her life, though she still loved him. Time would help her to forget him and she would go on with her life.

She went to the kitchen, opened the fridge. No more ice-cream, no chocolate, she noted. Doing a half turn, she opened a cupboard door, took out a bottle of brandy and examined it. A good shot should help me to relax, she thought. Her eyes moved to the window again. The rain had stopped and the sun was shining.

Sarah couldn't remember when was the last time she had a good night sleep and she was exhausted. She poured some brandy in a glass, gulped it down and refilled the glass. This should do the trick, she thought, as she stepped outside.

She made her way down the small rocky slope and to the beach. The air smelled fresh and clean, the trees shimmered with water droplets. She sat down on a rock, finished the glass of brandy. She still hadn't decided what to do about Brandon. The future gave no guarantees. What if they got back together and he gave her up for the sake of his family?

An unsettling thought snaked it's way into her mind, a thought that she hadn't dared entertain before now. How could Brandon be friends with a man like Ralph? That had shocked her and still did. She closed her eyes and forced dark thoughts away, pulled herself back from a place she didn't ever want to go again.

She sat there for a long time, thinking of the good times she had with Brandon, told herself it was over,that every good thing had an end, and it was time to go back to her original plans. She stood up, feeling rather unsteady, and headed back for the cottage. She lit a fire in the tiny fireplace, poured herself some brandy and sat there enjoying the gentle warmth. The cell phone rang and she ignored it.

There was a loud knock on the door. Sarah sprang to her feet, scared. Who was at the door? No one was supposed to come here and there were no cottages nearby. There was a knock again.

"Sarah."

Her heart stopped. She would recognise that voice anywhere. It was Brandon! How did he find her? She walked over to the door and hesitantly opened it.

"May I come in'" he asked.

Anger sprang up in her. There was Mr. Perfect, the guy who did no wrong. He had accused her of being cold and heartless because she had given her child up for adoption. Did he have any idea how hard she fought to keep her baby? What she had put herself through? Who was he to judge her?

"Why are you here? How did you find me?" She was surprised at the hardness in her voice.

He did not move, he just stood there and looked at her.

"Come in." She moved aside and he stepped in.

"Tim told me where to find you." He pulled uncomfortably at the wet shirt stuck to his chest.

"Tim!" She stared at him in disbelief. Why did he do such a thing? There had better be a good reason!

"At first, he didn't want to tell me. I went to your place several times and he eventually told me where you were." His eyes went to the bottle of brandy sitting by the fireplace, then back to Sarah, a questioning look in his eyes.

"Want a drink? That's all I have," she said, pointing to the bottle. "Cheap stuff. Can't afford anything expensive."

He shook his head, the puzzled look still on his face.

"Since when do you drink brandy?" He watched her with obvious concern.

"Since today." She was trying to be tough and so far she was doing a good job at it, but deep within, her love for Brandon still burned, and it hurt her to treat him this way.

"Why are you here?" Her eyes met his with a quiet look of challenge. She smiled. "I'm waiting for an answer."

He looked ill at ease, and after a full minute, he held her gaze. "I can see right through you, Sarah. Quit the act."

The alcohol, for the moment, had given her a certain courage that she normally did not possess. Her determined eyes held his. "This isn't an act! You are seeing the real Sarah. You don't know me at all." She wanted to hurt him, like he had hurt her. "What were you expecting? Do you want me to fall into your arms and cry? Beg you not to leave me, plead with you to love me?" She felt unsteady, she had had too much brandy. "Let me tell you something. I did that years ago, with a boy name Jake and I swore to myself that I'd never do it again. I intend to keep my word. By the way, do you want to hear about, Jake?"

"I don't." His voice was cold, unfriendly. "I didn't come here to talk about Jake!"

"So you don't want to hear about my steamy little romance?" She felt bad saying those words. She still loved Brandon, but wasn't going to tell him that. She tilted her head and looked at his angry face. He still hadn't told her why he was here. Better hold on to whatever dignity she had left.

"I came here to tell you that I'm sorry about the way I treated you." His blue eyes were intense. "I love you, Sarah."

His words took her speech away. She stared at the man standing in front of her, recovering some of her equilibrium, she asked, "Are you sure?"

He looked insulted, anger clouded his eyes. "I'm sure, Sarah."

She walked back to the fireplace, sat down, poured more brandy in the glass and brought it to her lips. She knew that she shouldn't, but liked the courage and strength it gave her.

"I think you've had enough, Sarah." He moved towards her.

"How would you know that? By the way, where is Stacey?"

He sat beside the fireplace. "I know that you're hurting. I'm sorry for what I have put you through. As for Stacey, we never got back together. She kept coming over to the beach house, hoping that we would be able to work things out. I know that you were sitting outside in your car and you saw her. I swear, nothing happened between us."

"And you expect gullible Sarah to believe that?" She laughed. It was a dry empty sound. She fought her feelings, forcing her mind to stay in control. She was starting to feel fragile again and didn't like it one bit. She studied the strange expression on his face and wished that she could read his mind. "It doesn't matter to me what happened between you and Stacey." She shrugged.

"Can you forgive me, Sarah? I know that I have hurt you. I'm sorry." His voice was mixed with sincerity and pain.

Her resolve to stay strong, to act like she didn't care, was slowly crumbling. Why did he hold such power over her?

Why was she doing this to him? He didn't deserve to be treated this way. She had, afterall, lied to him over and over again. He had a right to be angry, yet, he was here, telling her that he was sorry.

His eyes searched her face, a lost look lingered in their depths. He opened his mouth to say something, but didn't. He placed a hand on hers.

She looked at him through narrowed eyes, her eyes slid to his hand covering hers. "What do you think you're doing!" His hand remained on hers. "Let me see," she pretended to be concentrating really hard. "After that, you're going to slip your hand up my arm, you're going to kiss me and try to take it further. Forget it!"

He pulled his hand away, shock written all over his face. "Sorry I touched you," he whispered.

"Sorry." She laughed. "What do you want from me Brandon?"

"I'll tell you what I want. You. I…"

"Right. You want me. Where, honey? In bed?" She sprang to her feet, looked down at him. "Rich guys, like you and Ralph. You like games, don't you?" She sat down on a chair, her legs way too unsteady and her stomach felt queasy. The brandy had really done a number on her.

"I'm not Ralph!" His eyes were stony, but his voice very gentle, "He was not nice to you and I'm sorry for all that you went through with him."

"What! Who told you that?"

"Tim."

"Tim!" What on earth was going on with her brother? He used to keep her secrets. Why the sudden change? She hoped that Tim hadn't gone into any unpleasant details. She shook her head and muttered, "My brother has gone crazy."

He stood up. There was pain in his eyes. "I wish I could erase your pain, Sarah."

"Now you even sound like Ralph." She stood up. How many times had Ralph said that to her? Too many and everytime it was a lie. "What is the game tonight? Am I the stripper? The hooker? The servant? Let me choose for you." She started to unbutton her shirt slowly. "The stripper it will be. You know Ralph. Are you like him? When were you going to show me the real you?"

Brandon looked at her, anger splashed all over his face. "You want to strip,go ahead, lady. I'd would be stupid not to watch."

Hilda St. James

She continued to unbutton her shirt, ignoring what he had just said. The shirt came off. Sarah wanted to laugh at the look of frustration on his face. She opened her pants button.

Brandon walked towards her, scooped up the shirt lying at her feet. "Get dressed."

"Oh, you don't want me to play those dirty games until you get tired of me and move on to something fresh?"

He placed both hands on her shoulders and shook her. "Stop it!" His face was a mere two inches from hers. "I am not Ralph! Do you understand?" He fell quiet, still holding her. "I think you had too much to drink. Go to sleep and we will talk tomorrow."

She wriggled free of his hold. She was starting to feel sleepy. Why on eath did she drink so much? "I have to go to bed. You can leave now."

"I have nowhere to go. I'll sleep on the couch."

"No way! You're leaving!"

"I paid the owner of a private boat to bring me over here. I didn't think about reserving a room somewhere. I don't even know if there is a hotel on this island."

"Sleep on the couch, but don't come near the bedroom." She walked to her room, slammed the door and leaned against it. She knew that she was being really mean to Brandon, but she couldn't help it. It seemed like the past and the present, somehow got mixed up and she felt rather confused.

Mentioning Ralph had brought back so many nasty memories, especially one. The night he had left her tied up for most of the night. She had been terrified, pleaded with him to untie her, but he hadn't. He had told her, "See it as part of the deal for me helping you

282

to keep your baby." After that, she was really scared of him, but continued the relationship, because it was the only way she knew to keep her child.

For a moment, she thought that she was going to throw up. How she despised Ralph! Why was she even comparing Brandon and Ralph? Why had she talked to him about Jake and Ralph? They were not the reason she and Brandon had split up. All her past pain seemed to be flooding in, like dark storm clouds. She closed her eyes and said, "Stop it!"

She made her way over to the bed and climbed under the covers. She could hear Brandon moving around the cottage. She closed her eyes, knowing that she did not need to fear this man. She fell into a deep sleep

****

Brandon placed another log in the fireplace and sat down, his heart heavy with pain. Tim had told him about Sarah's relationship with Ralph and even went into a few details. The only reason Tim had done so, was because he had wanted Brandon to know that Sarah did fight to keep her child. He had promised Tim not to say anything to Sarah, but he had slipped and mentioned it.

He turned to look at the closed door, no sounds could be heard, she must be fast asleep. After all that she had gone through, Brandon was scared that Sarah wouldn't want anything to do with him. He would have to find a way to convince her that he still loved her. In fact, he had never stopped loving her. His love for Sarah had pushed him to find out about his biological mother, to make peace with a woman who didn't deserve to be hated, a woman who loved him deeply. Though she loved him, she had had no other choice but to give him up for adoption. She wasn't cold and heartless, like he had thought for most of his life.

Now, he understood Sarah. She had tried desperately to keep her child, but her efforts were futile and she was left with no other choice but adoption.

Fury filled him as he thought of what Sarah had gone through with Ralph. He forced his mind away from that path, the thoughts were unbearable.

He stared at the fire, his mind drifting back to Rebecca. If only she had met someone who really loved her, someone to make her happy, even if it was only for a few months of her life, before she passed away. And his father, whoever he was, how could he treat Rebecca that way. She was just a child, a child with a sad life. His heart overflowed with pain for the woman he never knew and for Sarah who had given up the last bit of her dignity in hopes of keeping her child. All he wanted now, was to love Sarah, to take care of her for as long as he was granted life.

He walked to the door, pressed his ear against it and listened. There were no sounds. He turned the door knob, opened the door slowly and quietly walked in. Sarah had told him to keep away from the room, but he had to sure that she was fine. He looked down at her peaceful face, at the gentle rise and fall of her chest. He longed to hold her, to comfort her, to tell her that he was sorry for the way he had treated her. He turned, walked out the room and closed the door.

He walked around restlessly, doubts gnawing away at his mind. What if Sarah told him that it was over? What would he do then? She had a stubborn streak to her and once her mind was made up, that was the way things were going to be.

He stretched out on the couch, thinking about Tim. He loved his sister with all his heart and she was lucky to have a brother like him. He had told Brandon, "I will tell you where Sarah is. Go to her because she could take forever to make up her mind. I know you too love each other." Tim had given him a serious look and said, "If you have any intentions of hurting her, please don't go. She has suffered enough."

He stood up, walked to the bedroom door, started to open it and stopped. He felt like shaking her awake so he could talk to her, convince her that he loved her.

He stuck his hands in his pants pocket and pulled out his grandmother's diamond ring. He opened the bedroom door and crept in quietly. Sarah was fast asleep. He leaned over the bed, took her hand and slipped on the diamond ring on the same finger with the pink stone ring. He let go of her hand, she stirred but did not wake up.

"Damn it," he murmured. "Wake up." He looked at her for a while then went back to the couch. If she woke up and saw him, he would be in real trouble.

Brandon awakened to the gentle warmth of the sun on his face. He turned his head and looked towards the bedroom. The door was open and the bed was empty. He sprang off the couch and made his way around the small cottage. There was no sign of Sarah.

A feeling of despair settled upon him. "Sarah, where are you?" he called out.

There was no answer. She can't be too far away, he thought. He slipped on his shoes, went outside and walked towards the beach. This place was quiet, way too quiet, except for the gentle whispers of the waves. He scanned the area around him. There was no one in sight.

He felt angry. Why did she have to disappear? Why didn't she stay and talk things over with him? He stopped for a while, stuck his hands in his pockets and stared out at the vast expanse of water. No matter what, he was going to find her.

He headed further down the beach and that was when he saw her. She was sitting on the sand, half hidden by the trees. His steps quickened. "Sarah," he called out.

Her head snapped up and she turned in his direction. She stood up and walked towards Brandon, her head bent.

They stopped a few feet away from each other. Brandon looked expectant. Sarah looked withdrawn, unfriendly. She looked into his eyes, then lowered them and stood there in silence.

"We have to talk Sarah." His eyes slid to her hand. She was wearing only the pink stone ring.

"I left your ring on the table. I had asked you not to come into the room. Why did you, Brandon?"

"I wanted to see if you were okay and...to give you the ring."

She looked up, a smile on her face, coldness in her eyes. "It's better if we go our seperate ways."

"That's not what I want." He reached out to hold her hand, then pulled his arm away. If he touched her, it would only make her angry.

"That is what I want." Their eyes held, cold determination in hers, pain in his.

"Sarah I was wrong to judge you, to think of you as a heartless person because of your past and I'm very sorry."

She nodded, her face serious.

She had lost weight, there were dark circles under her eyes but she was as pretty as ever. He longed to see her smile again, to come alive. He looked at her for a long time, she had become like a stranger. He wanted back the Sarah he knew.

"I'm sorry that I've hurt you so much. That night on the beach when you told me that you disliked your natural mother and women like her, I thought I was going to die. If I had told you the truth right away, it would have been over. I just wanted to have your love for as long as possible. I think that you are the only person who ever truly loved me, with the exception of Tim. I thought that if you loved me enought that you would have a change of heart. I know that this sounds stupid, but I'll say it anyway. By lying to you, I was gaining time, time to find solutions. I never meant to hurt you. I had lied to you before. The people before you, they never really loved me, probably what they felt was pity, because they knew what my life was like. With you it was different. You knew nothing about the mistakes I had made, or about my family, it was like you had formed your own image of me, an image of someone perfect, someone who didn't have a bad past and I loved it. It made me feel so good and I wanted things to stay that way, even though I knew you would one day find out. It was so beautiful while it lasted. I'm sorry for hurting you, betraying you."

Her words sank into him and he realized how fortunate he was to be loved so deeply, to be so important to someone.

"I love you Sarah. I was angry with you but I never really stopped loving you. I want things to be the way they were. Do you want to give us a second chance?

"You have met my father, you have seen the kind of person he is. When Tim was younger, he spent some time in prison. My mother is the only one with a clean slate. My family is not like yours, we are so different. Can you handle that?"

"Yes, I can." The wind played in her hair and he longed to reach out and brush it away from her face. He wanted to take her in his arms, just hold her, feel her body close to his.

"Ralph has seen us together. The two of you are friends. What if he tells your friends about the affair I had with him?"

Her eyes were dark with anger, her face tense.

"Ralph had better not utter one word of it! He should have gone to prison for that. The man is about twelve years your senior. I'll make sure he dosen't say a thing." Brandon felt rage building up within him. How could Ralph had done such a thing? "Ralph is not a friend, he is an aquaintance. I met him from time to time at business meetings."

It started to rain, and they walked back toward the cottage.

Once they were in the cottage, Brandon turned to face her. "Please, Sarah, give us a second chance." She didn't answer.

"I know that I've hurt you," he said.

"I've hurt you too Brandon. After all the lies I've told you, how could you trust me?"

"Let's leave all that in the past. I just want to have you back."

"That's what I want, too."

Sarah walked towards him, her arms circling his waist. He pulled her closer.

"There's one thing I forgot." He said, letting go of her. Brandon walked to the table, picked up the diamond ring, took Sarah's hand and slipped it on the finger with the pink stone ring.

Hilda St. James

About the Author

Hilda lives in Edmonton with her husband and two sons. She has worked as a nursing assistant for many years, in Quebec, Alberta and the jungles of South America. She first discovered her love for helping others when she was sixteen and became a volunteer at an orphanage.

She has written and published several short stories and this is her first book.

Hilda loves writing, reading, painting, but most of all she enjoys spending time with her family.

Printed in the United States
1460900002B/118-132

9 781410 797506